Nick Garnett spent seventeen years on the Financial Times as a reporter and feature writer. He was born and brought up in Yorkshire and took a degree in history at Cambridge University. He now lives in London.

1954: A CRIME NOVEL

Nick Garnett

1954: A CRIME NOVEL

AUSTIN & MACAULEY

A CIP catalogue record for this title is available from the British Library.

Some of the crimes referred to in this novel were real. The names of the victims have been altered. The book's main plot is an invention, all characters portrayed in the story are fictitious and any resemblance to real people is entirely coincidental. The scope and organisation of the local police force have been altered.

ISBN 978 1 905609 77 2

www.austinmacauley.com

First Published (2009)
Austin & Macauley Publishers Ltd.
25 Canada Square
Canary Wharf
London
E14 5LB

Printed & Bound in Great Britain

For Anne and Tom

ACKNOWLEDGEMENTS

The following people and organisations provided me with assistance in the writing of this book.

Eugene Nicholson, curator of Bradford Industrial Museum
Anders Clausager, Jaguar Cars
Jim Davies, British Airways' Museum
Eva Mansfield, Omega Watches
Mike Cartwright, Bradford Chamber of Commerce
Victor Murton, Imperial War Museum, Duxford
Roy Masini, historical department of the Metropolitan Police
Nick Vandervell, UK Petroleum Industry Association
Sara Slinn, Borthwick Institute, York
Bradford city librarians, especially Anita Thompson
Michael Stainer, Grand Hotel, Folkestone
Barbara Westlake, Rolls-Royce Enthusiasts' Club
Sarah McKee, Bettys
National Media Museum, Bradford
Richard Charlesworth, Bentley Motors
Lydd Airport
Vince Johnson, general manager, Hotel Majestic, Harrogate
Ruth Staples-Rolfe, Kent Wildlife Trust
Bradford Camera Exchange
Museum of Brands, London
Tony Pingriff and Ian Leggett, Standard Motor Club
Keith Crampton and Bill Smith, Armstrong Siddeley Owners' Club

Gerard Darcy, National Treatment Agency

Vicky Lowe, Scarborough Tourist Information

Confederation of British Wool Textiles

National Rifle Association

Stella Jones, The Crown Hotel, Scarborough

Brian Radam, The British Lawnmower Museum, Southport

Keith Bill, technical manager, Wilton Carpets

Betty Koppa, North Curry historical society

Iona Hames, Jaeger

City of Westminster Archive Centre

Judy Glossop and Ken Hutchings for their knowledge of Somerset, Julie Ivanov for her keen eye, Michael Hanlon of the Daily Mail for encouraging me to write this book, Selma Ross-Smith and Sharon Ives for typing, Helen for all her support, help and encouragement.

Special thanks to Andrea Derungs.

Books on Yorkshire which have been particularly helpful include those written by George Sheeran, John Ayers, Arnold Kellett, Stephen Wade and John Stolarczyk.

Ian Fleming's Casino Royale is published by Penguin Books.

She gripped the lamppost for support. Feeling a little funny, not like herself at all, she screwed up her face and looked out of one eye. Just like the admiral with whom she shared a surname. Moira giggled at the thought. The hotel was boring and she had slipped away from there without telling anyone, seeking out more fun but with no clue where to find it. Exuberant now and light-headed and confident, she heard the man's voice over the sound of the engine and turned to face him.

CHAPTER 1

April 1954

The body's head and torso hung out at an angle from the hole. It wasn't really a body, more a fleshy skeleton, facing out and down, eyeless eye sockets scrutinising the floorboards as if seeking a lost sixpence. Brick and plaster dust coated the stump in a floury blanket, giving it an almost clown-like appearance. Clinging precariously to the sooty sides of the chimney breast from where it protruded, the bony corpse oscillated gently in the fierce draughts of air funnelling through cracks in the abandoned house.

Detective Inspector Ray Stafford took a step back from the fireplace and looked around at the grim confines of Number Three, Back End Villas. Small rivulets of water trickled down one wall, fed by a dislocated rain gutter shoving through a broken window. Like rotting teeth, remaining shards of glass jutted up from the base of the window's rotting frames. A thin shaft of weak light coursed from a crack in the ceiling, directly below a gap in the roof slates. Dust particles whirled in the shaft like tiny midges trapped in an invisible tube, but as the sun disappeared so did the beam, plunging the room back into its dull complexion. Enough light was left to reveal vestiges of the room's wallpaper, a kind of rose pattern still visible through the blotches of green mould. Some of the paper had slipped away from the walls in curiously uniform strips. Small pools of something brown lay close to the skirting boards. Once a robust if mean dwelling, the house was crumbling into compost.

Stafford turned back to the body, shoving one of his hands into a raincoat pocket to protect it from the dwelling's dank insides while pushing his trilby back with the other. The sight seemed more bizarre than grotesque.

"It looks a bit like one of those dummies at a seaside ghost train ride. I've never seen anything like it." He rested a very large shoe on the hearth. Tattered remains of blue overalls covered the thin and patchy coating of skin on the waxworks figure. A bobble hat encased the top of the head, a tin badge displaying an engraving of a railway engine pinned to it. "Flying Scotsman", it read.

His colleague bent forward to take a closer look. "I was wondering, sir, if it might be Father Christmas. Maybe he got trapped in here delivering his presents. You know, his sack got too fat or something."

Batting away bits of brickwork escaping into the room from the ruptured wall, Sergeant Norman Feather twisted his body and peered into the flue shaft. "A giant Meccano box could be wedged in there or even a train set." Stafford had often noticed how agile the sergeant was, despite a body shaped like a boiler. In a city of thin men, Feather's chubby physique, immune to the last fourteen years of food rationing, strained both his surname and the fabric of his uniform.

Feather stepped back. The first police officer called to the site, the sergeant had been filling in some of the details about the grim discovery.

"The whole road was condemned and boarded up about four years ago, so the site foreman says. The road is only now getting the demolition treatment from a wrecking crew. Before the bulldozers get to work, each house it seems is inspected by one of the workmen. Something to do with gas and electricity safety. The bloke is over there."

Feather nodded towards the end of the upstairs landing. Standing next to a constable, the man was dragging on a fag in between bouts of bronchial coughing so violent his body buckled into a question mark. Small and elderly, the workman did not seem much taller than the sledgehammer resting against the fireplace. He was wearing grey trousers and an ordinary white shirt. Dust plastered his wispy hair as if a ceiling had collapsed in on him.

"Anyway, he has seen a bulge in the chimney breast and, for reasons best known to himself, has swung his sledgehammer at it. The body probably caused the brickwork to bow outwards over time. I'm only guessing. The hammer punctured the chimney. He got a big surprise when your fairground attraction, sir, stuck his head out for some fresh air."

Stafford glanced away from the bag of bones in its gruesome mortar coffin and surveyed again the first-floor room in which they were standing. A wooden ledge, possibly once a bookshelf, sloped down the back wall, an end still attached by a solitary nail. One corner of the room was missing a section of floor. A bell-shaped lampshade, wrapped in years of dust, still enveloped the ceiling light bulb. Some rags and used tin food cans were piled up in a corner, as if a tramp had tried staying here but had found the lodgings too odious, even for a down-and-out. A rank smell, like putrefying vegetation, pervaded the air.

Even by the impoverished standards of this part of the city, Stafford knew Back End Villas were an especially nasty example of the city's sub-standard housing. These particular mid-Victorian hovels were built in enclosed, airless courtyards, hapless residents forced to trudge across cobbles to dry ashpit lavatories. The middens had long been replaced by water-flushing outside tipping toilets, but Stafford couldn't help for a second juxtaposing these ratty dwellings with the new age of television, jet engines and affordable fridges.

"We'll set in motion the required searches," Feather was saying. "The town hall should be able to tell us the name of the house's last owner, if we cannot find a neighbour to tell us that is. There aren't too many neighbours left around here to talk to."

"What about the police surgeon?"

"McCrone was telephoned at home but it seems he was called out on some other police business. I've been told to wait here for him."

Stafford pushed a toecap through the detritus. "I suppose we better check this rubbish in case it's got anything to do with the thing over there." He nodded at the dead stump that had once been a man. He then took a couple of steps closer to the window. The draught from the smashed glass encouraged him to hitch his coat collar further up the neck. The dirty fog of the morning had largely evaporated into mizzle, that gloomy mixture of drizzle and mist. It was the type of weather where rain was so fine it lulled you into believing there wasn't any, until your overcoat was reduced within minutes to a shapeless lump of sodden cloth.

Blackened terraced houses, tightly packed in rows, slunk down the hillsides. The regimented lines resembled the teeth of a giant fire grate. Mesmerised by the close-knit strips of pitched roofs, he knew this type of view triggered the melancholy which often engulfed him. He couldn't take his eyes off the sight. It was like a self-provocation.

The imposing structure of a nearby mill stood out in the pitiless gloom, its chimney one of three hundred factory stacks in the city, pointing heavenwards like long dark fingers. Thin stone flutes, vaguely similar to spires he'd seen in photographs of Asia, protruded from the top of the mill's frontage. It was a slab-faced mass of stone finished off with an incongruous Alice in Wonderland flourish. Like an over-sized prize fighter in a silk top hat.

"What's that building?"

Feather walked over to the window, the floorboards complaining under his weight, and pushed his nose closer to the condensation-soaked glass. His stomach rested on the sill. "That's Shaw's mill. Built by Esau Shaw, one of the local wool industry's founding fathers. It has that funny frontage. That's why I know."

A crowd of women had formed across the road, near a hoarding advertising Melbourne Ales and "Tizer the Appetizer". They were peering at the house, their eyes drawn to the scene by the two bobbies standing guard outside. Some of the women wore the large headscarf come shawl which, fifty years before, was common attire throughout the city but was now confined to a few within the elderly working-class poor. The two officers heard the workman sidling back into the room but did not turn away from the drab vista laid out in front of them.

"Take a dekko at those houses," Feather eventually said. "I bet hundreds and hundreds of people have lived in them while working at Shaw's." The sergeant extracted a packet of Mackintosh Rolos from a pocket and offered the detective inspector one before popping two into his own mouth. "Coming from where you come from, I don't suppose you know too much about local history, Mr Stafford."

"A little, but only bits and pieces. Life and the past seemed somewhat softer down there in Somerset."

A dull but noisy creak escaped from wood joists deep within the house. It was as if the dwelling was talking. They both looked round and then turned back to the blackened cityscape folding away to the horizon.

Stafford placed a foot on the windowsill and stretched a calf muscle. "The solution to this crime is going to be dead simple or very tricky. I guess the silver lining is that we might be able to delete someone from our missing persons list. By the way, the last time I looked at the file some idiot had drawn a Biffo the Bear on the front cover."

"I saw that," Feather chuckled. "I hope it doesn't reflect the limit of our officers' reading habits. I mean fancy going for the *Beano* rather than the *Eagle*."

A bulldozer came into view on a patch of wasteland a street away. Plumes of smoke jetted out of its vertical exhaust as the machine lurched forward in small hops. It then clattered across a pavement into the cobbled road and its motor died. Under the dozer's rusting metal cage, the driver wore a flat cap twisted the wrong way round and a boiler suit well-percolated through with rainwater. In the distance, a mobile crane with a wrecking ball attached to its arm inched forward over a mound of rubble. Feather launched another Rolo on to the back of his tongue.

Water was penetrating the house so assiduously daylight perforated the disintegrating window frames in a myriad of dull pencil beams. Even this close to fresh air, the stench of damp was pervasive. The windows rattled.

A new Pathfinder suddenly appeared around the corner and rolled to a stop across the street. The RT officer was leaning across the front seat, talking on the car's Pye radio telephone. The driver climbed out of the big Riley, then slipped his head back into the car, spoke a few words to his colleague, slammed the door shut and approached the house. The eyes of the women tracked his steps, soaking up details to pack and embellish the gossipy chats they would embark on during the coming days while scrubbing down their front door steps.

Stafford idly wondered about the condition of the timber. Five men would soon be standing on a floor already bowing in the middle. Parts of the house downstairs were clearly visible through the large tears in the half-perished boards.

A minute later the police driver, reed-thin and immaculately uniformed, emerged from the landing into the first-floor bedroom. A look of bafflement stole across his face as he caught sight of Number Three's unexpected guest.

"Anyone you know, constable?" Feather snorted air into his nostrils in a stifled snigger.

The driver paused for a moment in front of the bones and skin sticking out of the brickwork. He then turned to Stafford. "The chief super wants you up on the moors now, sir. I'm here to take you. They've found the body of a girl there and it looks like someone has done her in badly."

A sudden quietness enveloped the room. Two bodies in one day. Even the workman stopped wheezing. Without sound, the dust particles seemed to be everywhere. Stafford could even taste them now. The metallic rasping of the bulldozer's engine started up again, breaking the silence, and Feather detached another chocolate from the tubular packet of sweets. "That's put this old ghoul into perspective. You go up now, sir, and I'll look after this sorry devil."

Suddenly, a loud crack pierced the room. A couple of bricks spilled from the chimney breast and the cadaver dipped forward a few inches, a clicking noise issuing from the bones as a skeletal arm hit the side of the fireplace. The movement twisted the head, turning it sideways. Eyeholes now stared at the wall, inspecting what was left of the wallpaper. It was as if the body resented its new status of second billing. The bobble hat pulled away from the head and soot sprinkled from the skull, freeing a tuft of hair which jumped up as if starved of Brylcreem. The dust prompted the workman into another fit of spluttering until he eventually spat out a large blob of phlegm. Stafford could see now that the workman wasn't old at all. It was just that he had virtually no teeth. Top or bottom.

CHAPTER 2

Earlier that same day, Jennifer Shaw crawled down the valley side behind the immense steering wheel of her Jaguar saloon. The atmosphere outside was so murky, the chrome bonnet strip on the bulbous car acted like an aiming device.

Trillions of soot particles, spewing from the surrounding mass of coal-fired chimneys, were being snared in the wet air. With so much grit in the soup, a filthy, medium-dense fog had taken hold. She edged closer to the windscreen, wipers on fast speed, in an effort to discern more of the road. Her hands, sweating a little in their beige leather driving gloves, gripped the wheel a tad tighter.

A cheese grater of an accent diffracted from the car's speakers, the BBC Light Programme broadcasting a variety show from Manchester's Palace Theatre. "Did I tell you, Arthur, I've developed quite an attachment for my mother-in-law. Yes I have. It fits over her mouth." She twiddled the sound knob on the factory-fitted Radiomobile to raise the volume, and then effected a rapid check of her make-up in the rear-view mirror.

Less than half a mile across the city, a badly-decomposed corpse would soon be unearthed behind the wall of a chimney breast. Jennifer Shaw knew nothing of this. She had never been to that exact part of the city. In fact, her long, lithe and fashionably-clothed body had never, ever set foot in a house as wretched as Number Three, Back End Villas.

"Funny thing, Reggie, how men meet their wives. I met mine in the Tunnel of Love. She was digging it."

Shaw chortled quietly. Arthur, whoever the comedian was, owned a screechy working-class voice. She imagined him with

21

poorly-fitting false teeth and the hollow cheeks and skinny limbs of the long-under-nourished.

Visibility perked up a little as the Jag nosed down the slope of the Pennines and the temperature rose a notch. A concentration of lit shop windows as she approached the centre of the city offered extra illumination in the gloom. Buildings were materialising unreal and ghostly. Feeble vehicle lights emerged dimly, but suddenly, like spectres. The heavy air suppressed noise to an eerie mute, the only sound a subdued 'swish' as the tyres of the biggest saloon the company made rolled over the wet tarmac.

She punched in the cigar lighter. Resting wrists on the rim of the steering wheel, Shaw flicked open her solid silver cigarette case and popped out a Pall Mall. The decanter, attached to a special rack under the dash, was brimful of Hennessy. If she had a free limb, she would have knocked back a snifter. Diffused beams from a set of street lamps revealed advertisements, in old withered paint, on the blank end of a row of terraced houses. Brobat cleaner and Rowntree's confectionery she could just make out. She casually blew a stream of cigarette smoke at the windshield, realising too late it blunted forward vision even further.

"I'll tell you, Arthur, I was married by a judge. Knowing what I know now, I should have gone for a jury."

Someone in the audience bellowed one of those jagged laughs, rising above the others like the cackle of the deranged. Shaw wondered whether the radio people wheeled the same nutcase with the crackpot squawk from one show to another. A suspiciously similar high-pitched laugh always featured in those shows.

Shaw's breezy disposition was on maximum wattage. It usually was. Not for nothing did her pals nickname her Blithe Spirit. Even her husband's vague exasperation at the size of her last clothes bill, admittedly whopping, could not deflect her naturally sunny outlook. She thought about the conversation they'd had that morning in their temporary kitchenette, slumming it while the builders butchered their existing kitchen before installing the new one. There was nothing wrong, of course, with shopping at department stores and local outfitters, as Stephen kept suggesting, dreary though some were. But like all ex-mannequins, she viewed top clothing as a non-negotiable must, and that meant couture. Jennifer 'the Sphinx' Garland they used to call her in the tertiary reaches of the magazines. For heaven's sake, it wasn't as if she and her husband were short of a few bob. They were as rich as Croesus.

A parked lorry loomed in view and Shaw swung her bulky motor further into the road. "Where did they find the Irish woodworm, Reggie? Dead in a brick." She turned the sound up further.

The last Knightsbridge trip had proved a wallet buckler, no getting away from it. But there was a good reason for that, Shaw silently explained to herself. She felt her outfit at the last wool industry knees-up had been a yawning let-down. Now she had rigged herself out with the best and, as the Yanks might say in their curious colloquialism, all the bases were covered. The Dior sheath with strapless bodice would be perfect. So would the Chinese silk number from Balenciaga, the top half crafted like a single-breasted coat, or the Jacques Fath frock with inverted pleats and two-tone sash.

"Now tell me, Arthur, what's the difference between a Scotsman and a coconut. You can get a drink out of a coconut." A dribble of static coursed through the radio reception and she leant over to adjust the station frequency.

Shaw considered her love for all things Fath, specialising as he did in clothing for tall women. She had loaded up the bill with another of his skirts. Now well past her mid-forties, the Sphinx knew she carried a bust a little too large for some of Jacques' clothes, but she also knew that she could still wing it. Just. Anyway, Chanel was about to reveal her comeback collection so Stephen could expect another tranche of bills. The famed French couturier's cardigan suits, previewed by *Vanity Fair*, did look odd she conceded. But, I mean, Chanel. Closed down in the Second World War and now back in business, it was history in the making.

The Jag ploughed on into the clogging air, a brew of toxic ingredients belching from Bradford's mills and its one hundred thousand coal-heated houses. Dirt was layering on the segments of the windscreen the wipers never reached. Lights on some vehicles emitted an illumination little brighter than a Swan Vesta. Yet a dense pea-souper it was not. She could just make out the billboard for Hitchcock's *Rear*

Window as the car weaved past the Gaumont cinema. Jimmy Stewart's startled face stared down at her from an advertising frieze. Damp soot was starting to line her mouth and she slammed shut the driver's door quarterlight as a logjam appeared up ahead.

"I took my wife to the waxworks museum, you know, Reggie. When the manager clapped his eyes on her, he said we'd better keep moving as they were stocktaking." Shaw laughed out loud at that one as she eased her foot on to the brake pedal.

Vehicles were backing up at a narrow junction, a small, broken-down van with a Sharp's Super-Kreem Toffee legend on the side the obvious cause. The driver was peering in at the engine. A policeman stood alongside, directing traffic with rigid arm jerks like a clockwork tin soldier. Shaw waited patiently. Even in the mist, her Jaguar, sprayed ivory, stood out among the tar-barrel colour of other cars. It even sported whitewalls. She liked feeling a bit Hollywood. As if she was Joan Crawford. Or Hedy Lamarr. Shaw gave the policeman a raised glove as she eventually slid passed the stricken vehicle. A formal salute was offered in return, the policeman's white armlets almost luminous in the light rays of the street lamp.

Plenty of gaps were visible outside the imposing Italianate Gothic pile housing the Wool Exchange, the place where material was still traded and prices set and which still exerted an influence, though waning, on the world wool market. Slipping the three-speed automatic gearbox – specially ordered – into reverse, she expertly backed the sixteen-foot long car into a slot.

"I can always tell, Arthur, when my mother-in-law is coming to stay. All the mice in the house throw themselves on the traps." She giggled again as her hand switched off the ignition.

The Exchange, a fantastical confection with a one hundred and fifty foot, pinnacled clock tower, was constructed out of local sandstone, its honey hue long metamorphosed into pitch black under the remorseless attack of pollution. Ten thousand tons of carbon and ash and sixty thousand gallons of tar tumbled down on the city every year, her husband had once told her. The figures were so monstrous they had rooted in her memory.

Into this lung-busting filth, Jennifer Shaw strode quickly, snuggling into her Jaeger camel hair and nap cloth coat with slanting front and huge petal collar. She had plenty of time for some shopping before meeting her brother. He seemed troubled and had pressed her to meet him. Not that she ever harboured much sympathy for Anthony. He was too much of an empty vessel for her liking, and too much of a chancer.

A welcoming warmth enveloped her as she strode into the dark-wood, Dickensian interior of Rimmington, the chemists. She passed the banks of drawers with their labels of mysteriously named potions and concoctions, and the marble notice board advertising antitoxic serums, and arrived at the cosmetics counter. The face of the Sphinx was starting to reveal a few cracks and that required remedial masonry work. Luckily, the counter was free of customers.

"Hello. Have you got any Pan-Stik." Her voice was cheery.

"We certainly do, madam. Let's see. Small jar?"

"Er, no. I think we need a big one."

"Alright. It says here Ann Blyth recommends it but I wasn't sure who she was. An actress I now know." The shop assistant pointed at a cardboard cut-out of the American starlet promoting Max Factor's foundation cream. Shaw could hear a man behind her, with a nasty croak, ask for a bottle of Owbridge's cough syrup. She needed lipstick.

"Have you got any Revlon 'Love That Red'?"

"We don't, I'm afraid. I don't know when it's coming in. We've got Revlon's 'Red Tape', if that will do?"

Purchases in her bag, Shaw doubled back past the Wool Exchange. As she sauntered along the pavement, the obituary of Henri Matisse she had read that morning in the newspaper slipped back into her head. She recalled seeing his paintings somewhere, odd twisted figures in searing technicolour. Various shades of black and grey were all that confronted her now as she turned up towards the Midland Hotel where she was meeting her brother.

Two men on ladders were vigorously propelling long brushes as they pasted up a large advertising poster against the side of a building. "Ride the Sunbeam" it said, a man in white mac and black homburg resting his hand on the roof of the car and beaming himself, as if he'd scooped the Pools.

Passing by the Midland's tall dome sat atop an octagonal tower, its arches decorated by dragons, Shaw entered the hotel. Designed by the chief architect of the Midland railway as a showcase of the company's authority, it was a testament to untrammelled Victorian confidence. On one side, a corridor led guests to the magnificent Princess Ballroom with its colossal chandelier. On the other, wide U-shaped stairs, reminiscent of a baronial mansion, pointed to the French Ballroom containing a ceiling so ornate it looked like the work of a wedding cake maker.

Shaw headed straight on into the busy lobby, wafting her way through the smoke of a hundred Capstan Full Strengths. Anthony was standing with his back to the bar, drink and small cigar in the same hand. Even from a distance he looked supercilious, a lanky and handsome streak of contemptuous disdain with no backbone. He saw her and offered a small wave. Even that simple movement seemed loaded with sarcasm. She shouldered her way through the crowd.

Anthony was wearing a deep mustard-yellow jacket, cravat and black slacks. "Hi, sis. Dressed to kill as usual. Always a bit too exotic for this town. What can I get you?"

Only one barman was on. Sweat beaded his forehead as he struggled with the orders. She caught his eye and he migrated over.

"Hello, Mrs Shaw. What would you like?"

"Yes, hello. Now let me see."

"This has just arrived." The barman held up a bottle of Chivas Regal. "They've resurrected this brand just this year after God knows how long. It's a twelve-year-old."

"Fine, I'll have it with some water please."

A booming noise engulfed the bar, a formless, flat-pitched din born out of countless conversations about piston rings, worsted shipments and golf handicaps. Tobacco smoke billowed in layers, reminding her of those peculiar formations referred to as mushroom clouds that occurred when they set off an atomic bomb.

"So what's the trouble?" Shaw turned to her brother. "You sounded worried on the phone. Not blown your last thru'penny bit on a horse?" She extracted from her handbag a silver lighter, with the Shaw name engraved on one side, and tossed it on to the bartop.

"Surprisingly, no. I'm managing alright at the moment. Never thought flogging cars off a driveway would be my forte. I'm turning quite a few pennies, thank you very much. You've got to do something for yourself when it's not laid out for you on a plate."

Anthony always delivered his lines with a touch of spite, his sister thought. After following her up from the family home in Surrey, he had wasted most of his adult life in the West Riding, apart from the war. Her husband had given him several jobs, but he'd shown no interest and even less aptitude. She had forked out to buy him a small house in a nice area on the edge of the city, and he'd eked out a life, financially supported by her husband. In her view Anthony was still chasing rainbows, like a starry-eyed teenager but with a streak of delinquency. Only he wasn't much younger than she.

The whisky arrived, the barman neatly placing a coaster on the bar top then ruining the moment by plonking the glass on the coaster's edge so it nearly toppled over. "Sorry, madam."

"That's alright." Shaw knocked back a good mouthful. "So what is it Anthony? Another scheme to make a mint? Only you need a suitcase full of readies from somewhere." Her brother pulled a face. "What was the last plan? Holiday trips to see the old Japanese prisoner of war camps? Except no-one could afford it. Oh, and no one wants to go back to the hell holes where they were starved and tortured. Can't imagine why. Apart from all that it was hunky-dory."

She was being cruel and apologised. Her brother stuffed a packet of small cigars back into a pocket of his Italian car coat that was draped over a bar stool. "Forget it, sis. Anyway, that wasn't a plan, just an idea that came and went."

Some of her husband's business pals were starting to circle, grinning in her direction as if practising for one of those ghastly Cumberland gurning contests. Most of Stephen's chums were gentlemanly in that rather old-fashioned northern way she had come to respect, but a few were not so kindly. Why were they always the ones with pencil moustaches and oily hair?

"It's nothing to do with business." Anthony threw a mouthful of beer down his throat. "I got myself into some trouble yesterday and I wanted to check where I stand on the legal side. I wonder if you could set up a meeting tomorrow with your solicitors and come along with me."

"Is this a police matter? I mean, what have you done?"

He stubbed out the remains of the cigar, then pulled out from a trouser pocket a pack of Senior Service. "I don't want to talk about it today. Let's just talk it through with the solicitors tomorrow."

"Well, is it business or criminal? Maurice Black will need to know."

"It's more on the criminal side. Let's leave it for now."

"Honestly, Anthony, you could have just told me on the telephone this morning and saved me the journey in."

"I thought it would be nice to meet up. Anyway, I do have a commercial idea I wanted to put to Stephen this afternoon and wondered what you thought of it."

"I knew it."

Her brother did not seem to be in too much of a funk after all. If he wanted to talk double Dutch that was his business. She had a nice day planned for later on and wasn't going to let Anthony's worries put the kibosh on it. She needed to be at that meeting with the solicitors though. Her husband did not cope well with bad surprises.

She took a long slug of the whisky and lit another Pall Mall, blowing smoke up to the ceiling in a long stream. Swivelling on the stool to scan the room, her attention was distracted by a blonde woman negotiating her way through the bar in the direction of reception. Shaw didn't recognise her. A blue satin sleeveless dress with wide front pockets adorned her rake-thin body which soon disappeared into the middle of a group of men from, whence a loud collective laugh followed seconds later. The dress was one from the upcoming Hardy Amies collection. There was no doubt about it. Where the hell had she got that from? Shaw asked herself. Obviously the Sphinx wasn't the only one shelling out a bundle to acquire an unforgettable look.

CHAPTER 3

If that day had been a clear one, and if Ray Stafford had trained the Kershaw binoculars – always kept in the boot of his car – on the city as he stared through the bust window of Number Three Back End Villas, he might have noticed a tall man looking out at the world. This was a rather patrician-looking figure with a slightly beaky nose and wearing a suit made of the best worsted money could buy. Standing at one of the five windows in his gargantuan oak-panelled office, Stephen Shaw was deep in thought as he eyed the rectilinear blocks of nearby rooftops, baleful in the soggy dullness.

The chairman of one of the city's proudest companies felt uneasy. His slight tetchiness over his wife's clothes bill was not the source of his discomfort. God knows though, the tab was big enough. Maybe the state of their temporary kitchen while the builders were in was getting him down, he thought. No. What was feeding his anxiety, he knew, was the report by time and motion people on the mill's future manpower needs.

"Cost effectiveness of new machinery expenditure versus labour recruitment in the Indian subcontinent" was the report's to-the-point title. He had read the report twice, then deposited it in a desk drawer for a couple of months before extracting the twenty pages of close-knit typing and eventually acting on the recommendations.

That the wheels were now in motion gave him a sense of relief, mixed with a feeling of disquiet. That was not a welcome state of affairs for someone who normally steered a path through life as rock-solidly sure as the stone with which Shaw's mill was built.

There was a gentle knock on his open door, and he turned from the window to see his secretary, the bird-like Miss Holroyd, march straight in. "Production schedules for next month, Mr Shaw. Worsted figures are on the top, then casement cloth and silk."

"Thanks, Barbara. Any chance of a tea with some biscuits?"

His secretary wore horn rims that, rather curiously, gave her an Oriental appearance. That, and her flinty manner, earned her in the typing pool, the nickname Hirohito Holroyd.

As he looked back through the window, Shaw told himself that all that mattered was the survival of the company. In truth, that is all that did matter. An image briefly appeared in his mind, a scale with shiny new equipment carrying a mammoth price tag on one side and a map of West Pakistan on the other. There was no arguing the sums. Or was there? There was certainly no question something had to be done. A commercial tornado was about to dump into the dustbin a big chunk of the city's woollen industry. And then screw down the lid for good measure and boot it into the gutter. Cheap foreign competition and man-made fibres. The twin devils from Hades.

His task was to ensure that Shaw's was one of the survivors. A pivotal slot in the lofty history of the company beckoned, and he was the man for the challenge. His son, Alan, taking his time joining the business but now on an Australian sheep farm learning the trade from the ground up, ensured that the family line was intact.

From his vantage point on the fifth floor, it seemed perverse to be so pessimistic. The yard teemed with activity. The company's lorries in their smart green and blue livery readied themselves for the road, fully loaded. The ageing Hattersley looms and the semi-automatic Northrops were working flat out. Shaw's was proud to be one of the shrinking number of so-called vertical mills. It did everything, taking in the fibres, washing, combing and spinning them, then weaving top quality material in weights never seen before.

In his luxurious eyrie, Stephen Shaw scanned the immediate horizon his predecessors had created. Designed by Lockwood and Mawson, the same venerable local architects responsible for the Wool Exchange, the mill was another example of boastful Victorian swagger. Its chairman never took for granted the mill's massive architectural power. He loved it too much. He often stood and admired its features, like the bold cornice with large dentils and panelled parapet encircling the whole structure like steel bands. The walls of the two staircase towers, each capped by a squat pyramidal roof, had been demanded by his grandfather, Esau Shaw, so they would project like castle bastions.

Directly below his office, polished pink granite columns standing on corbelled bases flanked Shaw's main doors. The entrance was designed to intimidate. Along the mill's frontage and above the entrance, Stephen Shaw's father, Jeremiah, had added a colonnade of spikes mimicking a mosque he once visited in Sarajevo. The mill's chimney included a high parapet with chamfered stone openings designed to ape the spire of a cathedral. It was a legacy his ancestors were entrusting to him from their grave.

Bradford's wool magnates felt such vast monuments of wealth were as symbolic of the potency of their businesses as were skyscrapers for New York's bankers and industrialists. Stephen Shaw was well aware that the company, and the family for that matter, were not in the same league as the most powerful wool dynasties, like the Illingworths, Fosters and Listers. Shaw could just make out through the gloom the two massive blocks making up Manningham Mills, one of the world's biggest industrial complexes when the Listers built it. A fifth of a mile long, the mills enclosed sixteen acres of floor area. They were topped by a chimney two hundred and fifty feet high whose construction consumed eight thousand tons of stone.

Alright, Shaw and Sons might not be the biggest fish in the pond but it did employ over a thousand people. The future of those workers and that of the company rested on his shoulders. Remember the tough decisions previous generations of wool barons must have made, he said to himself as he contemplated the new course of action the company might take.

He watched a driver down below munch through a breakfast teacake as he rested against the cab of one of the company's new, eight-axle Albions. It was extraordinary how some of the company's workers dressed like vagabonds. Shaw wondered whether the company should give the wagon men uniforms, then dismissed the idea. The mill would be laughed out of the wool association and, anyway, the drivers would refuse to wear them.

Shaw turned away from the window, sat down at his desk and pulled the production schedules over towards him. In one of the desk's large tooled-leather insets, the company's chairman kept a selection of pens from his Parker collection.

They included a Cordovan brown 51 with sixteen-carat gold-filled cap, a 51 in Nassau green with jewelled cap and a standard 51 but with a handcrafted barrel in hammered silver. He selected a Parker Flighter and worked down the production schedules. He then signed them off and slid the sheets into his out tray. The Flighter, bought in New York three years earlier during a week-long holiday, always reminded him of that trip – flying to and from Idlewild in the Stratocruiser with its full-size beds, and sipping manhattans at twenty thousand feet in the plane's lounge below the main passenger deck. He was even wearing the Boeing 377 tiepin at that very moment, a nice memento of the Pan American clipper service.

He looked around his office, his eyes resting on the two identical George the Third mahogany longcase clocks made in Scotland, the trunk doors sporting a Masonic plaque (a nice touch, considering). One of the office's corners housed a burr-maple desk inlaid with rosewood and brass. Another corner was taken up with a very large work desk fashioned by the company's own carpenters. With his door open, Shaw could see beyond the Biedermeier-style walnut ottomans in the inner office to the tiny, brittle figure of Miss Holroyd. She was operating her own secretarial control centre from a large office, also expensively panelled and carpeted.

Stephen Shaw pulled towards him the time and motion report which he'd been taking another look at.

"To meet current demand, maximise productivity and reduce unit costs, the company needs to run its machinery twenty-four hours a day," the report said. "However, the labour pool is not capable of meeting this demand. Scores of hands from the Ukraine, Poland and Yugoslavia have recently been absorbed by the company. They have settled in well and proved themselves hard working and able. Some, like Zibby Dabkowski, have a toehold in junior management already. Yet it is becoming increasingly difficult to attract people to work night shifts. The company needs to employ people who will work night shifts, or consider a technical, machine-based alternative."

Miss Holroyd walked in, depositing a tray of tea and ginger biscuits and removing the production schedules. He tried to imagine her Japanese goose-stepping but couldn't quite picture it and returned his attention to the papers in front of him. "As this report has outlined, a possible alternative to new labour would be new equipment offering greater automation and productivity. Here are the figures." He inspected again the cost of more automated Northrops, and the probable expenditure required to purchase very advanced Sulzers now under development. The prices were enough to burst a blood vessel.

Shaw's chairman deposited the report into his office's small Chatwood safe and, out of habit, tapped the face of the mahogany barometer by Agnew & Zanetti of Manchester before returning to the window. He contemplated his decision to press the 'go' button, at least to get the ball rolling. The decision had already been taken. That was why Tommy Nelson was, at that very moment, airborne. That was why the company's production manager was on a mission to meet local agents and discuss the type and quantity of labour Shaw's might require. That was why Tommy Nelson would soon be touching down in Karachi. The news was not always good from West Pakistan. The chairman imagined the manager as he jetted over the Arabian Sea. Good luck, Tommy, he thought ruefully.

CHAPTER 4

The broken carcasses of houses under demolition filled the immediate neighbourhood as the Riley pulled away from Back End Villas and steered towards the pretty township of Ilkley. Detective Inspector Ray Stafford stretched his legs in the back of the Pathfinder's roomy cabin, took out his mottled-green Conway Stewart fountain pen and jotted down a few notes about the chimney skeleton. He then put the notebook away, his mind drifting to the crime he had been called out to on the moors. Very soon he would experience the intoxicating mixture of tension and adrenalin policemen thrived on. Especially those with his particular psyche.

The car worked its way down one of the main arterial routes out of the city. It passed the Essoldo, the gaudy lettering above the cinema's doors advertising *The Creature from the Black Lagoon*. It motored along the front of Busby's department store, its milky-coloured frontage, punctured by dormers, turrets and circular, corbelled pinnacles, resembling a seaside version of London's main law courts. City's soccer ground loomed down the slope, great slabs of industrial-size wood and tin sheds, hemmed in by ranks of cobbled streets sliding into the gloom.

"I don't think English football clubs are going to join these European competitions," one of the officers in front was saying. "Maybe they think it's beneath them or something. The newspapers seem to think Scottish football teams will sign up."

They had ground to a near standstill behind a small lorry crabbing forward at a slug's pace. Its chassis was buckled and twisted, deformed by years of heavy work. The vehicle's rear suspension had virtually collapsed on one side, its load of rusting industrial barrels, tied loosely with rope, tilting over at a treacherous slant. "Maudsley Haulage. Secure Handling" was painted on the back. The police driver activated the gong, the noise of the bell making the wagon stop. As they overtook, the driver peered at them out of his side window and stalled the engine.

The oppressive atmosphere of terraced back-to-backs quickly gave way to grander homes and tree-lined streets in the suburbs. The city seemed to breathe a sigh of relief as it spread out from its cheerless inner core.

"I've been reading about this attempt they're going to make in the summer to break the four-minute mile. Seems beyond belief they could do that. What do you think, Mr Stafford?"

The radio telephone operator, behind whom Stafford was sitting, seemed a bit unkempt to the detective inspector's eye. That couldn't be said of the young driver. His uniform insignia shimmered, even with no sunlight, as if dunked for a week in a tin of Brasso. The uniform itself appeared steamed clean. Creases were knife-edged. He wondered if he used one of those Corby clothes presses found in upmarket hotel bedrooms. He could see too that the driver's hands were encased in non-regulation gloves. Instead of standard issue leathers, these were much longer, a stubby version of the gauntlets favoured by police motorcyclists.

The call sign for their car came over the Pye's open broadcast channel, and the RT officer took down a few instructions about the precise location of the body. "Turn where? Is it signposted? How wide is the track? I mean, can we get the car up there? Blimey, Madge, if we're not back by next week send out a search party will you?"

The Riley filtered off at an unmarked fork in the road and descended into the valley of the river Aire. The hefty bulk of Salt's mill hove into view, surrounded by the company village of solid, stone buildings its Victorian founder, Titus Salt, created. The scene was partly obscured by a decrepit hoarding resting on wood stilts, some of which were splintering to the point of breakage. Adverts for Thelson Oils and Mullard radio components – "Careless Listening Costs Valves" – peeled away in soggy chunks.

Stafford reluctantly offered up some conversation. "How do you find the new car?"

"It's big and comfortable, sir, but I'm hearing it's getting a nickname in the motor trade. Ditchfinder, not Pathfinder, because it doesn't handle very well. I think they've got a point. This one is the constabulary's first under trial. Plenty of space I'm sure in the back though, even for you."

Curling its way up from the valley floor, the road weaved past sturdy houses of doctors, accountants and factory and mill managers. The driver worked hard with the stubby gear lever, down to the right of his seat, as the car fought the steep inclines.

Air was sweeter up here. Yet every pore of the stones making up the walls criss-crossing the fields stored a century of soot. Tentacles of smoke reaching out from the city below had left them monochrome black.

As the car rose up on to the hilltops, a wild expanse of open country appeared suddenly. Small fields gave way to uncultivated land, sandstone replaced by diamond-hard gritstone. The lonely stretches of wind-tortured moor and the overheated cabin lulled Stafford into another bout of self-absorption. His wife's death at thirty-four, less than two years before, had left him rudderless. With his parents long departed, taking their calming practicality with them, he had backed himself into a cul-de-sac. A blanket of private lethargy, punctured by obsessive, if often unproductive, work had descended on him during the past two years. He stayed in the office too long. At home he slumped in front of the television, watching the limited programmes the BBC transmitted. He occasionally went down to the pub. When he could be bothered. On free days he walked in the Dales, sandwiches, a flask of tea and the Kershaws in a rucksack. Would it have been better if they had had children? He didn't know. He was stuck in quicksand from which he knew he must escape. Yet he couldn't wind himself up to make even a cursory stab at that.

"We had a reasonable time in Blackpool last year but the digs were rubbish." The driver was off again. "We're thinking of going to Filey this time. The bed and breakfast we had, right on the seafront, had the worst grub you could bloody imagine. The gravy always came out in a congealed lump like brown blancmange. I like a bit of grease with my cooked breakfast but the fried eggs were floating. Everyone in the dining room just about stopped eating, but we all kept turning up as it was already paid for."

Overtaking a steam-powered traction engine, they all looked round at the antique machine, still in work harness, tugging a trailer loaded with scrap iron.

"Then there was a right muck up with some tickets. My grandparents had booked for all of us to see Edmundo Ros at the Winter Gardens. My uncle had even bought a yellow shirt with pineapples on it to get into the calypso mood. Don't know where he'd got it from. Trouble was, the grandparents had got the date wrong and it turned out to be Winifred Atwell. Uncle sat in the crowd, looking like a light bulb, as she banged away on the piano keys."

The Riley was now plunging into Ilkley Moor. An oval-shaped piece of wilderness stretching over seventeen hundred acres, the moorland was an outcrop of sombre and hard millstone grit. It occasionally took on a persona of sullen intimidation. In poor weather, the atmosphere could turn spooky. This was a quality stoked by ancient monuments and peculiar Bronze Age markings left by unknown tribes. The most common of these were circles made around small depressions in the stone and called 'cup and rings'.

The driver steered the car past the cluster of rocks known as the Cow and Calf, then turned on to a single lane towards Hebers Ghyll. A mile or so along, the car swung into a dirt track feeding back into the centre of the moor. The track degraded into soft mud after a few hundred yards. Here, a number of vehicles were parked on a large grass-surfaced rock overhang.

They halted alongside one of the local station cars, a Wolseley with pre-war style running boards and stand-up headlights. Stafford got out and walked over to the police surgeon. Gordon McCrone was sitting on the edge of his car seat, legs dangling out of the open driver's door. A tartan travelling rug was wrapped across his knees and a doorstep sandwich filled one hand. The other hand gripped the cup top of a hot drinks flask in which the elderly Scot always kept a pint of Grant's Standfast whisky. Stafford could hear classical music flowing from the Humber's interior. The car's His Master's Voice radio imparted a heavy bass tone. McCrone's nickname in the force, Mac the Knife, had never seemed less appropriate.

The doctor lifted the cup in greeting. "Nice view, detective inspector. Well it would be if you could see a bit more through this bloody mist." He took a bite from the sandwich. "I've given the subject a cursory inspection. It's definitely murder as any ten-year-old playing Cluedo would know. I'll make a further examination in situ before the body is taken away. Then I'll be down in the city to examine your chimney sweep. That one sounds like a candidate for the McCrone casebook."

He gulped down a mouthful of alcohol. "Don't get your feet wet up there, laddie." A grey and green patina of mud and grass covered the bottom half of McCrone's wellingtons.

Stafford exchanged a few pleasantries with the doctor, then went across the track and over to Ron Twelves. The local plain-clothes sergeant was huddled in a raincoat which was clearly failing to offer enough insulation against the damp chill. He had pulled his shoulders up into his neck. Like the detective inspector, Twelves served in the Fleet Air Arm during the war. They hadn't met then, and crossed paths only occasionally now.

"Morning, sir. This is a bad one." Twelves raised an ankle-high hiking boot and rested it on a clump of rock. "The body was found by a couple out fell-walking. The two are pretty ancient but they were kitted out for a strenuous trek. They came back down to their car and told someone, who was just arriving, to drive back to the telephone box on the main road while they waited for us to arrive. They are still sitting in their car over there. I've told them they can go home but they haven't moved."

Their brisk constitutional having been abruptly terminated by the work of a killer, the pair were clearly stunned into inactivity as they stared out bleakly through the windscreen of their little car.

Stafford went over and tapped on the side window. The woman, with a strikingly blotchy complexion, wound down the glass.

"Please go home now. Thanks for your help. We have a lot of work to do here."

"Ooo, sorry." He watched their old Ford Prefect putter off down the track, springs creaking.

Stafford walked back and pointed at the cars on the site. "Look, Ron, why have all these vehicles been allowed in so close to the site?"

"There's just no possibility, sir, of getting an imprint on car tyres." Twelves stared up at the fell. "The body was almost certainly left here sometime yesterday, according to McCrone. Far too much water flooded down the hillside last night and this morning to get anything on that front. The track is either too marshy or too stony."

The two set off up a gully, the boggy turf seeping water within seconds into Stafford's brogues. "Christ Almighty. How far up here?"

"About a hundred yards, sir."

"Christ."

By the time the two had hauled themselves up to the gully's head, Stafford could not feel where his feet ended and his sodden shoes began. Several officers, all in waterproof footwear Stafford noted irritably, stood around a large mass of rock. It was split almost in two by a wide, shallow crevasse. The body of a fully-clothed girl lay in the fissure, one leg bent backwards and the head lolling loosely over a stone. Some kind of cloth bag hung off the top of her head, and what looked like electrical cable was tied round her neck. The cabling was thick with odd-looking outer striping in orange and green.

"She looks about eighteen or nineteen." Twelves took out a notebook but didn't open it. "The bag was tied loosely around her head with another piece of cable. The first officers on the scene lifted the bag off. There's no sign of identification, jewellery or handbag. However she got here, someone probably dragged or carried her a fair distance. She would hardly have walked up here of her own free will, given what she was wearing."

He pointed behind them. "There's a long grassy slope descending towards us as you can see, and there's a track on the other side up there, but the track is not wide enough for a car."

Twelves turned back to the rock crevasse. "You can see her shoes. It looks as if they weren't on her when she was pushed down there. The shoes seem to have been chucked in separately."

Stafford knelt on the boulder to get a closer look. The dead girl was snub-nosed and probably pretty, with natural blonde hair. To his untrained eye, she was dressed rather well in a dark blue skirt and light blue blouse. Despite the cabling, he could see that her neck was a mass of bruises and striations.

He turned away and gazed over Ilkley below. Phantom-like in the light fog, the town was the home of the wealthy, and those not so wealthy, but lucky to be living there. Its reputation as a spa town rested on a simple cold stream oozing from the hillside rather than proper sulphurous water enjoyed by its neighbour, Harrogate. The tops of the town's huge hydropathic establishments, Craiglands and Ben Rhydding, and the complex roofs of Ilkley's more imposing homes created a serrated skyline, even in the mist.

Stafford looked back over the moorland. Desolate and threatening, it was a terrible place to die, if this was where she was killed, and to die so violently. Was it any worse than a lingering death from the disease whose name most people were too squeamish to speak? Stafford's colleagues baulked at inquiring into his state of mind. Stafford wondered if that was because of the type of illness that took Diana's life. Maybe it was because he was so uncommunicative at the best of times and they thought it wasn't worth the bother.

Stafford took out his notebook. Even though the investigation could not slide into overdrive until they knew her name, he decided his men must be up and running, right from the off. He wrote out a list of everything he could think of, from the chain of command to responsibilities for press relations, and methods to get local townsfolk involved at the start. He gave instructions for the kind of search he wanted around the site and where the extra manpower to tackle the job would come from.

Once satisfied that everyone at the site knew what they had to do, he headed back along the gully. Half way down he met McCrone on the way back up. The doctor raised a hand to a sweating forehead. "The bastard could have been a bit more considerate about where he left the poor lassie." He was puffing heavily as his wellingtons fought for grip.

At the bottom, Stafford flipped open his notebook again and wrote down a few items he had forgotten up on the fellside. He then crossed the track to his car. A quizzical look was written across the face of the RT officer. "Sergeant Feather has been on, sir. He says he's identified Father Christmas, whatever that means."

CHAPTER 5

She was back now on home territory, her magnificent house in sight on the hillside.

The Mark VII Jennifer Shaw drove was one of the first Jaguars equipped with double petrol tanks. She had run down one tank some days ago and, having thrown the dashboard switch to the second tank, was on the point of running entirely dry, according to the car's single fuel gauge. The Shaws used Dibb's garage on the edge of Ilkley as much as possible as the operating manual in Stephen's Bentley recommended its Fina brand of petrol. She was relieved to reach the garage with a dash of juice to spare.

Distracted by thoughts of her brother, she mistakenly halted at the standard grade pump, then nudged forward to the premier grade, switched off the ignition and slid out from the blue leather upholstery. Hers was the only car there and the pump attendant had almost reached the vehicle from the service hut, despite his pronounced limp.

"Good afternoon, Mrs Shaw."

"Afternoon, Harry. Fill her up, please, both tanks. They are almost empty."

"Right you are." The elderly attendant, whom she had known for years, flipped up the closest rear wing flap and activated the pump. Shaw walked away a few paces and stretched her back, pondering the position her brother had got himself in. No clue about her brother's discomfort had been forthcoming. She wondered whether she'd even get to the bottom of it at the solicitors. As Bogart might say, the chances of Anthony coughing up the whole truth were none and slim and slim had quit town. She pulled out a cigarette and lit up.

Acres of school playing fields stretched away in the distance behind the garage. A dishevelled line of children on a cross-country run snaked across the grass, all the kids wearing white vests and black plimsolls. On the pavement outside the garage, a man, walking his dog, was wrapped up in a duffle coat, all the toggles tied. She recognised the coat as one of the new Gloveralls.

A red British Road Services flatbed wagon, its load covered in tarpaulin, pulled up outside the petrol station, partially blocking the exit. The driver clambered down from the cab and walked into the cafe next door. Visibility was much improved now and the drizzle petering out. The far distant slopes of the Yorkshire Dales were visible. An occasional shaft of sunlight came and went. It was still rather dark though and would soon be getting darker.

Harry closed off the second flap and slammed the nozzle back into the pump. "She took almost seventeen gallons. That'll be three pounds, thirteen shillings and tuppence, Mrs Shaw."

Handing over four one pound notes, she trailed his awkward, swinging gait to the hut. She pondered how ordinary people could afford well over four bob for a gallon of petrol, but then thought that, of course, they couldn't. She also wondered how Harry ever found anything in the hut, it was so congested. Things for sale – oils, cleaning fluids, cloths, gauges, batteries – reduced space for customers to an area not much bigger than a doormat. A stack of new tyres, under a "Dunlop" banner, looked as if it might topple over. An advert for re-treads hung from the ceiling. Shaw focused on Harry's grubby hands as he wrestled with the cash register, and she slipped off a glove to accept the change. Her sweet tooth played up. Right now she could demolish a Fry's chocolate cream bar, but couldn't be bothered walking across the road to the sweet and tobacconists.

"Thanks, Harry. See you soon."

"Bye, Mrs Shaw."

The air was turning sluggish and she was glad to be back in the warm, cavernous interior of the car. She stubbed out the cigarette in the Jag's ashtray. The BRS lorry still obstructed the exit as she moved away from the forecourt. The driver exited the cafe, a filled teacake the size of a plate wedged in his hand. Catching sight of the blocked Jaguar, the driver broke into a trot. Shaw signalled him to slow down but he didn't notice. A cloud of dense black smoke belched from under the vehicle as it moved forward. She drove into the road, tooting her horn as a courtesy.

*****

Pennymore, Jennifer Shaw's palatial home, was a product of the motor car. Yorkshire's wool magnates once built some of Britain's biggest private houses. Milner Field possessed the bulk of a large city hospital, with power architecture on a "Wagnerian" scale. All of the twenty-eight bedrooms at Oakworth House boasted hot and cold running water. Heating for the mansion, glass houses and winter garden depended on six thousand feet of cast iron piping, a range of furnaces and boilers and three specially-made reservoirs for water supply. Encrusting vast Cliffe Castle were so many domes, pinnacles and towers it looked like the architectural ravings of a delusional Bavarian king. Some of these "brass castles", as remarkable as the palazzos of northern Italy, had already been chopped up or demolished, ghosts of an even more extravagant era.

Esau Shaw poured a chunk of the early profits from his mill into a substantial mansion on the edge of Bradford's Manningham district, a handy fifteen minute clip-clop away by carriage and pair. But once the car arrived, Bradford's wealthy, including the Shaws, moved further out. The Shaw's new family home was constructed in Scots baronial style. With nine bedrooms, four reception, a "motor home" for four cars, and set in three acres of landscaped grounds, Pennymore was a compact take on the massive Littlemoor. That mansion had been created for one of the Foster family of Black Dyke Mills. To Littlemoor's armoury of crow-stepped gables and towers, the Shaws added a theme of bartizans which dominated every corner.

Into the long gravel driveway of Pennymore, Jennifer Shaw turned her car. The builders replacing the kitchen were using part of the garage for storage, so its doors now stood open. She eased the Jag alongside her other motor and got out, noticing that one of the chocolate brown front wings of the Armstrong Siddeley had changed colour. She frowned, took off a glove and ran her finger through what was obviously cement powder or some such builder's material. Fortunately, the hood of the large drophead was up or else the leather seats would have been coated.

Striding round the side of the house, she spotted Archie Tyzack's building team sprawled out under cover of the monumental drive-through porch, tucking into a very late lunch. They all tried to get up at once.

"Take it easy, chaps. We all need to eat. How's it going, Mr Tyzack?"

He was on his feet now, brushing crumbs off his front. "Fine, Mrs Shaw. We're staying a bit longer this evening, if that's alright. We're having an early tea."

"Oh, right. No, that's grand. Just let Mrs Williams know your movements. No problems up to now?"

"None that you don't know about." This prompted a few smirks from the rest of the team. A shutter in Shaw's mind briefly opened and took a snapshot of the scene in front of her. Five men of about the same height, that is about two inches less than hers, all wearing white overalls with a rule poking out of a back pocket, and a pencil stub wedged behind an ear. They were like extras in a Laurel and Hardy movie – one of those shorts in which a house under renovation suddenly tumbles into a pile of rubble as the incompetent duo breezily obliterates one structural wall too many. Fortunately, the Archie Tyzacks of this world were as dependable as concrete, she thought, as she strode past the men, a cloud of Elizabeth Arden's Blue Grass descending on the potted meat sandwich prepared that morning by Mrs Tyzack.

Tossing on to a divan in the hallway her crocodile skin bag with brass trimmings, she walked down the corridor to the second hall, turned left down another corridor and then right into a third corridor, poking her head into the kitchen on the way. What used to be the kitchen, that is. She had told Stephen that morning that it looked like the Luftwaffe had returned on a revenge raid. The Aga, installed by Stephen's deceased mother, was now a memory, along with all its attendant pipework. The stubborn sod virtually needed dynamiting before they could shift it. That was "the problem". The auxiliary coal-fired oven was gone, no loss there, Shaw reasoned, as well as all the cupboard units, tiles and sink. The old Thomson-Houston fridge was plugged into a socket in the temporary kitchenette next door.

Jennifer Shaw was going for an American-style fitted kitchen. Only it was German. She'd examined a few English ones but, unenthused, latched on to Janet Tomlinson's Poggenpohl. Altogether too modern for Stephen, so Janet, the sport, shot some photos of it and handed over the brochure. Archie was basically copying it, but in teak. She had wanted a modern work surface but couldn't understand the brochure's reference to Resopal until Archie informed her it was German for Formica.

What was it about the Krauts, Shaw considered. How come they were turning out kitchens like this? She seemed to remember they had lost the war, or was she missing something? She was even buying a German front-loading washing machine. An enjoyable Rhine cruise two years ago had revealed a Germany beginning to look gorgeous again. Yet photographs of London's East End seemed to show a desolate, bombed-out landscape, still frozen in time somewhere around nineteen forty-two.

The kitchen though was not of first importance to her. All things culinary were the preserve of Mrs Williams. Where was Mrs Williams?

"Mrs Williams," she shouted. No answer. Shaw backtracked and headed into the main living room, its grand picture windows overlooking the little lake. No sign of Mrs Williams' husband who performed the duties of handyman, nor the gardener, nor Phyllis, the maid. It was like the *Mary Celeste*.

Shaw manipulated, to the letter 'B', the chrome marker on the gold-coloured telephone organiser, pressed the button, read off the number, and dialled Maurice Black, the family and company solicitor. While she waited for the phone to answer at the other end, she pondered the idea of buying German equipment and using Jewish services, but her brain couldn't fabricate anything amusing out of the obvious juxtaposition. The Shaws' dentist, doctor and accountant were also Jewish. There was a synagogue somewhere in Bradford, she knew, but wasn't sure where. Her thoughts were interrupted by the voice of the receptionist.

"Hello, Miriam. It's Jennifer Shaw. I wondered if Maurice was free for a minute?"

"Hold on, Mrs Shaw, I think he might be. I'll just check."

Mrs Williams' sturdy frame crossed in front of the window, a potted plant in the housekeeper's hands. She had obviously fled the house now her kitchen lay in ruins.

"Hello, Jennifer. Maurice here. What can I do for you on this bright, tropical day?"

"Oh, if only. Look, Maurice, I wondered if you had a little time free tomorrow. My brother, you know Anthony, is worried about something and needs to see you about it, with me in tow."

"Can you give me a clue about what it's about?" Maurice Black's voice owned a singsong quality, rather high pitched for a man.

"He wouldn't tell me."

"Sounds a bit mysterious."

"Oh I'm sure it's not really, but he just needs to make sure he's okay with whatever it is he's worried about." That useless sentence about summed up her non-existent grasp of Anthony's troubles.

"What about twelve-thirty tomorrow? At my office, I assume."

"That would be absolutely fine. I'd have tried to see you today only I had another appointment. We'll be there."

She put the phone down. Another appointment, my eye. Stephen was eating at his club in Bradford, and she was meeting up with some of her girlfriends in the Regency bar of Harrogate's Majestic Hotel, followed by dinner with them at the Old Swan. She could nearly taste the first pink gin slipping down her gullet. She switched on the French ormolu side lamp and flicked through the second post deposited by Mrs Williams on the side table. Still no postcard from Alan. Why couldn't the boy keep in touch a bit more?

Shaw scooted upstairs, dived into her own en-suite bathroom, upturned a fresh Cussons Imperial Leather from its box, and enjoyed a quick wash. She was running late. She dowsed herself with another blast of Blue Grass. Most of her pals opted for Chanel No.5 or Joy but she could stomach neither of them. Back in the bedroom, she considered changing her twin-set in lupin blue, decided against it but kicked off her medium heels and chose a pair of Roger Vivier with three inch, steel-tipped stilettos. The Sphinx liked people to hear she was coming. On the way out, Shaw grabbed one of her full-length minks and draped it loosely over her shoulders.

The builders were finishing up their food. She had another word with Mr. Tyzack and then headed off to the garage, divesting an even more pungent trail of lavender and bergamot, this time enveloping Archie's packet of pink wafers. At the car, she slipped off her heels, eased on her driving shoes, then turned the Jag around in the drive, the wheel rolling easily through her fingers under the influence of its power steering.

The town was full of school kids, many of them toting hockey sticks or chucking rugby balls. She negotiated her way vigilantly. At one junction, a group of girls stared at her, a few of them smiling at the big white automobile that they imagined could be owned by a film star. She smiled, gave a little hand gesture and got a few waves back. Once on to the main road, Shaw opened the cigarette case, teased out another Pall Mall and floored the accelerator.

CHAPTER 6

Two men, both connected in one way or another with the dead girl on Ilkley Moor, were going about their quite different lives.

One of them knelt on the floor of a factory whose owners had just gone bust, destroying his job that had at least provided him with a regular place in the world. Jowett had made vehicles in the city for almost fifty years, but now the manufacture of its streamlined Javelin saloons, curious commercial vans and tiny Jupiter sports cars was terminated forever.

As he squirted oil into the recesses of the machinery he was maintaining, the man already knew he would be pocketing his last pay packet within a week, nine years of service to the company binned in the blink of an eye. It was made worse by knowing that the company purchasing the factory was keeping most of the workers on. But not him.

A generally docile disposition governed the man's behaviour, but the cogs and wheels of his brain were not as smooth running as they should be. Those cogs and wheels sometimes fouled up, allowing him to wallow in very bad thoughts.

He blamed schooling for much of his predicament, the memory of those years often leaving him tense and sweating. Symbols for words never made any sense to him at school, nor did they now. Sentences used to leap off the page, dancing like those broomsticks in *Fantasia* he'd seen at the pictures with his mum. Everything was a jumble of lines. In class, he tried copying from the blackboard, but when he did that and then looked up from his exercise book he could never find his place again on the blackboard. His brain simply could not recognise the letters.

Sometimes a teacher responded by clattering him with a rule and everyone laughed. Once a teacher flung a wooden blackboard duster at his head. He occasionally imagined Mr Pickles, and other tormentors like him, dissolving slowly in barrels of sulphuric acid or crushed under the wheels of a steam roller. What did they know? They could not even guess at how clever he was, a fact he needed to keep secret though he couldn't quite explain to himself why.

The shift over, he left the factory alone, ambling past the company's grand office entrance with its striking power motif, a car engine underneath bird wings. He walked along the road and climbed down into his three-wheeler car, so tiny the canvas roof rested on his head. The car rocked a little from side to side as he tried to make himself comfortable.

The vehicle struggled off from the kerb side into the semi-darkness, but it wasn't as turbid as the morning. He trundled along the ring road, his usual route home. He was humming a tuneless tune. It was chilly but the car was not fitted with a heater. Lights illuminated front room windows but people were already drawing curtains. He switched on the single screen wiper.

Held up at a traffic light junction, he watched a group of schoolgirls chatting and laughing, swinging school satchels and kicking with their heels the wall on which they were sitting. He stared at them, kitted out in pale brown blazers and pleated black skirts, happy-go-lucky teenagers with no care in the world. He wondered so often when he was young what it must be like to inhabit a carefree slot in the universe, but he never received an answer. He had let his eyes roam away from the girls, and when he concentrated his vision on them again, he saw that one girl did not project the good humour shared by the others. She was returning his gaze, looking right into his eyes. He quickly turned away and squinted at the sky through the windscreen. He chanced another peep but looked away again when he saw her staring at him. Counting out five seconds, he swivelled his eyes in her direction, keeping his head straight. She had jumped off the wall and was still peering his way. He held her eyes and then looked out directly ahead. Counting a few more seconds, he turned again, startled to find her face right up against the side of the car. She banged the roof.

"What are you looking at, you perv?" she screamed. "Haven't you got 'aht better to do, you sad bastard? Don't you fucking stare at me, you pervert."

The lights changed and the man moved off, his brain in a swirl. The girl slapped the rear wheel arch. He dared a glance and she was still standing there, hard-faced and scowling at the disappearing car. He had never seen her before.

He drove through Laisterdyke, an ancient pre-Norman name for an area now worn and disfigured, then past the long perimeter fence of the rugby league ground at Odsal. Calm again, his hands were still clammy and he felt nauseous. He didn't know if that was because of the schoolgirl, reminding him of what had happened the night before. Perhaps it was the lingering smell of Vim and disinfectant he had used that morning to scrub out the car's insides.

The feeble motorcycle engine fitted to the single front wheel tugged the funny little vehicle up to the village district of Wibsey. The car then turned in and bounced up to the entrance of a snicket, a narrow pathway running between garden hedges. He climbed out and pushed the car back into the front garden of a house the man shared with his mother. The street lamp, still gas-powered, cast a spectral glow over the vehicle.

"Mum, it's only me." He entered the hall, slipping off his windcheater and hanging it neatly on the clothes hook on the back of the front door.

"Hello, Henry." His mother always greeted him from the back of the house at this time of day.

He pushed open the sitting room door. She was hunched up next to the smart Bush radio in white bakelite he had recently purchased for her, listening intently to *Mrs Dale's Diary*.

"I've put your tea out," she half whispered. "Talk to you later on."

A tin of salmon was open for him in the kitchen but not emptied out. A plate with cold boiled potatoes and tinned peas lay next to it, together with another plate supporting several slices of white bread covered in margarine. He tipped the salmon into a bowl, took down a Sarson's bottle from the shelf and poured vinegar on to the salmon, mixing it in with the back of a fork. From the larder he brought out a large bottle of Dandelion and Burdock, changed his mind and took out instead a half-full bottle of white wine from the coldest part of the little room. He poured the Burgundy into a cut glass goblet, one of two he had bought at Lewis's department store in Leeds. Scooping the salmon on to the plate, he opened the cap of the Crosse and Blackwell bottle and used a knife to lever out some salad cream.

He munched through the food quietly, looking at the wall with its calendar and one small painting of Scarborough. He knew every brush stroke of that picture. *Mrs Dale's Diary* was not to his taste. He preferred the new *Journey Into Space*, at least now the spaceship had blasted off on its journey and all the boring chat had stopped.

A typical evening was in store. His mother always patiently read to him the business pages of the papers and had herself developed a knack for picking news items useful to him. For the past five years he had used a stockbroker in Leeds, starting off in a small way but becoming increasingly bold and knowledgeable with his share selections. The money in his bank accounts mounted now to the point where he could probably buy up all the houses in the street. Relishing his secret, he would have liked to buy a new car but people would then get to know more about him.

He finished the food and meticulously cleaned the plate and bowl in the sink, dried and put them away, neatly folding the tea towel before hanging it on a rail. He then wiped down the draining board, rinsing out the cloth and leaving it carefully aligned at right angles to the sink taps.

Access to the stairs in these late Victorian houses was through the living room. His mother was sitting in the rocker, knitting and now listening to Billy Cotton's band.

"I'm going upstairs for a bit, Mum. Then we'll go through the papers."

"Right you are, luv. I've made a pie from rhubarb I took out of the garden this afternoon. We'll have that with our tea."

The house was bigger than most other types of terraced dwellings in the city but the front bedroom was tiny. His mother had foregone the large bedroom so he could spread out his equipment. He looked out of the window, down the long garden with the vegetable patch they both tended, and out into the park on which the garden backed. It was too dark to see anything distinctly. After drawing the curtains, he switched on the ceiling light and sat at his workbench. This was covered in old radios, valves and tools. He was dismantling and rebuilding a pre-war Philco People's wireless.

The shape of the small speakers near the top of its face made it seem as if the radio was crying. It was one of his favourite wireless sets. Gathering up a pair of pliers and some wiring in his surprisingly delicate hands, he started to work.

*****

Just off that same ring road the little car had travelled, another man scanned the landscape from the window of his back bedroom above the cheery grocery shop he owned with his wife. Percy Barraclough was a very confident human being. Always had been, endowed as he was with that quiet aura of assurance people took to, his size adding an extra dimension of certainty, and sometimes threat.

Down below him in the one-acre plot with sheds and its own water supply, Barraclough gazed at the pint-sized pigs gobbling through the slop he'd shovelled into their sties. He loved those animals. He'd bought them as a single job lot from a farmer who bred cross-Blacks for smallholdings, then transported them over in his brother's van. They ponged a bit when it was warm but no one complained.

In the far distance, he spied kids biking on the big expanse of wasteland bordering the colossal engineering factory that was as big as an airfield. A large pond filled one corner of the open ground, disused chemical barrels heaped up on one edge. Their residual loads leaked into the water, converting it into multi-coloured runnels of industrial effluent. Machines used for heating tar for road laying and resembling baby elephants but with their chimney 'trunks' facing upwards, rusted in pools of hardened pitch. In summer, kids picked at the softened tar with lollipop sticks. There was no doubting it. This was a champion place for children to play. Just as it had been when he was a kid.

The only blot on this typical marriage of industry and housing, in Barraclough's eyes, were the gypsies at the back of his land. He wished a hole would open up and swallow those didicoys, taking with them their manky horses and dilapidated scrap metal carts. Why were their dogs so fucking nasty? The terriers had been bothering the pigs again. He'd tried to reason with the headman. Why couldn't people take responsibility? Twice he'd been told to sling his hook. He felt like taking a two-by-four and driving the bastard bloke's Adam's apple through the back of his bastard neck, the bastard.

Now Percy, calm down, Barraclough thought. Take it easy. Don't let it get to you. No point in letting your blood boil. Anyway, there was no time to dwell on all that. There was work to do and that needed concentration. It would soon be time to do one of the things he really loved doing. He liked the word 'transmute'. He'd read it somewhere in a science fiction story. To transmute into his alter ego, he liked to think, and, for at least a few hours, turn himself into the Black Night.

A professional wrestler for seventeen years whose modest career was dribbling to a paltry end, Barraclough had been tossed a lifeline. Persuaded by his manager to fight in a leotard with a full face mask, he'd also taken a new moniker. He looked brilliant. Even had a cape. Another plus was the garb partially hid the bulge where a million gallons of Tetley's bitter had found a transitory home over the years. The leotard was a bit itchy round the crotch, Barraclough thought, but this full uniform was streets ahead of the mask worn by one of his wrestling heroes. He looked tons better than Count Bartelli.

They'd spent ages hunting for a suitable name. The Great Nemo. The Malevolent Marauder. The Grim Reaper. Young Micky Driver, who helped out the manager, suggested the Petrifying Pig Breeder and received a clip round the ear for his trouble. They'd sent off to London for the costume and it had arrived by post, but there was a mix-up. Yellow with a wide pink stripe across the chest was the colour of the garb in the package. A bit of an obvious problem that, but they'd eventually got it sorted out and the all-black ensemble which eventually turned up was just the ticket.

He hadn't even hinted to his manager that every time his head disappeared into the mask a surge of excitement rippled through him. Its velvet touch definitely made him feel unnatural. Edna once caught him staring at himself in the bedroom mirror, wearing just the mask and his underpants. They'd both giggled. The new face of the beast, she'd said. Grand lass, Edna. She knew all the rumours about professional grapplers and their women fans, but she never brought it up. Still, it was getting a bit lean on that front. He still owned the barn-door shoulders and Desperate Dan arms of the super-heavy, but age was taking its toll. Maybe new avenues for his stuttering sex life would open up, thanks to his new friends at the drinking club. His first and so far only visit had not ended well, so he wasn't sure.

Barraclough's wife popped her head round the bedroom door. "Are you ready, luv? You better be off if you're using the bus."

She was short and petite, with a bottle-blonde mop of hair and a face still pretty and virtually lineless at her age of forty-three. He still loved her. "Have you packed the new tub of liniment?"

"Yeah, I've got everything, luv. I might have a drink at the Ring O'Bells afterwards, but I shouldn't be too late. Have you found a new potato supplier? It's a disgrace what Crowther's are giving us."

"Don't worry about all that now, and don't get hurt tonight. No bruises on the face as it'll spoil the wedding photos."

Their seventeen-year-old daughter was getting married on Saturday, much to Barraclough's annoyance. But what could he do? At least their son, Douglas, doing his National Service in the army, wasn't going to fly the coop. He zipped up his Slazenger tennis racket bag, slung it over his shoulder, kissed Edna on the mouth and headed out into the street. His flashy Zephyr, just bought from a local garage, was parked next to the shop, but as he was fighting locally he'd decided to use public transport.

It was a three minute walk to the bus stop. He arrived there at the same time as an old woman in a heavy blue overcoat and red woollen carpet slippers. One of her stockings had partially rolled itself down a leg. What was left of her hair was tied up in bright pink rollers, visible under a transparent headscarf. They waited quietly. Barraclough stared up at the high-level wires, suspended from roadside steel poles, that carried electric power for the trolley buses. The system was the very first in Britain, city councillors having taken an all-expenses paid trip to Vienna and Milan before plumping for it more than forty years earlier. Yet Barraclough had read somewhere that the days of the trolley bus might be numbered. That he couldn't understand, especially as they were just opening the country's first electrified railway line, between Sheffield and Manchester.

Soon the bus arrived, virtually soundless, electric power sucked up from the wires by twin booms attached to sliding trolleys on the roof. He followed the woman on board and sat downstairs near the front. The vehicle, in its blue Corporation livery, took off in a surge of power, an acceleration the city's diesel buses could never match. The conductor asked the destination, set the rollers in the heavy Universal machine strapped round his neck, and punched out a ticket.

On the way into town Barraclough practised the moves in his head. His opponent was an old mate and the fight would go to plan, the masked man winning by a submission in the fifth. He certainly didn't want a re-run of what had happened in Morecambe at the weekend. Anton 'pretty boy' von Marco, the bastard, drop-kicked him from the first bell which was not in the script, and then used a forearm while he was lying on the canvas. When his senses unscrambled, he'd reverse-posted von Marco, smashed his skull into the canvas with a pile-driver, split open his nose and mouth with an elbow jab, locked him in a sleeper and then chucked him through the ropes, the bastard dislocating a knee on a spectator's chair. No more "pretty boy". Anyway, what a poncy moniker. Von Marco? What was wrong with the name Rodney Lillicrap?

Barraclough sniggered to himself as he tightened his grip on the top of the metal frame of the seat in front. Calm down, Percy, and concentrate on the fight tonight. Within a few seconds, the Black Night was rehearsing in his brain the moves that would notch up another victory in the late blooming of his wrestling career.

CHAPTER 7

Another man whose life would be altered forever by the murder of the young girl found on the moor reclined in rather more comfortable surroundings than those housing Percy Barraclough's jumbo frame. Watching the world scurry by at five hundred miles an hour, courtesy of the British Overseas Airways Corporation, Tommy Nelson relaxed in his armchair seat and sipped a Martell. Shaw's production manager could see sunlight bathing the white-cloudy sky as he peered through the nearest porthole of the BOAC Comet jetliner. The Rolls-Royce Ghost engines issued a low rumble as they thrust the plane, sleek as a torpedo, through the rarified atmosphere above the Arabian Sea.

Nelson smiled to himself as he thought of the privileges he was enjoying, flying in the world's first jet-powered passenger aircraft. The return flight ticket cost two hundred and eighty-two pounds and twelve shillings, but he wasn't forking out a farthing. He took another swig from the glass goblet. The sun's rays danced across the candy-striped curtains, pulled open around the windows. He glanced at the flight map and thought they might still be over the Gulf of Oman.

He wasn't enamoured with his mission. Recruiting Pakistanis to work in a British textile mill seemed to him, instinctively, bone-headed. As an engineer loving all things metal, he put his trust in technology, not cheap labour. Nevertheless, if they were going to hoover up manpower in the Indian subcontinent they might as well get it right. As he knew more about Shaw's production needs than any living human, it was right he was in the dominion to check out the local agents and help them recruit the right kind of worker.

There was no arguing that this wasn't a nifty opportunity, even though it would last only a week. Not only was he relishing the ride in this marvel of British aeronautics, he was also determined to pack in as much sightseeing as he could while in Karachi. Not bad for a boy who left school at thirteen. He'd managed to get his mitts on a Baedeker and marked in the German guidebook the pink Mohatta Palace as a place he must see, though he wasn't sure he could as it seemed to be a government building. The Empress Market, a covered bazaar built by the Victorians, was another. Designed to look like a market in a British town, he wondered whether it might resemble Bradford's. His thoughts turned to his homeland but didn't dwell there very long.

Flight BA774 had departed London Airport at one in the afternoon, stopping off for refuelling and food supplies at Rome, Beirut and Bahrain, and was due to land in Karachi at seven-fifteen in the morning. Final destination for the plane was Colombo, Ceylon. A two hour hold-up in Bahrain to let a storm pass knocked their schedule, but who cared, Nelson thought. A full complement of thirty-six passengers was on board.

The mid-air breakup of a Comet three months earlier had made him a touch edgy. Was that the second or third fatal accident? The whole Comet fleet was subsequently grounded but the jet was now back in service, its maker reassuring everyone that it was as safe as houses. He took another drag on his Craven "A", blowing smoke towards the cabin ceiling, and re-opened the book he'd selected from the small library at the rear of the plane. Stretching his lower limbs in the ample legroom between the rows, he settled back for another dose of danger in the South of France:

"'Banco', said Bond, pushing out a wad of notes. Again he fixed Le Chiffre with his eye. Again he gave only a cursory look at his two cards. 'No,' he said. He held a marginal five. The position was dangerous. Le Chiffre turned up a knave and a four. He gave the shoe another slap. He drew a three. 'Sept à la banque', said the croupier, 'et cinq', he added as he tipped Bond's losing cards face upwards. He raked over Bond's money, extracted four million francs and returned the remainder to Bond."

Nelson directed his eyes through the plane's window and drifted off into another world, imagining himself as a British secret agent, duelling with Smersh across Europe. Before he got on the plane he had never heard of *Casino Royale*, nor its author, nor James Bond for that matter. But the book was gripping. Bond obviously thought his companion, Vesper Lynd, too feather-brained for the task ahead. Nelson read on: "This was just what he had been afraid of. These blithering women who thought they could do a man's work. Why the hell couldn't they stay at home and mind their pots and pans and stick to their frocks and gossip and leave men's work to the men. And now for this to happen to him, just when the job had come off so beautifully. For Vesper to fall for an old trick like that and get herself snatched and probably held to ransom like some bloody heroine in a strip cartoon. The silly bitch."

Two very pretty women with their own pots edged towards one of James Bond's new fans, so he closed the book and stubbed out his cigarette in a seat ashtray. The two food trolleys were loaded. One of the stewardesses first served Mrs Amies, his travelling companion since London. She jammed her book of Somerset Maugham short stories down the side of her seat and accepted the plate.

The stewardess turned to him and smiled. "Have you chosen from the menu, sir?"

"Yes, I have. The lamb, please."

"Very good." She placed a glass of orange juice on his tray then, at the trolley, levered the meat and some roast potatoes on to a porcelain plate.

"Cabbage and carrots with that?"

"Definitely." He wondered whether they had switched the food order as the plane was running late, so they were getting a very early lunch rather than a breakfast.

"There's spotted dick and ice cream for the sweet and cheese and biscuits after that."

She had very white and surprisingly even teeth. "Tea or coffee, or would you like some wine?"

It was just like the Pullman service on the railways. He took a glass of white wine and thought he caught the woman across the aisle raising an eyebrow as she glanced his way. She probably thought it was too early for alcohol. He took a gulp, the acidity making him wince, and tucked in.

The flight had been marvellous so far. Mrs Amies had simply introduced herself as that. He still did not know her Christian name. She was visiting her son who had been in the colonial service in India and had stayed on in some advisory role. Well into her sixties, Mrs Amies had also lived on the Indian sub-continent with her husband, recently deceased, a specialist medical man of some kind. She was taken aback at the idea of recruiting workers from Pakistan and kept throwing out snippets of apparently random information.

"West Pakistan, unlike East Pakistan, is basically arid. Some places get less than five inches of rain a year, you know, though the canals and barrages the British built have helped. Apart from Urdu, which is a mixture of Persian, Hindi and Arabic, there are lots of regional languages like Sind, Balochi and Pashto. Honour and revenge, prestige and hospitality all go together for these people. I think they imported a caste system when they were part of British India but I don't see how that sits well with Islam. Since Liaquat Ali Khan was assassinated three years ago, the government structure looks very rocky."

Nelson couldn't quite remember who Mr Ali Khan was and questioned whether a better grounding before he left might have been useful. Was the Baedeker up to it?

Mrs Amies kept slipping back into the school classroom where she had spent all her professional life. But what did any of this tell him about qualities a mill needed from its workers? Like dexterity, physical endurance and the ability to withstand brain-freezing monotony, not to mention one hundred and ten decibels of constant clatter in a weaving room. What would prove relevant in the enclosed world of warp and weft? Anyway, helping Shaw's sort all this out was what Saleem Nazaruddin and Sons were now under contract for.

She had asked him what he planned to see in his spare time, and he mentioned sights he'd earmarked in the little red guide.

"Outside the centre of Karachi, go and see the Dhobi Ghats where they do their laundry. It's quite a sight. And try and keep away from the meat. Stick to vegetables. Hygiene and sanitation are, how shall I say it, a bit on the under-developed side."

A lot of the flight was absorbed by Mrs Amies' stories of her trips to Tanganyika and Nyasaland, pre-war walking holidays in Bohemia, café society in Alexandria. It left Nelson contemplating his one foreign passport stamp – that of Austria for a business trip. How pathetic was that?

There was a whole world out there, and now holidays were on offer where the flight and hotel were included together so you didn't need to plan anything. That still left the slight problem of not having anyone to holiday with now that he and Emer had gone their separate ways after more than twenty years of marriage. She had moved to her parents' house with their daughter, Moira, while he stayed in the family home. Sad, but not too painful. As Catholics there was no question of a divorce. They didn't know anyone who had divorced, Catholic or not. The houses were so close he still saw a lot of his girl. Just as well, Emer said. Moira was becoming a bit unruly, not that he had noticed. She was the apple of his eye.

The sound of the stewardess broke into his thoughts as she cleared the tray.

"Now, what else can I offer you?"

He selected a Montecristo from the cigar box and she clipped the end. He lit the cigar with his own Dunhill London Rollalite with its easy-on-the-thumb action, and sucked in a good lungful of Cuban tobacco tar before blowing smoke up to the cabin ceiling.

"Another drink, sir?"

She poured him a second Martell in a different tumbler and slotted a spare cigar without asking into the top pocket of his shirt. You didn't get this treatment at Harry Ramsden's. Nelson ate at least once a month at Yorkshire's most famous fish and chip restaurant. He earned enough now to eat where he wanted, not that he did, and was proud of himself, the way he'd worked up from the bottom. He was almost on the board. Stephen Shaw demonstrated an egalitarian streak not shared by many mill owners. The company's chairman also believed in engineering, notwithstanding this Pakistan malarkay.

Nelson thought engineers were the key to civilisation and reflected again on the marvellous aircraft he was flying in. He knew the world's first turboprop service was now operating between London and Nicosia, thanks to British European Airways' Viscounts. He'd read that the country's 'V' bombers were due to be delivered soon, first the Valiant, then the Vulcan and the Victor, all capable of carrying a nuclear bomb. With a dozen or so aeroplane makers, it felt like Britain could rule the skies.

Nelson's daydream was interrupted by an announcement from the flight deck that Flight 774 was an hour from landing. He thought of Karachi, dwelt again for a second on how few places he had visited in his life, and decided there and then to swing into a holiday frame of mind. The work would still get done. He stood up, yanked his travel bag from the open luggage rack, and headed off down the dark blue, thick pile wool carpet to the back of the plane. He took a quick drink from the water fountain and stepped into the gentlemen's "dressing room".

Mrs Amies informed him that the ladies' room incorporated a fixed seat and dressing table with face lotions and hand creams. The gentlemen's wasn't quite so lavish but, rearward of the light alloy wash basin, it offered a small table with receptacles for shaving cream, talcum powder and hair lotion. The self-flushing Vickers toilet was actually in a separate compartment at the back of the dressing room.

He washed and shaved quickly, changed his shirt, removed his trousers and replaced them with a pair of gabardine shorts, then crammed his brogues into the bag before slipping on a pair of sandals. He strolled back through the plane, stowing his bag back in the rack. When he turned to take his seat, he definitely caught the same woman cocking an eye at him across the aisle, then frowning severely in a clear look of disapproval at his shorts. She was togged out in a flower-print dress and had not removed her hat or gloves during the whole flight. Nelson flopped into his herringbone-weave upholstered seat, lit the second Montecristo he had transferred to the pocket of his changed shirt, and stuck his nose again into Ian Fleming's first outing for Double O Seven.

What Nelson did not know, nor any of his fellow passengers, was that the stewardesses were nervous, despite their generous, toothy smiles and ready laughs. So too was the rest of flight crew 774 and all the other crews that manned Comets. Every time the plane lurched or the fuselage emitted a noisy creak, hearts beat a little faster under BOAC's stylish dark blue uniforms. The crews did not trust the plane. They didn't know quite yet just how right they were not to trust it. As Tommy Nelson sped towards his destination, another Comet was disappearing from radar screens, BOAC Yoke Yoke exploding and plunging into the sea near the Bay of Naples.

Yet for Tommy Nelson, it had proved a spell-binding journey and his Comet touched down quietly and safely in West Pakistan's major industrial port. He wished Mrs Amies a pleasant stay with her son, retrieved her bag and his, and then edged towards the rear of the plane.

"No chance of keeping hold of this, I suppose?" he said to a stewardess as he handed back the copy of *Casino Royale*.

"I'm afraid not. Got to think of other passengers. Is it any good?"

"Not bad at all. I've just got to an exciting bit."

"You can finish it on the way home."

Slotting the hardback into the bookcase, she looked relieved to be on the ground. Must be tough on the old pins, Nelson thought.

He was now in the rear "vestibule", as referred to in the plane's brochure, with its hat rack, curtained wardrobe, radio, and luggage compartment with a door in weathered sycamore veneer. He poked his head into the open air and the heat hit him like an oxyacetylene torch aimed at his skull. He blurted out an involuntary "Bloody Hell". The fashion plate behind him in the flower-pattern dress raised another eyebrow.

CHAPTER 8

"You'd only been gone five minutes, Mr Stafford, when the whole bloody thing came crashing out of the hole and his ration book dropped to the floor. The stupid bugger had gone out burgling with identification stuck in his top pocket. Billy Draper. He was known all over Bradford for it. We used to call him the smoke-hole sneak. Stupid bloody bugger."

Merriment written all over his face, Sergeant Feather tossed the document on to the table. Stafford fingered the dusty booklet.

"On His Majesty's Service", it said. "Issued to safeguard your food supply."

Holder's Name	Billy Draper
Other Names	Frederick
Address	34 Sutcliffe Lane, Bradford 4
Nat. Registration No:	AHAW 323 2
Date of Issue	Feb 4, 1949

"If found, please return to the Bradford food office."
Serial number of book 728578

It was becoming a hazy memory for most adults, but in nineteen forty-nine, almost everything was rationed. Now it was down to bacon, butter, margarine, cooking fat, cheese and some meats. Stafford chucked the booklet back on to his desk. "Let's get this straight. Some years ago, Bradford had a house burglar whose favoured method of entry was down chimneys? Why didn't he go through a window?"

Feather pointed a stubby finger at his forehead. "It might be something to do with old Billy being bonkers. He had two spells in a loony bin. Some kind of disorder where you keep doing the same thing with the same bad result but you can't stop yourself. Personally, I think he just liked robbing honest people. He occasionally jemmied a window and got in that way, but he preferred the funnel method." Feather slid a stubby finger into a pencil holder on Stafford's desk to emphasise the point.

"Every time there was a burglary and a pile of soot on the carpet we knew it was him. It was like he'd left his bloody signature. I was looking through the files and we did him over ten times. He once went down a chimney too early in the night and burnt his feet and ankles. Where the chimney had an especially narrow aperture, he used to prise off the top by breaking the masonry. A lot of the time people never heard him. He was helped by the fact that there are types of houses in the city that have chimneys with unusually wide vents."

"Nevertheless, he must have been a very thin individual?"

"Thin? He was built like a wood shaving. I think he must have taken his holidays in Belsen."

Stafford had spent seven years in Yorkshire, three of them in Bradford, and had never heard the beat of this. "I'm guessing you had an idea who it was right from the start."

"I thought of old Billy straight away," said Feather. "Now Draper was reported missing by his sister on October seventh, nineteen forty-nine. We are trying to find her now. Both his parents are dead, not surprising as Billy was in his sixties back then.

"Of course, that doesn't explain why he was burgling an empty house, if it was empty. We know he wasn't the full shilling, but he was crafty at casing houses that were worth thieving from. We're assuming it was empty because, if it wasn't, how could he remain dead in the chimney unnoticed? It would have started to smell. Anyway, as soon as they lit the fire the smoke would have backed up. Everyone uses their fires in October."

Stafford mentally checked that it wasn't April the first. "I don't suppose there's any chance that he wasn't burgling and was actually the victim this time?"

"No chance of that. The demolition foreman said there was no sign of the wall being replaced from inside. It was original. It's no loss, sir. He was a dyed-in-the-wool-thief."

An officer leant his head around the door to inform Stafford that all available officers were now on site, so he and Feather moved off down the corridor to one of the station's large incident rooms. About twenty-five feet long and almost square, the room was painted in a dull, now dirty, yellow. A scattering of metal and wood desks and larger tables filled the centre. Thirty or so uniformed and plain-clothes officers were sitting or mooching around. Small groups had formed, a low murmur of talk punctured by the occasional laugh. One officer, his jacket partly off his shoulder, was performing a mock striptease. Some of the younger constables sat quietly at single desks, paper and pencils at the ready like schoolboys. Stafford took a seat at a table facing the gathering and extracted notes from a jacket pocket. Everyone started settling down and finding a seat, or the edge of a table on which to lean. A paper aeroplane flew across the room, its delta wing transporting it all the way to the far wall before it crash-landed against a radiator.

"Right. Quieten down now," Stafford addressed the gathering. "We're hear to review the five main things we're engaged with. I won't keep you long so let's get on with it. Now, the dead man in the chimney."

"Skeleton in the cupboard," somebody said. "Body in the bath," someone else offered. "Corpse in the coffin." A minor revolt from the back of the classroom. Some of the officers were frowning, struggling to dredge up their own alliterative quips. No more were forthcoming.

"I took the missus to see *Creature from the Black Lagoon* yesterday. Bloke in a rubber suit but it scared the living daylights out of the wife."

"Alright, let's get on." Stafford was grateful of the banter, indicating as it did a closeness among officers and a collective spirit.

"Don't you get things like this in Somerset, sir?" one of the sergeants asked. "People mangled in cider presses, found dead in thatched roofs, drowned in those big tubs for making cheese?" Stafford could see now that most of the station were well aware of Billy Draper and his fate.

"Vats. They're called cheese vats. Now let's get on with it. Sergeant Feather is dealing with the case. We already know who the man is and we'll have more information this afternoon. We might be able to tie it up quickly. Right, now, the Queen's visit this month. Inspector Mapplebeck?"

Eugene Mapplebeck was one of the shorter officers and he tried compensating for this by sporting a bushy moustache, jet-black in contrast to his steel-grey hair. The moustache caused him trouble with the hierarchy and didn't suit his uniform. "As the county is handling most of it we are just liaising on the route she's taking."

"Have you talked to Buckingham Palace, and more to the point how are they coping with your voice?" Philip Drasdo spoke in a flat but painless local accent. Anyone who asked was told that his was a local surname, but no one could quite believe it. Especially as his middle name was Herman.

Mapplebeck's voice was broad and serrated, its texture akin to a rusty pipe. His accent required exaggerated movements of the mouth. This exacerbated the effect, stretching vowels like elastic. "Could they understand me? Could I understand them, more to the point. They don't all sound like Valentine Dyall down there, you know. Anyway, we have all the arrangements in place for cordoning off streets and we've agreed with the council everything necessary for them to put up flags before her visit. Staffing schedules for officers involved with the visit are sorted out. No problems so far."

A Black Maria reversed into the station yard, its motor's noise like that of a revolving barrel of nuts and screws, and Stafford waited until its driver turned off the ignition.

"Now, the third item. Samuel Reilly." This was a brutal one. Reilly and Arthur Pike, both itinerant workers, shared a room at the lodgings of a Mrs Tarpy. Pike was found dead outside the house, his body and head battered, with Reilly upstairs soaked in blood. "Inspector Lampton. Fill us in."

"Reilly is not going to escape from this one. The only plausible explanation is that he beat Pike senseless in their shared room, then lobbed him through the window to try and disguise the cause of his injuries. Reilly is a known violent drunk. We'll have enough evidence for a conviction. He could swing for this."

Stafford, like some of his colleagues, did not appreciate all the talk about abolishing the death penalty. He thought some people deserved the noose. Yet in a case like this, he knew Reilly would get a long stretch rather than the ultimate sanction.

"Next on the list. Katy Follows." A sigh that deformed into a groan spread through the room.

The case was troubling. Katy Follows' body had turned up the previous year in a local park. She had been strangled. Also known as Eileen Lennon, the mother of five travelled to the park by taxi, accompanied by an unknown man. She died close to a place called Lover's Walk. A male, described as knock-kneed and with a long nose, was seen hoofing it across a nearby golf course. Someone, with a lot of knowledge about the killing, later telephoned the police, the call traced to the city's Odsal district.

Stafford and his colleagues wondered if the telephone call was an act of remorse from a killer whose lust metamorphosed into murder. The unsolved case, dubbed "the body in the park" by the local paper, had squeezed the force's confidence. It more than crossed Stafford's mind that the Follows' murder and the killing on Ilkley Moor might be linked, yet other than a similar method of murder, there was nothing, in truth, to connect them. The bodies were also found fifteen miles apart.

"Anything further to report, Sergeant Rouse?"

"No." A few officers shook their heads.

"Well, where are we with it?"

"We've got some new bits and pieces of information that need checking but it's not much." Rouse leant back in his chair. "Maybe we should be put on other duties."

"Absolutely not. The public expect us to find her killer and we need to show we are doing everything we can." If he was honest with himself, he was losing heart like the rest of them. "Now, finally, the girl on the moor."

Stafford spent twenty minutes outlining what little they knew, what things they were doing in Ilkley to involve the public, and what steps the police might need to take once her identity was known. After the meeting, he returned to his office, gratefully accepting on the way a mug of over-stewed tea from a female police officer.

The huge cast-iron radiators were pumping out too much heat and he loosened his tie. His shirt, in one hundred per cent man-made fibre, did not feel good on the skin. He sat at a side table and slotted paper into his typewriter, an Imperial 50 from the nineteen-twenties. The station also used more recent Imperial 55s and 58s and had been supplied with one, just out, model 66. But the old 50 was sound enough, and he tapped out everything he could think of from what he knew about the murder on the moor.

At lunchtime, Stafford removed from his locker the point two-two rifle he had brought in from home that morning, and walked briskly out of the office. It was very bright outside, but cold. He ambled across town, spirits somewhat lifted now the station could focus on one, not two, new investigations. He entered the front door of Carter's, sauntered past the packed displays of Dinky toys, train sets and model house-building kits, and went through to the back. There the shop displayed its rifles and shotguns. He knew the salesman and the salesman knew him.

"Good afternoon, Mr Stafford. That's the gun, I presume." Mr Quarmby pointed at the weapon bag. Stafford extracted the BSA and handed it over the counter. Quarmby examined the rifle's workings and the telescopic sights in their separate pouch.

"Just as you described it, Mr. Stafford. It's not a Greener, of course, but for a BSA it's in grand fettle. I said nine pounds on the phone but I'll give you ten."

Stafford could see no future for the rifle in his hands. He'd used it only for shooting rabbits, mainly in his native Somerset, but the country's rabbit population was being savaged by myxomatosis. The myxoma virus killed its victims within a fortnight, rabbit carcasses, with swollen heads and pus-filled sores, littering farmland ditches in their thousands.

A much more modern-looking two-two rested on the counter, its telescopic sights attached, and Stafford couldn't resist fingering its loading mechanism.

"That's the latest Golden Marlin. I was just showing it to another customer before you came in. Go on, Mr Stafford, take it outside and have a good look at it." The salesman, stacks of cartridge boxes behind him, handed up the gun.

Stafford exited Carter's by its rear door. He stood at the kerb side, lifted the American-made rifle, peered through the sights, adjusted them, then panned along the side of the town hall. Another design by architects Lockwood and Mawson, the building was a mish-mash of French and Italian Gothic. Inspired by the cathedral at Amiens, it was dominated by a two hundred foot clock tower modelled on that of the Palazzo Vecchio in Florence, touches of the town hall in Siena thrown in. A striking feature were thirty-five statues, each seven foot tall, of kings and queens. They were carved in niches high above the pavement. Stafford trained his sights on the heads of the monarchs, lingering over Henry the Eighth before sweeping over to Oliver Cromwell, included by the architects as an offering to local nonconformist traditions.

"I hope you are nailing those fucking pigeons," a passer-by remarked as Stafford moved back along to Richard the Second. He contemplated, for a brief moment, issuing a warning to the individual for using offensive language, but thought of the words his officers often used. Fuck it, he told himself.

"Very tempting, Mr Quarmby." Stafford handed the Marlin back to the shop assistant. "I just can't justify it to myself now with all this myxa."

He climbed the stairs to the first floor and bought a Dinky Super Toys petrol tanker for his nephew's forthcoming birthday, and a tipper lorry. He spent four shillings and sixpence on three cars in the new Matchbox series of micro toys. He also purchased some goods wagons for Peter's Tri-ang model railway. That name always amused him. Tri-ang was one of those cleverly-named companies, set up by three brothers with the surname of Lines, three lines forming a triangle.

His sister, May, had revealed rising exasperation at his unwillingness to visit home. "We hardly see you," she had scolded him the last time they spoke. "Peter is nearly nine now and you've missed just about every birthday. Can't you come down this time? Just this once. He'd love to see you."

They had been kind to him since his wife had died, but it was such a long way to Somerset where his sister had always remained. By car it was like trekking to Pluto. Stafford was determined this time to get down to North Curry, and Peter's birthday was little more than a week away.

He strode up one of the small medieval lanes wriggling their way from the town centre and, on a whim, stepped into Arensberg's, the jewellers. It was stuffily warm. A couple of customers were being served and he could examine the contents of the glass cases in peace. Eventually, a middle-aged woman with black hair and make-up that gave her face the colour of Kiwi light tan boot polish came over, and he asked to look at a tray. He eventually selected, for his sister, a locket on a silver chain, wrote out a cheque and then left, crossing the road and entering a butchers shop.

Lita Roza's *How Much is that Doggy in the Window* was belting out of a doorway somewhere. He bought a hot pie, filled with gravy and some indeterminate meat, and sat on a nearby bench outside, scoffing it within a few minutes.

Bradford's streets were devoid of litter. Rubbish bins, which would have been largely pointless, were virtually absent. Eventually he found one outside a bank and successfully bowled into it the screwed-up pie wrapping. A Fred Trueman moment, slightly punctured by a young woman hurrying down the bank's entrance steps. "Easy when it's only two feet away," she pointed out. She looked over her shoulder after a second or two and mouthed "sorry".

Back in the office, there was a note to ring the police surgeon, and a report on the cables tied around Moira Nelson's neck. The wiring was of the type normally used in industrial premises for lighting and basic internal power supply. It was unusual, but not that unusual. He made a few calls within the station and set up a sub-investigation into cable suppliers, and a random check of industrial sites to ascertain just how common was the wiring's use. He then telephoned the police surgeon.

"Ah, good of you to call, detective inspector." McCrone's voice sounded guttural. "I wish we could all take a leisurely lunch break." As if McCrone didn't. Stafford thought a device attached to the telephone and measuring the alcohol level on the breath of the person at the other end of the line would prove very useful.

"Now then, the specimen in the chimney. More like archaeology than medical work. I should have studied Egyptology but I had no clue that could prove so handy around here. He has a broken spine, close to the neck. Your Sergeant Feather said he was a burglar who used the chimney as a means of entry. That's a new one on me. Whether he fell into the chimney head first or broke his back manoeuvring inside it, I couldn't say."

McCrone's words were not actually slurred but alcohol, Stafford had no doubt, was making the vowel sounds blurred. "I looked through the cavity and the flue has a pronounced bend. Obviously dead some years but nothing further on that yet. I can't give you a reading on his mental health but, as an educated guess, and using my extensive forensic experience, I'd say one hundred percent barking."

"He was reported missing in the autumn of nineteen forty-nine."

"There you go. Now, the young girl on Ilkley Moor. I trust there's no further word on that?"

"No."

"I would say late teens or twenty. She died sometime the previous evening, can't be more precise. No indication, I can see whether she was killed close to the spot where she was found or somewhere else." McCrone cleared his throat in a wet, phlegmy rasp. "Preliminary examination shows she was killed by strangulation. There is heavy finger bruising on her neck so it was done, most probably, by hands rather than those wires. In fact, given the nature of those longer marks on her neck, I think the wiring was used to drag her. A very violent attack, I would say. Thyroid bone broken. Neck injuries not caused by any fall. A few scratch marks at the top of her legs but no sign of intercourse. Some recent bruises on her face and on her hands but cause indeterminate. One perhaps significant thing is that the finger marks on the neck might suggest her killer had small hands even though they exercised a great deal of force."

"Like a woman's hands?"

"Highly unlikely given the power that was used. Anyway, that's only a supposition about the hands."

McCrone offered other details about the victim and her clothing, then brought up the obvious point.

"Nothing to suggest any connection with the unfortunate Mrs Follows. Let's hope you have a bit more luck, laddie, with this new one." Stafford noticed the "you" rather than "we" and detected a vague reprimand from the police surgeon. He could be imagining it.

"We still have sweet FA on the Follows' case," Stafford volunteered.

"An eight-year-old girl who was raped and dismembered."

"What?"

"F.A. Fanny Adams. A real murder case in the last century. It's also the name the Navy gave to its canned meat."

Stafford thought of the Scot as a bit of an over-confident know-all. He made a few more calls to ensure both the track above, and the slope leading down to the gulley where Moira Nelson was found, got a second thorough going-over. Perhaps the killer had somehow used that narrow pathway and then dragged the body down the slope, using the wiring. He had absolutely no idea yet.

He then typed up more of his notes and accepted another brew offered by one of the station's clerical staff. Sun was still streaming through the window, and he turned around in his seat to stare at the sky. Clouds were hardly moving at all. One cloud formed an unusual block shape, rather like the head from one of the *Flower Pot Men*, the peculiar string puppets on *Watch with Mother*, the children's programme he occasionally watched on his days off in that transfixed state of inactivity he adopted at home. His brain was emptying of its own accord when a knuckle-tap on his door broke into his daydreams. A sweat stain now circled the top of Norman Feather's shirt collar, at least where the collar was visible through the constantly shifting mounds of his flabby neck. He plonked himself on a chair.

"Bastard heat. The furnace must be stoked to the gills. I thought I'd be stuck in the town hall for weeks trying to find out who lived in Back End Villas." Feather used the back of a hand to wipe sweat from his forehead. "If it wasn't for a certain Mrs Triggle, I think I would have. She's so old I think she must have been around when the town hall's foundations were laid. Anyway, she went right to one shelf, took down a carton and had the names out in a jiffy." The sergeant leant forward and stared at his notebook.

"Mrs Lukina Vladyko, daughter Olena and son Burien. I caught Mrs Vladyko at her new address this afternoon. From the Soviet Union somewhere. Got displaced and came here at the end of the war. Now, Billy Draper was reported missing on October seventh but disappeared on the sixth. The Vladykos left on the seventh. It might be an incredible coincidence. Either that or Draper knew the house was about to be vacated, and also knew there was stuff in there to thieve and decided to get into the house before they left. I'm guessing the latter."

Feather looked at his notes. "They had some family jewellery and a collection of, now what is it? Oh yes, icons, some religious paintings or something. Most of this stuff the family have sold now. Mrs Vladyko said they had bars across the ground floor windows. I've been up to Back End Villas again, and sure enough you can see the holes in the brickwork for the bars. Someone must have half-inched them while the house stood empty."

A couple of papers fell to the floor from the file in the sergeant's hand, and he retrieved them with neat agility.

"As I read it, old Billy tried to burgle the house on the night of the sixth and the family cleared off on the seventh. She can't remember, but Mrs Vladyko said they probably didn't bother setting a fire on the day they left. No one knew Billy Draper was jammed in the chimney. The house was boarded up straight away. Unfit for human habitation. It's taken them all this time to knock it down. It's a rum old story, but when you get your brain round it, it would have to be something as queer as this to account for his body being there." Feather took out a pink sweet of some kind and bit off half.

Stafford gave him a rundown on McCrone's report. The sergeant dropped the file on the desk and opened the door to leave before turning round.

"Oh, by the way Mr Stafford, we're running a sweep, get it, on a newspaper headline for Billy Draper. You know, Bungling Burglar breathes his last in Botched Burglary at Back End Villas. Tanner a go." Feather slotted the rest of the sweet into his mouth. The sweet did not stop him whistling as he strode down the corridor.

Stafford immersed himself in paperwork, and on checking the moorland search was being undertaken as he wanted. It had thrown up nothing so far. Another detective inspector, a better communicator, had been handed the job of day-to-day dealings with the press. A copy of the local paper, the *Telegraph and Argus*, was handed in to his office. The story was on the front. There was, of course, no photograph nor a name for the victim.

Tired and burdened by a withering attention span, Stafford opened the *Daily Telegraph* and put his feet on the desk. He scanned the front page and then folded the paper, a story on page two concerning the inquest into the death of Alan Turing catching his eye. A mathematician who invented a machine that did complicated calculations, Turing had been arrested two years earlier for committing gross acts of indecency with a man, and had undergone hormone therapy. The inquest concluded that Turing committed suicide, dying after eating an apple coated with cyanide.

Underneath it, the paper reported the formation of a Home Office committee to make recommendations on the laws concerning homosexuals and prostitution, following a rise in reported homosexual crimes. The bespectacled face of John Wolfenden, the man chosen to lead the committee, stared up at the detective inspector.

Stafford read the paper for another ten minutes, then left the office to buy torch batteries. He couldn't stop his eyes wandering to the public toilets, surrounded by nice flower beds, in the square. Back in his office, he looked through a few files. The phone rang. The investigation into the murder on the moor took its first forward step.

CHAPTER 9

Stafford knew immediately it was the person they were looking for. The woman seemed a near-duplicate of her daughter, in features and colouring, though her attractive face seemed washed out.

Emer Nelson had walked into a police sub-station on the edge of Bradford that late afternoon and reported her daughter missing. Persuaded that this might be the mother of the girl found dead on the moor, sparse details of the case now with all local stations, the duty sergeant had informed Stafford he was bringing her over in a squad car. In the canteen, Stafford stoked up with a sandwich of Cheddar cheese whose vivid yellow hue he eyed suspiciously. It didn't stop him wolfing it down rapidly and then buying a second.

He and two officers walked across the police yard in time to see the woman step out of the car. Unsteady, she placed an arm on the car's rear mudguard. A constable rested a hand on her shoulder. She was wearing a brown overcoat, twisted out of shape. In her state of anxiety, the buttons had not been aligned correctly with their holes.

"Can I see her body now, please," she said in a dull, matter-of-fact tone. She obviously knew about the body on the moor and was expecting the worst.

The officers looked at Stafford. This was not the correct way of going about things, but why delay it, he thought. He nodded and let the other officers take her to see the corpse. The air had turned cold and he was glad to be back indoors. He followed the group, staying several feet away, while the woman identified the body. She was calm, her eyes steady and lifeless. Stafford sent a constable off to ensure there was a female police officer in the station.

The woman was brought in to one of the nicer interview rooms, where Stafford sat behind a desk. Dark clouds were blocking out the sun and he switched on more overhead lights. The room seemed too bare and he made a mental note to ask for more pictures for the walls.

He spoke as softly as he could. "Please sit down, Mrs Nelson. We are so sorry for your loss. We truly are."

Emer Nelson stared blankly in front of her, a handkerchief in one hand. But there were no tears, and no obvious signs of distress in her face, other than that of its pallor.

"My name is Ray Stafford. I am a detective inspector. This is policewoman Rosemary Worsman and constable Jack Swale." Worsman was a single woman in her thirties with a pronounced forehead, and a haircut that formed a uniform black frame around the top of her face. Swale was new and nervous and every part of his face was pointed – chin, nose and ears. Even his cheekbones looked chiselled. He sat a little away from Stafford's desk. "Would you like some tea or something else to drink?"

"Tea." A silence then "please." Stafford nodded to the constable. "And biscuits?" Swale enquired. Stafford shot him a glance of exasperation. He then checked a note he had made of the daughter's name, now that they knew it.

"Mrs Nelson, I need to ask you some questions. If at any time you want me to stop, just let me know." Further silence. A muffled shout broke from somewhere in the bowels of the building. Clearly the voice of a man, or else the juxtaposition would have proved very uncomfortable.

"Would you tell me when you last saw Moira?" Mrs Nelson displayed no reaction to the noise and spoke immediately in a dead, monotonal semi-whisper. "Monday evening, after tea, about six-thirty. One of her friends, so-called, came round to pick her up. Donald Wardle. Twice her age. Got his own business. A garage. He's picked her up a few times. I don't like him." An officer opened the door of the room, apologised and closed it again. The salty cheese had dried out Stafford's throat.

From the limited occasions he had talked to women forced into dealing with a violent death, he knew the spectrum of their reactions was wide. At one end was a near-indifference. At the other, it ranged from immediate despair to an apparent stoicism which really hid mounting emotional disintegration. Curiously, the first sign of this latter pattern were eyes that shrank further into the skull. Emer Nelson's eyes had started that little journey.

"Could I ask this, Mrs Nelson? Did you worry yesterday when Moira did not return home?"

"Of course I did. A bit. I should have gone to the police yesterday, but she's stayed out before without me knowing where she was. She's nineteen. She sometimes stays with her father. We are not..." She let the sentence hang. Then added, "We no longer live in the same house."

Moira's mother was now trying to stuff her handkerchief into a hollow made by forefinger and thumb, like a trick in a Robert Harbin magic show.

"I rang his works yesterday but he's gone abroad. I knew he was going but I'd forgotten the date. I knew she wasn't due in where she works on Monday because she had to work all day Saturday."

Constable Swale returned with a cup of tea and some custard creams. Mrs. Nelson's eyes receded further. She was still manipulating her handkerchief in and out of the aperture shaped in her left hand. Her face remained a void.

"I didn't sleep much last night. I went to Behrens and Earnshaw, that's where she works, but she hadn't come in. I took the bus home to see if she was there. Walked around the streets a bit. You don't want to admit to yourself that something bad could have happened. Going to the police. It's like accepting that she really has gone missing. I saw a copy of the paper at the police station with the story about a girl's death."

Stafford knew he should keep the conversation going, but a shift in Mrs Nelson's countenance made him feel uneasy. Her face was collapsing inwards, starting at a point between her nose and mouth. He could tell Rosemary Worsman was unsettled as she leaned forward with her hand flat on the table, searching intently into the eyes of Moira's mother. All of a sudden, Emer Nelson rose slightly off her chair, emitted a kind of low-pitched wail engineered in the back of her throat, and lurched backwards on to the floor.

Stafford left others to help the bereaved mother. A cleaner mopped up the spilt biscuits and tea, the food crumbs and Mrs Nelson's handkerchief swallowed up by the bucket. He checked around the station. People knew Wardle's garage. It sold second-hand cars, but no one remaining in the station that evening knew him. He rang the garage. No answer. It was well after normal closing time. He checked the telephone directory again. Too many Wardles to make speculative calls.

It would have to wait until morning. He would look in on the garage on the way home, just to make sure the owner was not on site.

Outside, the weather had suddenly shifted into dampness. Stafford climbed into his bulky beetle-backed Standard Vanguard and drove up to Wardle's garage. The gate was locked, the office hut unlit. Across the road, troops of Life Boys in their semi-naval uniforms were streaming in to a church hall. After pulling into the driveway of his semi-detached, he undid the padlock on the wooden garage and nosed the car in. The deceptively gentle drizzle had saturated the car's paintwork, acid rain eating into the already rusting crease running along the driver's door, damaged in a minor collision.

Stafford fried a pork chop and ate it with some tinned vegetables and a bottle of Mackeson. He dropped into an armchair in front of his television's tiny screen, about the size of a dinner place mat. Most people bought standard models from Bush, Pye or GEC, but his was a Fitton Ambassador. Manufactured only a few miles away, he'd bought it because it came in a wedge-shaped cabinet, fitting neatly into a corner of his over-furnished living room.

Tired, he dopily watched the black and white picture. *What's My Line* was on, a four-person panel of celebrities trying to guess the livelihood of people with the help of just a few sparse clues. A woman filled the screen, miming her job with a clutch of abnormal twists and turns of the wrists and fingers. She worked in a factory making sewing machines. The panel failed to solve the puzzle. Smartly dressed and coiffured, none of the television stars looked as if they'd been within a hundred miles of an oil can.

Stafford padded into the kitchen again and rustled up a corned beef sandwich. Back in the armchair, he relaxed for another half an hour with *Fabian of The Yard*. Played by the suave but solid Bruce Seaton, the nerveless policeman was now up against a particularly nasty poisoner. As usual, the fictitious murderer was depicted with a balding, sweaty head and creepy round-lens spectacles, a clone of John Christie. The Notting Hill murderer was becoming a template for every make-believe villain. Stafford fixed his eyes on Elspet Gray and drifted into a daydream about the handsome actress. She looked nothing like Diana but his mind concocted physical resemblances where none existed. That, he thought, was a peculiar way for his brain to deal with loss. The famed man-hunting machine eventually collared the criminal, and the real Fabian rounded off the programme, as usual, with his homily on the work of the police force. It was down to plodding routine, never to a flash of brilliant detection, the tough little copper informed the viewers.

"If only," Stafford said out loud as he thought of Katy Follows.

Back in the kitchen, he used the key provided to remove the lid from a tin of pilchards, cutting his finger in the process, and constructed a second sandwich. He opened the *Daily Telegraph* and spread it across the table. The big news was the disappearance of yet another Comet. He had never been on a plane, not even during the war. He was too sleepy to read the paper closely, so he left his eyes and mind to their own devices as they selected items at random. Page two offered a picture of a sailing ship he had never heard of, the Cutty Sark, a tea clipper heading into dry dock for restoration in east London. He glanced at the science column. This was a discussion of the discovery by Cambridge scientists the previous year of something called DNA, the material of heredity. It held no resonance for him, another scientific break-through that would mean nothing to the common man. The newspaper also reported on an American company offering a television screen that could show programmes in colour. Just like going to the flicks.

He skipped through the foreign pages. The British Army in Kenya was really sticking the boot in against the Mau Mau. Two apparently normal girls in New Zealand cold-bloodily murdered one of their mothers. A big future was predicted for the all-new Bic ballpoint pen. He poured another Mackeson and read a boxing report on the upcoming heavyweight championship fight between Rocky Marciano and Ezzard Charles. Below the story, another item said Jake LaMotta was finally retiring. He had never actually seen any of these great fighters fight.

Stafford checked the watch his father had bequeathed him, a gold-cased Swiss wind-up whose face contained no brand name, nor even a "Swiss made" legend, and then trudged upstairs. He undid his Clarks heavy-sole shoes and lay on the bed. Reaching over to the bedside table, he switched on the Bush and tuned it to Radio Luxembourg.

He was just in time. Dan Dare was embarking on another adventure in his interminable battle with the Mekon. Taken from the *Eagle* comic, the Captain of the Future was a broadcast he found exciting, the square-jawed British commander crossing space in the fictitious nineteen-nineties. Stafford knew some of the child still remained in him. Yet as the Mekon, supreme leader of the Treens, mounted another improbable escape, Stafford drifted off into his own world of unconsciousness.

CHAPTER 10

That same bright morning when Detective Inspector Stafford was informed of the dead burglar's name, Jennifer Shaw came awake rather too quickly. The Trans World Airlines eye mask, with its emblem of overlapping globes, had given up the battle staving off the rays of sun piercing the bedroom curtains.

She could hear Stephen in his bathroom, the sounds of a clogged throat being repeatedly unblocked drifting through the solid wood door. She lifted a corner of the eye band to scan the general scene, then let it spring back, slightly stinging her cheek. The bathroom door opened and her husband's voice intruded with the kind of direct language between long-standing spouses.

"Got any aspirin up here?" He sounded gravelly.

"In my bathroom. Top cupboard. Second shelf up. On the left. Next to the Four Seven Eleven."

"Any chance of the latitude and longitude while you're at it?"

"Very funny. What time did you get in last night?" She vaguely remembered a dead weight collapsing next to her.

"About midnight. The club was very busy."

Shaw dislodged the eye band and swung out from the bed, stretched, and peered through the window into the acres of garden. Stephen's car was in the driveway, slewed across at an odd angle. A few inches further forward and the famed 'B' wings radiator mascot would have penetrated the rhododendron bush.

"How much did you knock back last night?"

"A skinful. A dozen G&Ts probably. Or was that two dozen. Why?"

"The Bentley looks as if it is playing Eskimo noses with the foliage. You shouldn't drive with all that booze in you."

He took a peek through the window. "There's no law against it as far as I know. Anyway, I was fine." She heard a gulp as a tablet headed into his stomach.

Shaw slumped back on the bed and stared blankly at the window, then stretched her arms again and yawned. "There's a film showing locally I'd like to see. *Three Coins in The Fountain.*"

"What's it about?"

"American secretaries falling in love in Rome."

"Oh Christ."

"Jean Peters is in it."

"Ah well, we are definitely going then."

A minute later, her husband let out a groan, followed up with a "damn" and a "blast" as he sat on the edge of the bed. "Look at this." He held out his watch, a square Omega Cosmic, incorporating a moon face. A crack ran right along the glass.

"How did you do that?"

"I think I fell over when I left the club."

"Christ, Stephen."

"Can you see if Fats stocks a replacement while you're in Bradford?"

"Of course. Hand it over."

Stephen Shaw padded the thirty feet or so to the cupboard, angry with himself for damaging a watch he had carefully selected at a jewellers in Thun at a cost of eight hundred and ten Swiss francs. He extracted another watch, a three-dial Omega Centenary, bought in the US for four hundred and fifty dollars six years earlier and featuring a tachometer and pulsometer. Stephen Shaw never paid import duty on his watches. He just wore them on his wrist when breezing through Customs, and no one had ever stopped him.

"I'm off to the mill. I'll have breakfast there, seeing as the kitchen is eviscerated." She knew Stephen was fond of the Aga and there was a hint of peevishness in his tone.

"Mrs Williams is perfectly equipped to do you toast and eggs."

"It's alright. I'll get a sandwich from the canteen."

"I think you're enjoying this. Evenings out with your chums and scoffing buns with the hoi polloi."

"Got it in one. And it's skilled textile machinists, if you don't mind. Well, some of them. Oh by the way, the car is going in for a check-up on Friday. I'll need the Jag. Hope your brother is not in too much hot water. I'm on tenterhooks wondering what's up."

"I'll bet." Stephen showed so little regard for Anthony. Jennifer Shaw thought her brother could disappear up the lousiest cannibal-infested tributary of the Orinoco and

Stephen would view the search party as a fishing opportunity. She had telephoned her husband from the Majestic yesterday to tell him she was seeing Maurice Black. Stephen gave her a kiss and disappeared through the door.

Shaw enjoyed a lingering bath and, seeing it was sunny, decided to overdress. As if she needed an excuse, she thought to herself. She selected a jacket and skirt from Harry Popper, the Austrian couturier in London's Grosvenor Street. Popper sold directly to top stores like Harrods, but also offered his services to private clients. During her last visit to the fashion house, she had shared a short conspiratorial chat with Princess Marina.

Downstairs, Mrs Williams dropped a couple of slices into the Morphy-Richards in the temporary kitchenette they had thrown together near the large pantry. Shaw could see, through the window, Archie Tyzack's building crew measuring up wood. The same gang of men, stubby HBs behind over-large ears. She hadn't noticed that before. Their ears were all potato-sized. Was this something to do with the pencils? Christ, she was going doolally. One extra body had shown up. She'd seen him once or twice before. An angular young man sporting one of those new Teddy Boy-style haircuts. He seemed in a surly mood and lobbed his work bag against the French windows on the patio. Archie Tyzack directed some words towards him, she could not hear what. There was a delay of a few seconds and then everyone burst out laughing. Except the young man.

Shaw wolfed the remains of her toast and downed the last of the Liptons, snatched her newspaper, and headed off for the garage. In the Jag, she reached across to the glove compartment and extracted her cat's eye sunglasses with lemon frames. Once the car was in the drive, she slipped on the glasses and looked at herself in the rear-view mirror. With its rhinestone accents, it felt just a bit too Antibes that morning. She tossed them back in the glove compartment and pulled out another pair, Foster Grants with tortoiseshell side flashes. They looked better. The Sphinx eased her foot down on the throttle and drove out into the road.

The journey into Bradford was uneventful, though she did make eye contact with a somewhat unusual-looking individual. Near the Bradford School of Art, Shaw braked the

Jaguar at a zebra crossing, the Belisha beacons dispensing an orange glow even in the sunshine. The youth, black hair pitched over his forehead, was obviously an art student, a big hard-backed folder under his arm. As he crossed in front of the Jaguar, he stared into the car through oversized spectacles as if wondering who the woman could be behind the wheel of this white behemoth. She held his gaze for a second. He looked rather intense, as if he was storing up an image to relay on to canvas. She could see in her rear-view mirror that he was still watching as her car drifted away down the hill.

A large billboard on the Alhambra Variety Theatre proclaimed the arrival on their British tour of Stan Laurel and Oliver Hardy. She thought about the men installing her kitchen, then of the ersatz Poggenpohl. Should she have gone for a fridge even bigger than the Prestcold she had ordered? Forthcoming turns were also listed on the theatre's frontage. Frankie Vaughan she knew. Bruce Forsyth she did not.

Shaw parked the car and headed for the jewellers. The chill ate into her and she stuffed her silk scarf further down her neck. The scarf was a Hermès classic, using, as its design, symbols from Napoleon Bonaparte's army. It was, of course, totally useless against the Pennine cold.

Fattorini's or 'Fats' was the most celebrated jewellers and watch shop in the city. It had been founded by Antonio Fattorini from Bellagio on Lake Como, who came to Britain in eighteen-fifteen to help in the fight against the same Napoleon. It was too late by then, so he and his family settled down to trading, eventually creating in the city two of Britain's greatest mail order businesses, Empire Stores and Grattan. Fattorini, the shop, was an institution, and not only for the well-heeled shopper. Every Bradford bus displayed, on its front, an enamel badge bearing the city's coat of arms and supplied by Fattorini at two pounds, four shillings and sixpence each.

At the counter, she was greeted by one of the shop's friendly staff. "Hello, Mrs Shaw. Nice to see you. What can I do you for?"

"Well look at this, Mr Hardaker." She handed over the Cosmic.

"Uhm. Taken a bit of a beating. I haven't seen this time piece before. Wait a minute." He slipped his circular-lens spectacles back on and disappeared into a back room, before returning to the counter and informing her that new glass would have to be sent for from Switzerland.

She undid her Omega Sapphette with sapphire-facet edged crystal glass. "While I'm here would you change the strap, same colour if you have it, and give the watch a polish. Thank you, Mr Hardaker."

Jennifer Shaw slotted herself into one of the store's armchairs and opened her *Daily Telegraph*. She already knew about the crash of the Comet from the radio and, finding domestic news as dull as ever, rifled through to the foreign pages. Two couples came into the shop, one of the men with obvious plastic surgery on his badly burned face. Probably a pilot, she guessed. You didn't see those kind of injuries as much up in Yorkshire as you did in the south. "It's brass monkeys out there," she heard one of the women say.

Shaw looked down the columns of print. People were getting injected in the United States with the polio virus to protect them against the disease. West Germany would soon be allowed to re-arm. Wasn't that a bit soon? Nasser was taking over in Egypt. What a holiday that was. Super monuments but too much 'Delhi Belly'. What was the Egyptian equivalent of Montezuma's revenge? Her mind searched fruitlessly for a rhyme using Alexandria, eventually coming up with something unprintably rude. She smiled to herself.

The watch back on her wrist, Shaw hurried across the road to Brown Muffs department store. Peckish after the feeble breakfast, she had time on her hands for more food. She walked through the store, always too hot for her liking, and waited at the metal cage lift which would spirit her to the top-floor cafeteria. She let her eyes track the crazy spider's web of piping which circulated money and receipts around the building in rocket-like canisters. It was powered by some mysterious, unseen force. Compressed air, she guessed.

Seating herself at a corner table, she ordered egg and cress sandwiches on brown bread and a Russian tea. The cafeteria was quite full and even hotter than ground level. The waitress, in black and white, delivered the order, the tea coming in a long glass with metal handle and stand. A nice wedge of lemon usually floated on top, but perhaps the fruit was unavailable that day.

Shaw opened the paper again. A last-stand battle was under way in French Indo-China, the Viet Minh still attacking Dien Bien Phu, a name she was becoming familiar with. She briefly studied the map that went with the article. Algeria looked as if it was going up in flames. Goodness me, the Frogs were really copping it, she thought. Then she caught sight of the two paragraph short. Her arm, about to unload a chunk of food between her full lips, involuntarily halted in midair. She couldn't believe it. Not him. How had it happened? The story didn't say. He was too young. Her favourite dress designer. Dead. Poor Jacques. For half a minute Shaw was truly despondent. Then a thought light-bulbed in her brain. Where was she going to pick up more Jacques Fath couture? Perhaps Marshall and Snelgrove might have one or two pieces, though she doubted it. A plan for the afternoon was being mapped out in her frontal lobe.

She set off for the Swan Arcade, a covered sub-Italian style Victorian shopping thoroughfare housing forty-four shops and three upper floors of offices. Hunting for some flowers to give Maurice Black, only daffodils were on offer. Instead, Shaw purchased the biggest Rowntree's Dairy Box she could find. She knew he enjoyed, like her, a sweet tooth and had often wanted to buy him a Black Magic but thought it too obvious. Chocolate had got its old taste back, thankfully, now rationing was finishing and the makers had fallen back on their traditional recipes.

Shaw drove across to her solicitor's office. Most professional companies operated from buildings elsewhere in the city. Black's business was housed in an area largely built by foreign traders. German, mainly Jewish, merchants had started setting up trading houses in Bradford a hundred years before but, by the turn of the century, most had packed up and gone, leaving just a small nucleus behind. Maurice Black, she knew, was a descendent of Johann Schwartz, a dealer in dress fabrics with China and the Americas.

Even in such a short time, these merchants bequeathed an impressive array of buildings, many in mock-Italianate design, others with more like Grecian church fronts. As palaces of trade, their lowest storeys were frequently designed to exude an aura of power, often employing massive pieces of millstone grit. A common characteristic was the use of stone-carved serpentine markings. Black's office, once a cloth warehouse, was a magnificent creation, with polished grey granite columns down the sides of all its windows, above which the spandrels demonstrated elaborate stone carvings. The lower levels of stonework were heavily decorated with that characteristic serpentine vermiculation. Jennifer Shaw marched in through the wide entrance, framed in pink granite columns and overshadowed by a double-headed falcon.

"Hello, Miriam. I've got an appointment with Maurice."

"Nice to see you, Mrs Shaw. Please sit down and I will call him."

The receptionist angled her seat and attacked switches poking from a giant intercom box. Shaw inspected the magazines on a nearby table. Mainly devoted to law and accountancy, they looked specifically chosen to induce a coma. Not a *Vogue* in sight.

"You can go up now, Mrs Shaw. You know where it is. Second floor."

The height of each step was unnaturally low and, after half a dozen, she used her long legs to take two at a time. She was met by the short and immaculately turned-out solicitor, waiting outside his office door.

"My dear. Nice to see you." He reached up and gave her a peck on the cheek. "Come right in."

She threw on to a spare seat, her Italian blue leather non-branded shoulder bag, bought in Perugia, one of her favourite cities, and slid into a stiff-backed work chair in front of Maurice's oak desk.

"I'm afraid to say it's a rather wasted journey, Jennifer. Your brother called about a quarter of an hour ago. He won't be coming after all."

The second thing that day she couldn't believe, after her husband's inebriated stumble. What was he good for, her brother? "Oh no. What a pain."

"You can give him a call from here, if you like." Using Black's telephone, its maker's name tag, G.E.C., still occupying the dial where the number should be, a call to Anthony's home produced a long ring and no answer.

"I'm so sorry, Maurice. I just don't know what that brother of mine thinks he's playing at. Would you credit it?"

"Look on the bright side. It might mean there's nothing to worry about after all. Anyway, what's he up to these days?"

"He's always getting ideas but doesn't seem to put anything into practice. Stephen has subsidised so many failed ventures. Anthony's now got this plan to act as an agent for a company that makes an expensive machine for turning out cups of coffee."

"What's wrong with a kettle?"

"Well, I know, but they do look like a lot of fun in Italy. Gaggia or something. Stephen told him there were not enough milk bars up here to justify it, and Anthony said he could sell it to fish and chip shops. I thought Stephen was heading for a coronary, he laughed so much. Anyway, that's on the QT. How about coming for a drink? My shout. I could do with the company."

"To be truthful, Jennifer, I'm rather glad Anthony couldn't make it. I'm snowed under at the moment. Next time." The solicitor's desk did look like a paper depository, tall stacks of files threatening to topple at the first sign of a breeze.

She got up and leant across to kiss Maurice, rather catching him unawares as he was still looking down at his desk, and managed to leave a red imprint of her mouth on his forehead. She handed over the 'chocs'. Black beamed, revealing three gold teeth.

Outside, Shaw stood immobile on the pavement. What did she need? A stiff drink, that's what. She ambled up the hill towards the Victoria Hotel, making a short detour into the Exchange train station, a vast Victorian edifice featuring two great, semi-circular, wrought-iron arches, cast at a local foundry. A copy of London's King's Cross and only ten feet narrower, it handled ten direct services to the capital every day.

Like all stations of this size, the atmosphere reeked of an age whose time was almost up. The railways still used over eighteen thousand steam locomotives, almost as many as before the war, and the air was dense with the grit of burning coal and the hissing of super-heated water. But a strange-looking machine stood at a nearby platform and she surmised, rightly, that it was the new diesel locomotive, making one of its first appearances in the city, that she had read about. She purchased a couple of magazines, dodged the trajectory of one of the Scarab mechanical horses that transported baggage and freight within the station, and headed towards the Victoria.

An architectural take on London's Grosvenor, the hotel was warm and quiet and she ordered a Tom Collins at the bar. Finding a window seat, Shaw took a sip of the cocktail. She hadn't watched it being made and wondered what they had used to generate the citrus flavour if Brown Muffs couldn't get a supply of real lemons.

From her window seat, she could see a couple walking up to the hotel, a small girl with them carrying a multi-coloured metal spinning top. The girl was practising her hopscotch steps. Opening the *Telegraph* again, the first item taking her interest was a story about Disney, the American cartoon people, announcing their first fun park themed on their cartoons. Staff at the California location would all be wearing special costumes. On the same page was an advert for a smart, half-length 'dandy' coat for fourteen and a half guineas at Marshall and Snelgrove. That got her going again. Where was she going to buy more evening wear from dear, dead Jacques?

CHAPTER 11

When Ray Stafford awoke the following morning, his mind, even in a state of drowsiness, centred immediately on his dead wife. In the bathroom, he was thinking of her and Don Wardle. By the time he stepped out of his house though, his mind was concentrating solely on Wardle and the lifeless body of Moira Nelson.

It was seven-thirty, and Stafford sauntered down the hill and into Bairstow's sweet shop and newsagents. The single storey former weaver's cottage was typical of a kind dotted all around the city's suburbs. Many had long been converted to 'fisheries', serving up haddock and chips deep fried in beef fat that infused the batter with a distinctive flavour he had come to love.

Alfie Bairstow was trying to secure on the counter a big cardboard advert for a new strip in the *Beano* comic. "When the Bell Rings", it said, due for issue 604, and displaying a motley collection of pug-ugly characters called Erbert and Spotty and Plug among other silly names. "Morning, Alfie."

"Oh, morning. Will be right with you. I don't really have enough room for these promotions."

The shop owner tried again to anchor it, but the cut-out eventually tumbled to the floor and Stafford retrieved it. The elderly newsagent had once suffered from tuberculosis, and Stafford wondered if that was the cause of his bent back. He took the paper and strode up the hill. His neighbours now parked in their front garden a small, old-fashioned, corrugated caravan, right out of a Noddy and Big Ears adventure. It was beginning to irk him.

Stafford backed the Vanguard into the near-deserted road and headed for the station. It was Thursday, and the weather had carried on from where it left off the evening before. Dank greyness. Sometimes, the sun gave up on industrial places like this.

The most tangible item on his office desk was a note policewoman Worsman had obtained a recent photograph of Moira Nelson that her mother always kept in her handbag. The photograph had been spirited over to the local newspaper.

He took a quick look at the latest reports lodged in the incident room, then, with two officers in an unmarked police Wolseley, drove the short distance to Wardle's garage. It was a typical 'bomb site' operation, though bigger than most second-hand dealers. About twenty or so cars were parked on concrete, in rows behind a high fence. A proper, well-appointed sign was attached to the gate. A long wooden hut occupied the back, and next to it stood a V8 Pilot. A tallish man with a thin moustache leaned against the Ford, examining a piece of paper. He wore a boxy suit with extra wide lapels and wide-legged trousers, his trilby tipped up in a jaunty American-style slant. Stafford knew it was Wardle and took an instant dislike to him for no good reason, a bad trait in a copper Stafford was only too well aware.

"Mr Wardle?"

The man looked up and clocked the constable's uniform. "My goodness. The long arm of the law. What's my wife complained about now?" He had a Geordie accent and a very false smile.

"Can we go into your office? It won't take long."

The hut smelled damp but was surprisingly warm, two electric fires on with all of their bars glowing. Wardle must have been here very early that morning. The owner sat on a metal-studded chair and put his feet up on the desk, all the paperwork piled neatly in wire baskets.

"I'm Detective Inspector Ray Stafford. This is Constable Priestley. We are interested in Moira Nelson. Would you tell me, please, about Monday evening."

"Moira? What about Moira?" Wardle looked interested, but only in a vacant way.

"Would you tell me about Monday evening?"

"Monday evening. Well, yes, I picked her up from her house at about six-thirty or seven. It's her grandparents' house, I think. Why are you asking this?"

"Moira has been found dead. We are trying to trace her movements. Go on, Mr Wardle."

The muscles slackened in the garage owner's face, and he lowered his feet from the desk and sat forward. He placed a hand to the side of his head. Stafford could see the back of the hand was covered in matted black hair.

"I can't believe it. What's happened to her?" Wardle's look of surprise appeared entirely convincing. His face was draining of colour. Stafford knew this wasn't their man. He tried to ignore his disappointment but he felt his concentration slipping away.

"We went to the Talbot Hotel," Wardle continued. "That's all. Wait a minute. It wasn't that girl in the paper yesterday, was it? Up on the moor? My God. Look, I've got nothing to hide. We went to the Talbot. There's, er, a special room at the back there. It's private, like, where people can have a quiet drink. My nephew is the chief barman there. I slip him a few quid and we can use the room. Sometimes they are my customers. It helps business. If Lenny, that's my nephew, gets to know, them they can just go in."

"It's like a members' club?"

"No, no, nothing like that. It's just a room. Hey, you're not going to get Lenny in trouble. He's done nothing wrong."

"You were there on Monday evening?"

"I took Moira over. She's a nice kid. There was no harm in it. There were quite a few in there but I stayed only half an hour or so. She was still there when I left."

"You had a relationship with Moira?"

"No, I didn't." He looked peeved at that question. "I was just a friend."

"Where did you meet her?"

"Let me think. Yes. One of the pubs in town."

The interview continued on these lines for a while, and Wardle provided a list, with no argument, of the people he said he could remember at the Talbot that night, and a list of other people not there but who had used the room at one time or another. The total list ran to between twenty-five and thirty people. Wardle supplied details of addresses, using a flip-up holder. This took nearly an hour. No customer pitched up at the hut.

Dislike was still etched on his own face, Stafford knew, and despite a spirited effort, he was transmitting that across Wardle's desk. Wardle, he knew too, was receiving it, and began staring back at Stafford with a steady gaze. The colour was returning to Wardle's face.

Stafford walked around the office for the umpteenth time, floorboards creaking every time he moved. He peered at sheets of information, attached to the hut's plasterboard lining with drawing pins, and examined several times the same framed photograph of a bridge in Newcastle which he had first thought was the Sydney Harbour Bridge. That structure he had just seen in a television item on emigration to Australia by the "ten pound poms". He could feel Wardle's eyes on him. He turned back and said, "We will have to talk to your wife about Monday evening."

"Doris? Yeah, of course. As I say, I went straight home after leaving the Talbot."

"She doesn't mind you out and about enjoying yourself in the evenings, Mr Wardle?" Stafford detected in his own voice a sneer he failed to suppress, and was annoyed with himself.

"No, she doesn't." Wardle waited a few seconds. "Doris has been in a wheelchair for seven years. She had polio diagnosed before we got married. I look after her as a husband should. No, detective inspector, she doesn't mind me going out at all."

Stafford felt his chest tighten. Seeking fresh air, no matter how unfresh it was, he went outside, the other two men following. He looked around at the assortment of metal and found himself staring at the nose of the closest car which sported an extraordinarily large and elaborate horse's head radiator mascot.

"Interested, Mr Stafford? Virtually new. Only three hundred miles. Singer Hunter. Nice colour. Moss green under silver. Owner died. Just bought it from his wife. You can pick up a bargain when there's a bereavement." ·

"No, I'm not interested."

"Yeah, well, you need a bit of style to drive a motor like that." Wardle swaggered off to the office, hands in pockets and shoulders rolling. He was whistling the Blaydon Races.

On the way back to the station, Stafford called in on the radio and had an officer sent up to Doris Wardle. Then he had the car stop at a cafe. He and Priestley went inside for some ham teacakes. In front of them in the queue was a group of workers from the local slaughterhouse, blood and bits of bone dripping on to the lino from their rubber boots and aprons. One of them had a large serrated gutting knife hanging from a belt. Stafford looked at his feet. He was standing in a pool of liquefied gristle.

"Do you think Wardle's got a point about style?" Stafford asked.

The constable gave him a once-over. "Don't worry, sir. Not everyone can be a snappy dresser."

Back in his office, Stafford looked at a note on the conversation an officer had shared with Shaw's mill that morning. Moira's father was due to leave on Monday afternoon, the company confirmed, staying at the Park Lane Hotel, London, before flying to Pakistan the following day. The hotel said that a man of that name had booked in that evening. His bill showed he ate in their dining room. The airline said Tommy Nelson had caught the flight.

The Park Lane, on Piccadilly, sounded a bit ritzy for a mill manager. And why was he going to Pakistan? Not that that was in any way relevant. Stafford wondered whether Nelson had flown there in a Comet.

After ditching from his head those useless questions, Stafford took the same car, and two officers, to Behrens and Earnshaw. The accountants where Moira earned her living as a clerk was in Bradford's own Piccadilly, a far less dramatic road than its namesake in the capital. The accountants were housed in a drab, simply-faced building, except for an extraordinary piece of stone carving. Above the entrance, an ensemble of eagle-like birds with pronounced talons stood proud from the wall. As a coat of arms it would befit a minor Germanic royal dynasty. It was as if the building's original owners tried to combat its listless frontage with a fancy flourish.

The inside was a rabbit-warren of pokey offices and narrow corridors and smelled of wood. Selwyn Printer, Moira's rather young boss, sat in a leather wingback, swivelling side to side in quarter circles. His eyes swivelled too. It was like a constant flicker. Obviously an ailment of some kind, with probably a horrible-sounding name, Stafford guessed, but it didn't stop Printer holding down a good job. Printer had no complaints about Moira's work. Other members of staff added nothing of interest. She didn't have a close friend at the company, and no one knew anything much about her private life. The staff occasionally enjoyed a drink together and that was all. Stafford thought the inert spirit of the workforce at Behrens and Earnshaw ideally matched the ponderously stodgy building.

The officers headed off to the home of Moira's grandparents, where Moira Nelson and her mother had been living, the visit arranged that morning on the telephone. The drive took less than fifteen minutes. It was a lower middle class area, short of love and attention. Theirs was a joyless end of terrace in a nineteen-thirties development, with its own garage. A small, neat garden ran down to a well-maintained brick wall. Window frames and doors were newly painted, but in brown. This gave the dwelling a sad countenance. The word 'Kenmare' was written in loopy writing on a black nameplate near the front door bell. Across the road, a stern Victorian church glowered at neighbouring houses.

Leaving the driver in the car, Stafford and Priestly approached the front door and were met by the grandfather. Brian McGillicuddy's face was ruddy. Obvious musculature beneath his small frame perhaps spoke of a farming lineage. He retained a strong but soft southern Irish accent which, Stafford guessed, put him a long way from Dublin. The grandfather was courteous and matter-of-fact. His wife stood with her back to the kitchen sink and gazed down the hall at the policemen. Even from a distance she looked haunted.

Emer Nelson sat in the living room, her pretty face puffy and reddened. She looked tired and shrunken. Lipstick had been applied, but unevenly, and tears blotched her mascara. Stafford gave her shoulder a squeeze and then followed the grandfather up to the back bedroom Moira had been given to herself. The family's little terrier hurdled the stairs after them, struggling with the steepness of the steps. "Skedaddle, Bobby," Mr McGillicuddy said on the top landing. The dog ignored the command and lay down in the middle of Moira's bedroom, looking as forlorn as the rest of the family.

The bedroom was neat and filled with unremarkable items. A stack of *Picture Show* annuals "for people who go to the pictures" rested on a chest of drawers. Above the bed head, posters of film stars were pinned to the wall in a half-moon shape. Dana Andrews, Stewart Granger, Brian Keith and James Mason. Stafford noted the actors, somewhat older than might have been expected in a young girl's room.

A much smaller photograph of Laurie Anders was also pinned above the bed. A nice-looking blonde girl, with a black bow in her hair and a low-cut frilly top, smiled back at

Stafford. He had never heard of her. The legend was printed in fussy, loopy writing: "Born in Goose Egg, Wyoming, she was brought up in the saddle."

Mr McGillicuddy explained a few points about the bedroom and about his granddaughter. His accent reversed the 't' and 'th' sounds, "fifth" becoming "fift" and "thought" becoming "tort".

Back downstairs, the two officers were offered tea. A full packet of Peak Freans was tipped on to a plate. Stafford decided to get on with the interview straight away.

"Mrs Nelson, could I ask you whether Moira kept a diary?"

It was as if he had poked her with a stick. She stood up quickly and walked to the corner of the window, pushing a curtain to one side so she could see out. She was wearing very shiny high heels. "No. No, she didn't." She stayed there, quite still, Stafford looking at the back of her lime-green print dress. A very small child, on its own, pedalled past on a tricycle. It was leaning forward to gain as much purchase as possible on the pedals. The child did a couple of circles, then crashed the front wheel into a tree and sat there, unable to figure out what to do next.

"I don't think she was a girl that looked backwards," Mrs Nelson eventually said. She rested a hand on the window frame. "We were disappointed she didn't stay on at school. She passed her eleven-plus, you know, but left at seventeen."

Turning around now, Emer Nelson walked over to the fireplace and gazed numbly at the opposite wall. She had the five-hundred-yard stare of a person unhooked from reality by overwhelming loss. Then they all sat down.

Mrs Nelson spoke randomly about her daughter, Moira's friends and interests, the delivery as monotonal as the evening before. A picture emerged of an ordinary, nice-looking girl, gradually slipping away from the control of her family. Moira was not behaving badly, but was starting to lead an adult life quite apart from that of her mother. Perhaps her parents' separation unsettled her. That was so unusual for a Catholic family. Unusual for any family, Stafford thought.

His mind tramlined off for some seconds to his dead wife and absence of children. It veered back, latching on to a minor conundrum. A marriage spanning this exhausted woman in front of him and a mill manager important enough to travel to the other side of the world seemed odd. He looked closely at Mrs Nelson. It was impossible to make any judgement. The murder of her daughter had punched such a hole in her spirit.

After almost an hour, the two officers stood up. Stafford could see through the window that the child with the tricycle was perhaps fifty yards away now, still pedalling on its own. He also noticed, for the first time, that the plate had been totally denuded. He remembered having two biscuits. He turned to Constable Priestley who was masticating heavily and about to drop yet another cream-filled wafer into his rapidly-moving mouth.

"I'm sorry," said Stafford. "We seem to have demolished all the food." Sitting in front of the empty plate, Bobby looked especially fed up.

CHAPTER 12

From the McGillicuddy house, Stafford was driven into the city centre. It was busy and they had trouble pinpointing a parking spot. They crawled round the block housing the Talbot and settled on a space outside the Bradford Commercial Bank in Hustlergate. A stumpy, chain-sided brewery lorry was parked in front, a drayman rolling a wooden beer barrel off the back. A second drayman waited on the pavement ready to manoeuvre it on to a two-wheel push trolley. A gaping hole scarred the road surface. An iron tar-making machine was bellowing smoke, ready for road surface re-laying. A workman was lighting a kerosene lamp resting on a metal tripod, as a warning for approaching vehicles.

With Constable Priestley, Stafford walked up the hill, bought a *Telegraph and Argus* from a paper seller, checked that it carried a photograph of the dead Moira Nelson, and slipped under the renowned statue of a dog that marked the entrance of the Talbot. This was a commercial hotel, not to be confused with a superior establishment like the Midland. Nevertheless, it was proud to broadcast the word "commercial" with a permanent sign across its façade, partly to distinguish it from hotels that were merely pubs with rooms.

The first door on the right had the word "manager" painted on it. It was ajar, the tinny, jocular sound of *Music While You Work* was issuing from a radio. Stafford knocked, pushed the door right open, showed his identification and asked the man behind the desk if he was the manager.

"I am. Bruce Chew. What can I do for you?" He smiled at that practiced rhyme. Chew sported a gimpy eye in an incongruously podgy head, resting on top of a thin body. He spoke out of the corner of his mouth while he ate. A sandwich with a green-coloured filling lay on a willow pattern plate sitting in front of him. He got up and shuffled out of the office, pointing out Lenny Wardle, manning the beer pumps at the large bar. People were milling about in dense groups and three barmen struggled to cope. Thick with cigarette smoke, the room's atmosphere duplicated the outdoors. Stafford did not use cigarettes but his father had, and he accepted the smell and air-borne taste of tobacco tar as a normal part of everyday life.

Showing Wardle his police card, Stafford shepherded him over to the quietest corner of the room. He could see Chew was out of his office, observing him. Stafford eyed him back, and the manager retreated behind his office door.

"I want you to show me the private room that your uncle uses here," Stafford said.

"Why?"

"Because I'm asking you to. Please show me the room." Lenny Wardle was in his early thirties. With eyes unnaturally close together and a nose pointed like a pencil tip, he resembled a rodent. Stafford didn't know what he was expecting, but the room was quite small and quite ordinary. Built-in sofas in pale blue synthetic material that reflected the light filled the corners. The carpet was in darker blue and the walls entirely bare. Crates of beer were stacked up in a corner and a faint whiff of hot food drifted down from an air vent near the ceiling.

"What happens here?"

"We use the room for small-scale do's, you know, cheap wedding receptions and the like. We have a much bigger room for proper functions."

"No. I mean when your uncle uses it?"

"People just sit around and have a drink."

"Why don't they just do that at the main bar?"

"It's nicer in here. It's like they're in their own private club or something. My uncle says he gets a few more car sales from it. I'm sure it makes him feel important. Some bigwig."

Stafford got the feeling that uncle and nephew didn't always see eye to eye.

"Why doesn't the manager stop you doing it?"

"Both the day and night managers get a few bob out of it. They couldn't care less. Why should they? Anyway, I'm in charge of the bar. What's this all about?"

"You take drinks in to them?"

"Sometimes, or they just come to the bar, or my uncle will buy a few bottles of whisky or something and leave it for them. What's going on?"

Stafford showed him the picture of Moira in the paper. He recognised her, and a look of surprise registered on his face, ever more shrew-like the longer Stafford studied it.

"The place was really busy on Monday. There was a Chamber of Commerce do or something and they were all in the bar beforehand. I have no idea when she left."

Stafford thought of all those people in the hotel. The idea depressed him. They'd have to put out another call through the newspaper asking for witnesses. The manager eventually came over and pretended to collect glasses.

"Alright, Mouse?" he asked. No one offered a response and Chew sloped off, wiping crumbs from his mouth with the front of his hand.

The two officers worked their way through the staff, a task generating nothing recognisable as a lead. Stafford noted down a reminder to visit the night manager on the way home. He took one last look at the room. An opium den it was not.

Outside, he sent the constable back to the car. The paper seller was bent over, enduring a coughing fit that jerked his head to and fro, like one of those nodding dogs people were starting to place on their car parcel shelf. It reminded Stafford of the workman at Back End Villas. That was only a couple of days ago. It felt like a week. The old paper seller's raincoat might have been grey once and had somehow advanced to a mouldy green without passing black. Tape held his spectacles together on one side. Soles were parting company with the body of his shoes. The seller resumed his call. It obviously meant something – like "Telegraph and Argus" – but the voice authored a cry of utter mumbo jumbo. Incredible the raw lung power in such a weedy chest. And he was shouting with a fag still in his mouth.

Stafford strolled over to the big, Victorian, metal-structured Kirkgate market, the paper man's verbal hieroglyphics still within earshot. He entered under the figures of Flora and Pomona, goddesses of flowers and fruit and all things fresh and scented. The place was sweaty with bodies. After waiting in line at Watmough's, the butcher, he purchased a pig's cheek and steered a course back to the Wolseley down Bank Street. By the time he reached the vehicle, something squelchy was oozing from the meat and through the paper bag on to his hand. He stuffed the bag into the *T&A*. A second later, he realised he had done that across the photograph of Moira Nelson's face.

Stafford climbed back into the car, noticing a Mercedes-Benz saloon parked in the spot vacated by the brewery wagon. Interested in motors, he took time to admire one of the few Mercs he had ever seen. It was the same pale blue colour as the carpet in the Talbot, but on the Merc that colour looked classy and exotic. The steering wheel was in brilliant white. The owner had to be really loaded, given the price of these imports.

The Riley then pulled away. As it did so, the officers had no reason to clock a rather odd-looking individual, with a head too big for his non-symmetrical shoulders, emerge from the Bradford Commercial Bank. This bank, designed in French Gothic, included a tall tower, mitre roof, fretted balcony, and granite shafts around windows and the main door, all symbols of its importance to the city. Single cheques for more than a million pounds were occasionally handed over by the big wool companies to startled counter staff who never quite got used to it. The man with the rather large head was inwardly smiling at the size of the balance in his deposit account and, as usual, expending a few thoughts on the rich people who used that particular bank, just like he did. Then he saw the Mercedes. It annoyed him for reasons he could not quite put his finger on. He glowered at it. If the man had seen Moira Nelson's face in the *T&A* that day, a rush of other feelings would have overtaken him. But he couldn't read. So he never bought the local paper.

In the station, Stafford dropped the pig's cheek into the bottom drawer of his desk. The division of labour set in motion while he had been out was now well in hand. Officers were already interviewing people on Wardle's list. Others would soon be doing the same with shops near the Talbot. Another list, supplied by Moira's mother, of items she believed her daughter was carrying on Monday evening, was surprisingly long. It included a clover leaf pendant, a brooch in the shape of a butterfly and a cross on a necklace. They all had initials or inscriptions and were all missing. Her clasp, purse-type handbag in mauve had disappeared. The girl was wearing a pale blue coat, which the police needed to find, and probably a dark green scarf with blue stripes. He'd check those clothing items with the night manager of the Talbot.

Stafford hit the keys on the Imperial, writing up his notes destined for the central pool of information now mounting up quickly. He wrote a separate note of suggestions and, after pouring tea into a pint mug, wandered around to see what everyone else was up to.

Paying a call on the Talbot's night manager in the early evening produced nothing of note. The roads were so empty he never had to stop once before arriving home.

In the dated kitchen, Stafford luxuriated in a lengthy stretch, peered vacantly out of the back window on to the lawn and stalled in mid-thought. His body went rigid for a moment and then inwardly sagged. A feeling of helplessness swept over him. He almost lost the will to move. He had left the pig's cheek in the desk drawer.

Stafford was all too aware that the loss of his wife sometimes flicked a mental switch whose sole purpose was to exaggerate minor headaches into major crises. By the time he'd crossed the threshold of Mudge's fisheries, the pig's cheek was a distant memory. After ordering haddock and chips, scraps, and a cake which, in tat part of the country, consisted of a layer of potato and a layer of fish, he added to the order a full-size bottle of Tizer. Back in the kitchen, he buttered half a dozen slices of bread, and deliberately ate slowly. He took down a tin of Lyons coffee, thought again, and instead rooted out a Fry's cocoa canister he found behind a packet of Paddy washing powder.

Hot drink in hand, he moved into the living room and switched on the television. Stafford knew the Independent Television service would start broadcasting from next year. With some fanfare, the company had announced the purchase of an American series called *I Love Lucy*. For the moment, everyone had to make do with the one BBC channel. He drew the curtains and sat on the settee, stretching his legs out on the top of a three-table nest.

As soon as the television warmed up and the picture appeared Stafford cursed. He'd intended watching Peter Cushing and Ann Todd in *Tovarich*, but it was already on. He checked the *Radio Times* (North of England Edition) and saw that it was almost half-way through. He had a vague crush on

Todd. He watched it for a few minutes but didn't know what was going on.

It bemused him how he could show little interest in the women around him since his wife's death, yet could still develop an emotional 'thing' about a distant film star. He had begun to suspect that these distant 'things' were getting stronger. He had even stared a little too long at that poster of Laurie Anders on Moira Nelson's bedroom wall. Signs, perhaps, that his emotional drives were returning to normal.

Stafford studied the radio section of the BBC journal and, as luck would have it, Ann Todd was doing *Rebecca*. It was just about to start. He carried the cocoa upstairs, retuned the radio from Luxembourg to the Light Programme, took a sip of the hot liquid, and lay face down on the bed. He was just in time to hear Todd's clipped tones in the role of the second Mrs de Winter. Within a few minutes, Stafford was beginning to lose interest in the story, but the actress's voice gripped the attention of his mind and his body.

CHAPTER 13

In his suite in the Palace Hotel, Tommy Nelson stood by the window as he pulled the belt tight on his light-weight cotton trousers. He knew the shorts he'd donned in the plane were a big mistake as soon as he stepped into Karachi's airport terminal. All the local men were clad in traditional pyjama-style outfits or in Western business clothes, with or without a tie. He'd looked like a day-tripper on Morecambe beach. The passport wallahs had definitely displayed some reverse colonial snootiness when they saw his kneecaps. As soon as he entered the sanctuary of his comfortable hotel room he had changed clothes. It was now his second day in the city and the shorts were crammed into the bottom of his suitcase. They wouldn't see fresh air until his first stint of fell-walking in the Pennines, when the weather warmed up.

Shaw's production manager was enjoying a rather nice time in the Dominion of Pakistan's richest city. He certainly had not expended much energy on work. His hosts were too good at being, well, hosts. Still, it was only day two into a week-long trip. He'd have to get down to business at some point.

Nelson sat on the edge of the bed and relived that first afternoon with his new friend. Mr Nazaruddin, using his Morris Minor as a private taxi, ferried the Yorkshireman around the surprisingly airy and spacious city on a sightseeing tour. He had insisted on Nelson meeting some of his sons. "I am blessed with five. I hope you like them, Mr Nelson. They are going to be part of the new Pakistan."

Fazal worked in a book printers in Bunder Road, specialising in novels. Tea was served there in a small dusty office next to the printing presses. Noisy, but not the decibel levels of a weaving mill. Majid was an economist in some government agency or other and they had all shared another brew in a café next door to a tea merchant. A Lipton sign, attached to the frontage by a long rusting pole, hung over the merchant's doorway. A row of slow-moving ceiling fans, with exceptionally long arms, disturbed the stifling air but to little effect. It was like being in the film *Casablanca*, thought Nelson. He wouldn't have minded Ingrid Bergman as an addition to these all-male gatherings. They sat at a corner table below one picture of the Queen's father and another of Muhammad Ali Jinnah, Quaid-e-Azam. "Beloved of all the people", Nelson was informed. The founder of Pakistan, in shirt, tie and jacket, looked down in a rather kindly way. He possessed quite big ears.

The Nazaruddins wore western clothes rather than the pyjama or salwar. Most of the women out and about were donned in traditional costume, though Nelson spotted a few local women wearing frocks. "These are almost certainly Christians," Nazaruddin senior informed him.

Majid was a very serious man with a hectoring tone which Tommy Nelson soon found tiring. "You know, Mr Nelson, life expectancy here is only thirty-three and the infant mortality rate is one in five. We have so much to do. Three years ago, the economy shrunk by two percent and grew by less than two percent the year after, at a time when numbers are rising so quickly."

Nelson remembered seeing West Pakistan's population figure somewhere and noting it was about the same as Britain's.

"We think the population will double now every twenty-five years. Over the past twelve months, the economy rose by ten percent. That has helped."

Neat and clean-shaven with a furrowed brow, Majid continued to tick off the points, like one of those new adding machines.

"If you take people over ten years of age, Mr Nelson, less than a quarter of men can read and write, and it is about one in twenty for women. It's a lot less for those in the countryside." The countryside was precisely where Nazaruddin and Sons was planning to source workers for Shaw's. So that was not an entirely comforting thought.

"We've got so much to do in public health. The requirement for training more nurses and doctors is so great. You know, Mr Nelson, we have well over forty thousand cases of smallpox every year and, in three quarters of cases, people die. The numbers are still rising."

This got a little too much. Majid's father had also taken a bellyful.

"For goodness sake, Majid. This man is here for business and a bit of sightseeing." Nazaruddin senior held his arms in the air, palms outstretched. "Mr Nelson is not in school, plus you'll have him thinking he's going to come down any second with some horrible disease." That thought had lodged in Nelson's mind.

Majid flicked his spectacles on to his forehead and flopped back into the wicker chair.

"I'm sorry, Mr Nelson. I'm so enthusiastic about my new country. I get a little carried away. I just wonder whether we are going to handle it. You know, Jinnah wanted a separate state for Muslims partly because he felt we wouldn't be able to compete with Indians. He thought they had a gift for business we don't have."

"That's just great, Majid, just as I am trying to sell dear Mr Nelson here our services."

Majid slapped his hands together and apologized again. They began a conversation about last year's Coronation of Queen Elizabeth which Tommy Nelson's new friends had watched on some newsreel or other.

Fortunately, the rest of the day was taken up with sightseeing of the travel book variety. They had strolled along the marine promenade at Clifton, an upmarket area of the British-created city, and peeked at some of the grand colonial housing. The wharfs, further along the coast, were packed with boats and they had spent an hour watching the fishermen selling their catches. Nazaruddin proved an informative guide but his continual whistling became irksome. *Blaydon Races* was the only tune he seemed to know.

Nelson was already on his second roll of Kodak, the Voigtländer Bessamatic, with its powerful Helomar lens, almost permanently sprung from its case. Changing the camera before flying out had crossed his mind, and he had popped into the Camera Exchange, a shop whose frontage sported block tiling in a yellow so garish it belonged more to Blackpool than Bradford. He'd examined other German single lens reflex equipment, like the Zeiss Ikon, and had taken a close look at the all-new Leica M3 with bayonet lens mount. The cost of that was horrific. He decided in the end to stick with his trusty Bessa.

It was now the morning of his second day in Karachi and, from the bedroom window, Shaw's production manager took a last glimpse at the sky, somewhere in colour between Wedgwood blue and purple, and threaded his arm through the Voigtländer's shoulder strap. He was looking forward to breakfast. He was looking forward to the whole day. More sightseeing, a drink at the Metropole, which, apparently, was the social hub for Europeans, and then an evening at a club with jazz supplied by Goan musicians. In between, a visit to the Nazaruddin office was on the cards so he could at least pretend he was working.

He switched off his bedside wireless. Without the pleasant symphony music put out by the Pakistan Broadcasting Service, he could just hear the street hubbub down below. He took the stairs down the one floor to reception. The camera was again out of its case as he intended adding a couple of shots of the hotel's interior.

Hameed Khan, the Palace's manager, saw Mr Nelson walking towards him. Mr Khan had been dreading the moment. In his hand were two telegraph messages for the nice Englishman. He knew what they said. He wished someone else could do it, but it was his job. He was feeling anxious, now the Englishman was standing right in front of him, and wished the deputy manager had been on duty that day.

"Good morning. It's alright, I assume, to take a photo of the hallway here?" Nelson removed the lens cap. "The light is just right this morning."

"Of course." Mr Khan rested a hand on his arm. "Mr Nelson." There was something firm but fretful in the way the hotel manager spoke.

"Yes?" The hotel manager's forehead looked horribly creased.

"Mr Nelson, we have two messages for you." He passed over the one he thought should be read first. Nelson extracted the paper from the envelope into which Mr Khan had inserted it. It was from the British Overseas Airways Corporation. It informed him that, due to the crash of another Comet in the Mediterranean, all flights of the plane were being suspended until further notice. The company would be using other types of aircraft to fly passengers but some disruption to schedules was, unfortunately, inevitable.

Nelson knew nothing of this latest tragedy and stood rigid in surprise. He imagined the terror passengers must have endured and put himself momentarily in their position. Then he thought how lucky he was. He had travelled safely. He crossed himself. God was on his side that day. A fly landed on his nose and he waved it away.

Mr Khan handed over the second envelope. The moment he did it, the hotel manager wished he had invited the guest into his office. He silently cursed himself. Tommy Nelson opened the envelope. The message was from Stephen Shaw. Moira was dead, it said. Everyone was so sorry. The police were involved. He must return home on the earliest possible flight. A car would meet him at the airport. Again, everyone was so sorry and would do everything to help.

Nelson felt his knees give a little, and his shoulders slumped. The camera tumbled on to the unforgiving floor. The lens shattered and the film, with his carefully-crafted photos spilled out on to the tiles. Mr Khan again placed a gentle hand on his arm. Tommy Nelson could hear the fly buzzing around. It was the only thing he could hear. It sounded very loud, as if it was actually in his head.

CHAPTER 14

Friday began rather tediously for Detective Inspector Ray Stafford but ended up with an unexpected twist. For Jennifer Shaw, the same day started out fitfully, perked up noticeably, then nose-dived rather badly.

Stafford sat in his office making calls and reviewing police reports trickling in from the city and from Ilkley. He conducted an interview with a shoe shop owner whose premises were a short walk away from the station and who had bought his car from Donald Wardle. A picture was emerging of an entirely innocent drinking pool using an ordinary back room in a third-rate hotel. This line of enquiry offered little promise. Wardle's wife, in a wheelchair, told the police her husband had arrived home early in the evening of the day in question and stayed put.

Another report on the cabling showed that, though quite unusual, it was used by too many local companies, employing too many workers, to make an investigation on its own. They needed a suspect first who they could then somehow prove had access to that type of wiring. Fingerprinting and other scientific work, so far, had thrown up nothing worth a grain of salt.

During his lunch break, Stafford went for a long walk around town. A sliver of weak sun perforated the banks of grey cloud. It was definitely milder, probably in the low fifties. One shop that sold sledges was removing them from its window display as he walked past. They obviously thought winter was well and truly over. Sure sign the city would be up to its tonsils in snowdrifts by next week.

He stepped into a small cafe without actually being aware of having made the decision to do so. After ordering, at the counter, a lamb chop with peas and mashed potatoes, he found a seat on the outside wall. A window cleaner, on the pavement, was applying a final polish to the glass, using pronounced balletic sweeps of the arms. Across the road, bales of wool were being winched down the front of a warehouse on to a flatbed lorry. Stafford idly contrasted the spotless state of the window with the crumb-strewn condition of his table. A brown sauce smudge was visible, fortunately in the corner opposite to where he sat.

Sergeant Norman Feather walked three quarters along the length of the window before he spotted his superior. He retraced his steps and entered the cafe.

"Afternoon, sir. Sorry to disturb you." He rested a hand on the back of one chair while his stomach drooped over another. "Just to let you know, amidst the more serious business, that we managed to find an aunt of Billy Draper, so we can tie all that up now. I'll drop you a note. I didn't tell her that her nephew was found rotting in a chimney five years after he climbed into it. I think she'd have dropped off her perch."

Feather looked around as if he was only just now clocking where he was. "Christ, guv. You don't want to nosh in this place. Let's leave the kamikaze stuff to the Japs."

The waitress stood behind the sergeant, well within earshot. She stretched round his girth and slid the plate at Stafford with a squirt of venom. He was forced to use a hand to block its trajectory or the plate would have disgorged on to his lap. Feather looked down at the grey and green combination. "Anyway, no chance of picking up gut ache with niggardly portions like that." He made a point of approaching the front counter, peering over the top, then walking straight out.

Stafford scooped out some very vinegary mint sauce from a jar on the table and tapped it on to the side of his plate. The cafe's proprietor sat on a high stool at one counter end, oblivious to his customers. A low forehead retreated at an acute angle just above the eyes, the skull rather elongated and almost torpedo-shaped at the back. His nose was buried in a magazine. Stafford could see it was a publication about the food business. It included the word "Food" on the front cover.

Stafford could not know, of course, but the cafe owner was boning up on an article about a new style of catering. Sinclair Ratledge was initially interested. A company called Insta Burger King was just starting up in Florida. The McDonald brothers had begun franchising their Californian burger bar concept. This followed the peculiarly named Colonel Sanders, a company, the article continued, which, two years before, franchised its first outlet selling fried chicken to an old Kentucky recipe. The article finished up by referring to the first burger bar Wimpy was soon to open in Britain, a franchise taken by the well-known Lyons tea rooms.

All interesting to Mr Ratledge. But not that interesting. He folded the magazine, tossed it in a bin, and ran his hands down the side of his Brylcreemed hair. He then returned to the business end of the counter, lit a fag and began laying corned beef and potatoes into a 'cake' ready for the oven.

Stafford finished his meal, pushed his plate forward and took a gulp of strong tea. He laid out the *Daily Telegraph*. The front page included a big photo of the Prime Minister, Winston Churchill, looking forward to the final end of food rationing in July. A commentary piece down the side suggested people might be tempted to carry out mass celebratory burnings of ration books. All of a sudden, Stafford remembered the pig's cheek in his office.

After his lunch, Stafford strolled aimlessly through the town centre. The course of the enquiry turned over in his mind, interspersed with the homilies of the Scotland Yard detective on the goggle box. He wasn't sure they would get anywhere soon. Concentrating at last on his bearings, he loped down a side street to a music shop he occasionally patronised. He was not an avid listener of music and rarely purchased anything. But he enjoyed talking to the owner, and Mr Reiniger enjoyed talking to him. A former prisoner of war like Bert Trautmann, goalkeeper for Manchester City and ex-paratrooper, the German had remained in Britain and married a local woman. Reiniger relished chatting about police work, and Stafford imagined him as a policeman in Germany before the war. Mr Reiniger said he had been no such thing. He had worked in a music shop in a town called Mettman, but all his relatives had been killed, as far as he knew.

Unlike most shops, this one did not close at lunchtime. Stafford pushed the door. A big poster of Max Bygraves was taped to the inside glass, the sheen on the crooner's slicked hair obviously touched up to give it an extra bluey lustre. A few customers were inside, flicking through racks of gramophone records. Reiniger stood behind a small counter, examining a musical score. He looked up and smiled.

"Mr Stafford, nice to see you." Reiniger always regarded him with what Stafford thought was unnerving concentration.

"Afternoon. Busy as usual?"

The shop owner lifted a hand in acknowledgement. "Best music shop in town. What can you do?"

A very unusual type of sound was escaping from the shop's internal music system. Stafford frowned and glanced up at the ceiling to make the point.

"*That's All Right* by a character called Elvis Presley," Reiniger remarked. "Not my cup of tea, I have to say." One of the youths, sorting through the racks of long-players, snorted a disparaging grunt.

Someone came up to the counter to make a purchase, and Stafford wandered over to the section housing music equipment. He leant down and pulled open the front of a long Grundig radiogram. He did the same with the top of an HMV, then twiddled the jet-black knobs of a white wireless with a fan-shaped speaker. Above the equipment, a poster was taped to the wall advertising the Fender Stratocaster, a new electric guitar. Stafford made his way back towards the counter.

"Are you dealing with this dead girl, Mr Stafford?" the shop owner asked in a half whisper.

"Indeed I am, Mr Reiniger. Nothing to report at the moment, but you'll be the first to know."

"Well I doubt that, detective inspector, but at least the case is in good hands, I am sure. Very upsetting for everyone. Such a wilderness that moor. My wife said this morning, she didn't feel safe going up there for our regular Sunday picnic."

"Now don't let it worry you too much, Mr Reiniger."

"I know, I know, but what with the case last year. It reminds me of some of the famous murders in Germany before the war. They made a mystery film, you know, about one set of particularly nasty ones. Actually there was one man, Fritz Harmaan, who killed twenty-five people in not much more than a year. It was just after the First war. The government had him beheaded."

"Good Lord, Mr Reiniger, take it easy with these thoughts."

The shop owner seemed increasingly at ease talking about Germany and was clearly comforted by the speed at which his home country was now climbing back on its feet. He had started pointing out things Germany had given Britain. To Stafford's amazement, the Cumberland sausage had apparently been brought over by Germans working in the local slate quarries up there. Recently, Reiniger had taken to listing British companies founded by his fellow countrymen.

"Take Daimler cars. That was a licence from Daimler in Germany. Rolex watches were founded by a German and first made in London." That was a bit lost on Stafford as he had never heard of Rolex. Anyway, the watches were now made in Switzerland. Last week, Reiniger had pointed to a big display in his shop by EMI, advertising its new 45 rpm "extended-play" records. "A very important British company but one of its founding fathers was German. Actually an American born in Germany."

This time, Reiniger pointed through the shop's plate glass window. A man was trying to kick start a large motorbike.

"That's a Triumph." The shop owner adjusted his head to get a better view. "Yes, a Tiger I think. You know, Triumph, when it was just a car company, was founded by a German."

"No, I didn't know that. You certainly know a lot of things."

The sound of Elvis Presley died away, but their voices were then drowned out by a van passing by, its driver trying to double declutch but botching the job and crashing the gears.

"What do you drive, Mr Reiniger?"

"An Austin. A very nice car it is too."

The shop owner turned and began attaching to the wall a new poster for His Master's Voice, with its symbol of the dog in front of the gramaphone trumpet. "Dear old Nipper."

"We like our dogs," Stafford said. "The Lassie stories were actually set around here. Well, in Yorkshire somewhere."

"You know the original Rin Tin Tin was German," Reiniger replied. "Came from a German army trench in the Great War and was brought over to Hollywood to star in the pictures."

Stafford wondered why he liked talking to Reiniger. In his cut-off state of mind maybe it provided the right balance between distance and familiarity. Defeated by the German's persistence and knowledge, he said goodbye and left.

He walked around the corner, crossed the road, and went through the main door of the Midland Hotel. He turned down the passageway leading from reception to the platforms of Forster Square station. The passage was a wide, sloping tunnel, floored in polished wood and walled top to bottom in ornate tin-glazed tiles by Burmantoft of Leeds. A porter, on the way to reception, was wheeling luggage piled on a cart that ran on a specially-laid track.

He found a free bench and sat down. The station was busy, and he pulled his legs in so as not to trip people scurrying along the nearest platform. A railwayman walked along the length of a passenger train, stooping to tap the wheels. Steam suddenly hissed out of the nearest locomotive's outlet cock. The engine driver was leaning out of the cab, peaked hat looking too big for his head.

Stafford watched the hustle and bustle for a while but the soot, and the sharp clanks of carriages shunting together, started to annoy him. Prising himself out of his lethargy, he walked briskly back to the office. He again scrutinised some of the eyewitness reports of the area around the Talbot Hotel at the time Moira Nelson disappeared. A surprising amount had been going on for a Monday evening. A Tetley-Walker brewery lorry was seen parked at the top of the road. An amateur football club held a drinks 'do' at a nearby pub. A red, three-wheeler car was observed in a side street. Several other vehicles, partially or wholly identified, were also parked nearby.

Some motorbikes, possibly AJS, or Matchless or Royal Enfield, or some other makes, were seen close by, riders unidentified. One bike might or might not have been fitted with side-mounted carrying bags. Several people belonging to an association for radio hams went in and out of an upstairs meeting room of another commercial hotel. A very large, two-door car with a hood was seen outside a bank. A few people in uniforms and overalls were going to and from work. All these sightings embraced tiny individual stories requiring thorough checking. The investigation was generating a momentum of its own.

Across town, Sergeant Feather and a constable approached a grocery shop at the sharp end of a row of terraced houses in the down-at-heel district of Laisterdyke. The shop was open but deserted, and a call produced no response, so they went alongside to the house attached to it and knocked on the door. They heard the sound of water cascading down an outside pipe, and then a door closing somewhere on the first floor and feet hurrying down the stairs. The busty blonde introduced herself as Edna Barraclough and invited them in, a quizzical look etched on her face.

"I don't know where Percy is. Let me call him." Mrs Barraclough shouted upstairs but no reply was forthcoming. "He must be in the gym at the back. Follow me."

Norman Feather considered that as he followed the woman, while stealing a glance at what looked like a very nice firm, rounded bottom. Who in their right mind would have a gym at their house? Then, as an occasional grapple fan, he put two and two together. He had thought the ageing wrestler had hung up his boots. Feather followed Mrs Barraclough down a long corridor, then across a backyard to a sizeable shed with no windows. A definite smell of animals wafted in from somewhere. She knocked on the door and they went in.

The room was dimly lit and bare, save for two posters on the back wall. One was a piece of stylised artwork of a half crouching wrestler, arms out front in a semi-circle, a fake snarl on his face. The other was of a large black pig, its beady eyes staring straight at the camera. Right in front of the two officers, an enormous man, lying face up on a thick padded mattress, was lifting a bar with weights. He was naked save for white underpants and a fierce-looking, hood-type affair covering his head. At least the young officer thought it was intimidating, especially as the man's eyes widened creepily at the sight of the policemen. But Feather recognised straight away the regalia of the Black Night. He wasn't the least bit unnerved by the super-heavy.

"Now, Percy," he said. "I'm not sure that underwear really does justice to the mask. Or is it the other way round."

By the end of the afternoon, most of the Bradford police force knew of Percy Barraclough, and the cover of the Black Night was well and truly blown. More to the point, Sergeant Feather had returned from the backyard gym with a rather startling piece of information. Ray Stafford now needed to interview someone who might, or might not be, a certain Tony Garland. That name was certainly on the Wardle list. Stafford could do with knowing for sure. Another visit to the second-hand car salesman was required, and the detective inspector grabbed his coat and trilby and left.

*****

When Jennifer Shaw awoke, she lay on her side under the cover of her TWA eye mask and thought of the Nelson family. Stephen had told her the evening before of Moira Nelson's murder, after the police had visited the company. He'd sent off a wire message, on behalf of Tommy Nelson's wife, to the hotel in West Pakistan he was staying in. She'd met both the manager and his wife at company functions. A nice man, she thought. Moira she did not know. It was so awful it was impossible to get a handle on it.

Her husband decamped from his bathroom, ready for the day.

"Are you going up to see Mrs Nelson?" she asked.

"I thought I'd better. What do you think?"

"Of course you should. I know you've sent some daffs but take up an armful more if you can find any. I'll write you out a card."

She got up, stretched, and wearily draped herself in a Chinese dressing gown, purchased at Galleries Lafayette during one of her many trips to the French capital. Downstairs, in the hall corridor, she manoeuvred round the new Prestcold which seemed even more gargantuan than it had in the showroom. The awful end to the girl's life rather took the shine off the building work. The kitchen was taking shape, but she couldn't think about taps and cupboard handles right now.

Mrs Williams handed her a cup of tea, and she sat on a stool in the temporary kitchenette, holding the cup in both hands. Archie Tyzack's men were in the main kitchen. She could see them through a serving hatch. The young man was there, the one with the Teddy Boy haircut who appeared sporadically at Pennymore. It was the first time she had surveyed his face. He possessed a certain thin-lipped, high-cheek-boned meanness. Does he carry a flick knife, she wondered.

In the drawing room, she retrieved some letter paper and scribbled a note for Emer Nelson. She screwed it up and wrote a longer one. Through the window she noticed a shooting brake she didn't at first recognise. Then she saw it was from the Rolls-Bentley dealership, waiting to pick up the car for its service. The dealership had dispatched two mechanics, one to drive the Bentley, the other to take back their own vehicle.

Her husband usually bought his motors from Hoffman's in Halifax but the recently-purchased 'R Type' came from the local dealers. It was the most expensive car Stephen Shaw had ever purchased. His wife had been a little taken aback at its price. Her husband, or rather the company, had off-loaded four thousand, eight hundred and thirty-four pounds, made up of two thousand, eight hundred and seventy-five pounds manufacturer's price, purchase tax of thirteen hundred and twenty-nine and the dealer's margin of six hundred and thirty. About the equivalent of all the property in a medium-sized Spanish village, her husband had joked when he wrote the cheque.

She heard Stephen coming downstairs and walking to the front door. "Have you seen my Lobbs, the brown ones?" he shouted along the corridor. "In fact, what the hell has happened to all the shoes?"

"I moved them when they brought in the fridge." His wife poked her head around the drawing room door. "The shoes are in the second cupboard from the end. The ones you are looking for are third shelf down, last pair on the right."

"Why didn't they bring the refrigerator in through the annex door?"

"My mistake. I thought it was easier this way."

She kissed him and passed over the note for Mrs Nelson. Her husband tapped the face of the hall barometer, and she then watched him walk across to the garage and reverse the Bentley into the driveway. She saw one of the mechanics, wearing white gloves, toss a dust cover over the driver's seat and climb in. He committed the error Stephen frequently made. The 'R Type's' gear lever, a long angled rod, protruded from the floor to the right of the steering wheel. Stephen was continually banging his leg on it. The mechanic did the same. Stephen eventually drove away in her Jaguar, facing a task he was obviously not relishing.

Jennifer Shaw indulged in a lengthy bath and then slipped into a Jaeger double-breasted Jersey dress with four vertical pocket flaps in a *café au lait* colour. She carried downstairs one of the fanciful hats she owned by milliner Simone Mirman. This one was a swept-back triangle above a broad brim, in dark brown. She was just in time to catch the postman at the door.

Mr Thwaite was breathing heavily. "I'm sorry the delivery is so late, Mrs Shaw. I had to see to my wife this morning. She wasn't feeling too smart."

"No bother at all, Mr Thwaite. I hope she is alright."

The postman looked so old Shaw often referred to him with her friends as "the geezer who's been delivering letters since the Norman Conquest." He usually dropped in the first mail at about seven but it was now well after nine. Shaw's heart leapt when she saw a postcard from Australia sticking out of the small clutch of envelopes. It was a photograph of a kangaroo. Her son had written: "A picture of a typical local in the outback. Love, Alan." At least her son was alive, she thought a little bleakly.

She checked with Archie Tyzack that the building of the kitchen was turning up no extra unwelcome surprises. She then manoeuvred the Hurricane out of the garage and on to the Harrogate road, time in hand for her get-together with Janet Tomlinson. Janet had not managed the drinks bash at the Majestic a few days before, so Shaw was looking forward to catching up with everything.

She had fancied the Hurricane as soon as she spotted it for sale in a local showroom, simply because the Armstrong Siddeley's bonnet mascot was a sphinx. Stephen wilted under her pestering and eventually stumped up the money. Now that really was extravagant because the Hurricane was problematic to drive and hardly ever got an outing.

This wasn't because of its unusual gearbox, the one thing which the salesman seemed to be worried about. The box was a Wilson pre-selector which involved the driver pulling a lever on the column to pre-select the gear required. When the driver wanted to change to that gear, a gear-changing pedal on the floor needed depressing and releasing. Designed for battle tanks, it worked well enough and caused her no problems.

What really bothered Shaw was everything else – the visibility, steering and scuttle shake, three drawbacks the salesman had failed to point out. The car was spacious and quiet, if gloomy with the hood up, but a disagreeable blind spot, on the sides at the back, rendered parking a dreaded test of courage. A rear window, not much bigger than a domestic letter flap, heightened the tension. Power steering was not available, and to compensate, Hawker, the company that made the Hurricane and which once manufactured the fighter aircraft bearing the same name, designed the car with a large lock. In other words, you turned the steering wheel forever while in a state of partial blindness.

Harrogate was busy, and Shaw was forced to hunt for a parking space near Bettys tea rooms. Eventually one turned up and she backed in anxiously. During the manoeuvre, she alighted twice to check her relative position to the kerb. She could feel sweat threatening the surface of the Pan-Stik. A man she was blocking in a black panel van which said, along its side, "Knife-Sharpening on the Go", offered her a 'V' sign. A crass piece of behaviour she had never been subjected to before. She considered returning a Churchillian 'V', but by then he had snail-paced away in an exhaust cloud. The van backfired and she let out an audible laugh. Once out of the car, she patted the sphinx bonnet mascot, relieved the *Queen Mary* was safely berthed.

Bettys lay across the junction in Cambridge Crescent. Everyone was thankful to Fritz Bützer, the Swiss immigrant who changed his moniker once in Britain to Frederick Belmont, and who had set up the famed café more than thirty years earlier. With branches also in Bradford, Leeds and York, it dished up its own-baked cakes and pastries of a type almost unknown outside London.

Shaw was somewhat irritated to see Janet's drophead Minx parked right outside the entrance. To position the Hillman any closer, a slide rule would have been needed. It was doubly irritating because the Minx's chrome front always seemed to display a permanent, self-satisfied grin, rather matching her owner's.

She crossed the threshold and walked upstairs. Bettys still bore signs of the cumulative commercial impact of war and rationing. The carpets were pretty threadbare for a start. But the place was heaving and obviously on the road to recovery. She was glad to see that Janet had nabbed a couple of chairs at a four-seater table shared with two other women. On the head of one sat a hat with feathers as worn as the carpets and with a cluster of coloured beads in the shape of fruit, just like one of Bettys' summer tarts.

"Hello, darling. Great to see you." Shaw greeted her chum with a kiss on the cheek.

"Jennifer. I like the hat." In a long-sleeved wool taffeta shirt with U-shaped yoke, Janet was waving, in all directions, her black cigarette holder with embossed snake. The girls had been betting for years that someone would get an eye poked out, but it had not happened yet. Not as far as they knew.

Janet was only an inch shorter than her friend and was once just as lean. But in the past two years a certain sturdiness had overtaken her. If Janet had broached the topic they would all have had a laugh and no one would have cared a fig. But Janet had not. So Shaw kept her mouth buttoned.

"You're looking marvellous. Is that the new bracelet?" Jennifer Shaw asked. Janet tipped her arm forward. The wrist band was solid gold, about a quarter of an inch thick, and resembled a trinket from a Marrakech bazaar. It must have cost a bomb. It was several feet the wrong side of vulgar.

"You don't think it's vulgar?"

"Of course not."

The two women alongside were taking a peek. One of them peered over half-moon spectacles, her face pointing down at the table to get the right viewing angle. Meanly, Janet Tomlinson thrust a limb right under the women's noses. They jerked back into their seats. Shaw harboured a soft spot for Herbert, Janet's husband. She knew who wore the trousers in that marriage and who had the hurtful streak.

Janet started waving her arm again to get attention. The end of the cigarette traced grey patterns in the air, like Red Indian smoke signals in a cowboy film. A harassed waitress came over, and she ordered tea and a teacake. Shaw ordered a teacake, scone and a cauliflower, a sweet fancy cake shaped like the vegetable and served by Bettys since the cafe's inception. Janet made no mention of the disparity in food tonnage. If you had a sweet tooth but a body biologically committed to pulping fat, not to mention three-monthly teeth check-ups with the best dentist in Yorkshire, then stuff it, Shaw reasoned.

"Look over there." Janet nodded her head at some point in front of her. Shaw turned. A young, olive-skinned man was serving at a corner table. "They're getting Italian waiters in for some reason. That'll liven the place up."

The food arrived and they helped themselves from the silver cake holder, Janet Tomlinson being a little circumspect with the raspberry jam but her companion shovelling it on the teacake and then the scone in chunky red wedges.

"Now, Le Touquet," Janet said.

"What?"

"The new airport in Kent is opening in a week's time and we thought it would be fun if we flew over, taking the cars with us on the plane. A very long weekend. Spot of gambling in the casino, drive down the coast. You'll have to prise Stephen from behind his desk." She flipped a little brochure of the French seaside resort on to the table.

"Sounds wonderful. I'll get to work on him. When are you thinking?"

"In a few weeks' time. Let's check diaries."

The two other ladies at the table ordered a second pot of tea. The conversation next door was too good to miss, even if one of the tall women was a bit of a cow.

Shaw occupied the rest of the day with her friend, shopping in Harrogate, then visiting Janet Tomlinson's home in a small village north of the town. It was an Elizabethan gentleman farmer's house with a ring of gargoyles circling the top, just below chimney level. Shaw didn't like the gargoyles. They reminded her of the Imp on Lincoln Cathedral. But she loved the Poggenpohl and reacquainted herself with its modern fifties look, something her kitchen, alas, would slightly miss out on. The Poggenpohl though did seem a little incongruous on top of the stone flagging.

The rest of the house had just been floored in the heaviest and most expensive five-colour Persian-pattern Wilton with a unique border, specially ordered from the Wiltshire factory. Shaw knew Herbert's company made some type of electric control for machines. It was obviously minting it.

The two eventually ran out of gossip, and Shaw took the wild A59 route back to Ilkley. The dreaded scuttle shake started to disturb the Hurricane, the chassis flexing and slipping into a persistent shaking rhythm. A nasty tremble transmitted itself up into the steering wheel. Objects in the rear-view mirror shimmered as if suffering from St Vitus's dance. She knew that slowing down cured it and she reluctantly did so.

South of Bolton Abbey and travelling slowly, she had chance to admire countryside rolling in long sweeps with knotty hills in the distance. Some farmers were already out with their tractors, taking advantage of the improving weather. She noticed that one tractor, pulling a machine of some kind, was almost enveloped in white powder as it spread chemicals on the furrows. She wondered if that was DDT, and then thought that that chemical perhaps only came in liquid form.

By the time she edged the Hurricane into Pennymore's driveway she was a little weary. She parked the car, stretched her back and walked round the side of the house. Mrs Williams was in the drawing room window and raised her hand when she saw her employer. She was holding the telephone to her ear. She pointed to the telephone and mouthed "telephone". I wonder if I'm wanted on the telephone, Shaw asked herself.

"It's a Detective Inspector Stratford, I think." Mrs Williams handed over the receiver as Shaw eased out of her coat. "As in Shakespeare, Mrs Shaw." The housekeeper left the room but remained in the hallway, listening to the conversation, one hand on the heavyweight Hoover in case she was caught out and needed to look busy.

"Hello, Jennifer Shaw. Sorry, your name is? Stafford? Oh, right." Mrs Williams got about half of the names wrong. "Tony Garland? Yes, Anthony is my brother. He doesn't live here. I don't know why he gave this number, detective inspector. No. He's not here. Well of course I can give you his home number but I know he's not there. He went to Manchester a day or two back to see a friend. He'll be back very late this evening, or so he told me. Uhm, yes I could. You want to see him tomorrow morning? But that's Saturday. I see. Do I need to come? It's routine but he might like to have a solicitor. If it's routine why would he want a solicitor? Alright. What's the station's telephone number? Right. Can we park at the station? Thank you, Mr Stafford. Goodbye."

Shaw gently placed the receiver into the cradle of her white bakelite telephone. The policeman owned an obvious West Country burr, spoken in deep tones. So her brother had been up to something. Why hadn't the pea brain turned up for that meeting with the solicitor? She had better ring Maurice Black and see if he could come in tomorrow. Shaw flipped up the number holder and called him at work and at his house in Leeds. No answer at either. She could just see the whole evening swallowed up by dialling his home every fifteen minutes, probably to no avail.

Shaw opened the drinks cabinet and poured herself an inch of Teacher's, then strolled into the kitchenette. The day could not have ended on a worse note, she thought. Then she actually saw a note, left by Archie Tyzack. Written in pencil, it informed her that the refrigerator was too wide for the gap left for it between the meticulously planned cabinets. What did she want him to do?

"Oh that's just dandy," she said to no one in particular.

CHAPTER 15

The rain hit the Vanguard's split windscreen at close to horizontal, launched by a vigorous wind. Stafford had aimed to reach his office early so he could dispose of the pig meat, slowly putrefying in the station. He'd suffered an attack of amnesia for a second evening and had left it in his drawer again. He had been unaware of any smell originating from his desk, but that was fifteen hours ago. Now, instead of getting in early, he'd overslept, his body clock switched over to weekend setting. The rain propelling against the car only delayed him further.

In the station car park, a big Jag, so white it seemed luminous even in the grey light, was laid up in one corner, its prow against the wall. A small roadster sat next to it, the hood sodden into a glistening black. Stafford donned his trilby, dashed to the main entrance, but was soaked within a few seconds.

Through the side window of his office, he could see an elegant woman, possibly in her early to mid-forties, he thought, and a man in a modish three-quarter length coat. Both were perched expectantly on the edge of their chairs.

As soon as he entered the office, his nostrils picked up the distinctive whiff of decomposing sinews. The pig's cheek had clearly passed the point of no return. Tony Garland and his sister got up, and Stafford introduced himself. She was almost beautiful, so tall in her heels she was little more than half a foot shorter than himself. Her brother was slightly taller than his sister and owned a similar-featured face. Tony Garland's was drained of colour.

"There's an awful smell in here, Mr Stafford. Has someone left a potted meat sandwich in a drawer?" The woman's handsome face was questioning rather than sneering.

"I'm sorry about that, Mrs Shaw. It is Mrs Shaw? I think we're having a few problems with the drains. Let's go into another part of the building."

Seated opposite them across the desk in the interview room, Stafford could feel Shaw's gaze resting steadily on his face. She was attired in a dark blue jacket with enormous wing collars, as if shielding herself from the contamination of the station's grubby surroundings. Long gloves covered her hands and lower arms, even though the station was stuffy and unventilated. She looked like a temptress on the cover of a shilling novel. Stafford wondered if she'd ever been required, since leaving school, to sit on a bare wooden chair, as she was doing now. He offloaded those thoughts into the back of his cranium and proceeded with the interview.

"Have you a solicitor coming?" He directed the question at her brother.

It was she who replied. "Yes. He said he would be here but he's coming from his home in Leeds, so I guess the rain has delayed him."

"Do you want to wait?" He again addressed Tony Garland.

"Look, detective inspector, I think we can clear all this up now," she said, treating her brother as if he was a deaf mute needing protection from a bully. "Anthony did not know Moira Nelson was dead. I only told him last night. Then he told me he was in some dive with her on Monday night. I'm sure we can sort all this out now."

She was animated, her face expressive, brown eyes alive, a deep, accentless voice venting from a large, well-rouged mouth. The outburst would speed things up. Garland looked a little less tense. Perhaps he surmised that something nasty he expected was not, in fact, on its way after all. How disappointed he would be, Stafford thought.

"Your brother looks old enough to answer for himself, Mrs Shaw. Now, is all that true, Mr Garland. About you not knowing of her death?"

"Yes, it is." Garland sucked in a lung-full of air. "I haven't read the local rag for the past few days. I normally do. It's where I pick up most of the cars I sell. You know that? I earn a living selling cars. But I've been in Manchester for the past two days. You can check that."

For a man of his size, Garland's voice was peculiarly whiny. Stafford asked Garland where he had met Moira, how long he had known her, what his relationship with her had been.

"I know Wardle through the car trade. I started going to the Talbot. I took Moira to the pictures a few times. She is, was, an awful lot younger than me. It's a dreadful thing that has happened to her. I stayed at the Talbot for hours after she left that night. You can check that too."

The wind was making something buzz, like the sound a papered-over comb makes when blown on. Garland's sister was searching the walls, hunting for something interesting to fix her gaze on but finding nothing. Then she settled her eyes on the detective inspector, a kind of "so what else have you got up your sleeve because I could be somewhere else drinking a Martini" look on her face. Stafford stared back at her for a second. She didn't annoy him because her expression was a long way from supercilious. Her face was just a mixture of beauty and boredom.

Stafford left the room, then returned, as planned, with policewoman Rosemary Worsman. She also opened a notebook. Rain pelted against the windows in gusty blasts, making intermittent drumming sounds against the glass. The wind generated a draught behind him, just enough to unsettle the corners of the paper sheets on his desk. Stafford deliberately stared at the papers for several seconds.

"Right, Mr Garland. What did you give Moira Nelson that evening?" In between the bouts of drumming, Stafford could hear another buzz, this one clearly discharging from an errant light fitting. A door banged somewhere down the corridor. Garland looked at the floor. A bald patch was starting to take hold on the crown of his head.

"Give her what?" his sister asked, staring questioningly at Stafford. The frown gifted her skin a few extra creases. Stafford wondered how much she resented those. He thought now that she might be a little older than he first guessed.

"What did you give Moira Nelson? I don't want to repeat the question." Garland tipped his head further towards the lino and rested his hands in his lap, constructing nervously-precise movements by revolving his thumbs out and back, a nice little sign of insecurity and stress.

The sister angled her face towards her brother, then back at Stafford. He could see what was so disconcerting about the two faces. They shared most of the same features, but in only one were they assembled in such a way as to make the face determined and open. In the other, they appeared shallow and weak. It was as if Tony Garland's face had been fashioned from a similar recipe, but with a crucial ingredient absent.

"Mr Garland. I'll make it easy. I'm not interested in you. If I was, I would have been up at your house already, ransacking it for you know what. I'm only interested in the state of Moira Nelson's mind when she left the Talbot. Now. Answer the question or I'll have you charged with obstructing the inquiry." Stafford aimed a thumb in Worsman's direction. He noticed that Jennifer Shaw's head was poker-still. Rain was beating against the windows in ever more furious insistence.

Garland eventually relented. "Alright, alright. They're called strawberries. Anyway, that's the name the man I bought them from uses. In Soho. I don't know his name. They're amphetamine-based. That's what he says. They just give you a pep up. Makes a dull world a little brighter. I gave Moira a couple that evening. They don't really do anything serious to you. Look, she left the hotel long before I did. She was fine."

"And there was a man in the room who rather took exception to you handing out these sweeties, wasn't there, Mr Garland?"

"I didn't think anyone had noticed. We were in a corner. Yeah, some enormous Boris Karloff lookalike."

Stafford matched Garland's steady gaze, and knew the man sitting opposite him had said that quite deliberately, introducing a nasty little personal element. He ensured his own expression remained expressionless, though he thought a well-aimed ligament-rupturing kick under the table wouldn't go amiss.

"The gentleman's name, I gather, is Barraclough. An ex-wrestler or something," Garland said.

"He said what to you?"

"He threatened me. Said he had a daughter about the same age."

Norman Feather's notes lay in front of Stafford. "More precisely, he said he was going to strap your testicles to a light socket and switch on the current?"

"Something crude of that sort." Stafford caught the woman fixing her gaze at the ceiling. She then lowered her head, pointedly turning it away a fraction from her brother.

"And he said he was going to shop you to us. That didn't worry you?"

"It did for a day or two. I thought I might need legal help. Then I reasoned he wasn't going to do anything. Look, I know nothing of what happened to Moira after she left the Talbot. She just said she was going home."

Jennifer Shaw looked at Stafford but it was obvious she wasn't seeing him at all. Emotion leaked from her face in a curious transfiguration. It was like she had gone somewhere else. She seemed to have drifted into the clouds, as far away from her brother as possible. Her handsome features now projected as much life as a face on a Grecian urn.

It would have been nice to think Garland had just stepped across a threshold with gaol scrawled over it. That was not the case, Stafford knew. An officer poked his head round the door to say Garland's solicitor was here and should he be shown into the interview room.

"No. I'll get him. You two wait here please." With his back to the pair, he gave Worsman a wink.

As he walked along the corridor, Stafford contemplated the inadequacies of his country's drug laws. Police were normally required to bring an assault charge if a conviction was wanted against a small-time supplier. Anyway, he harboured few doubts the 'strawberries' were relatively innocuous. American pilots in the Korean war were said to have used similar types of stimulant, and rumours persisted during his war that hard-pressed RAF flyers, trying to keep alert, were supplied with tablets. Even stronger drugs, like crystal meths, were given to Japanese kamikaze pilots, so the stories went.

Anyway, witnesses who had seen Moira in the Talbot failed to notice any abnormal behaviour, other than a happy boisterousness. Others in the drinking pool confirmed that Garland stayed for hours after Moira had gone. Nevertheless, Stafford couldn't help wondering whether the uppers had lowered Moira Nelson's guard. No charges would be laid against Tony Garland. But Stafford liked the idea of keeping him in the station as long as possible, letting the contamination of its grubby atmosphere rub off on his lanky frame.

"Ah, Detective Inspector." Maurice Black greeted him in one of the anterooms. He was wearing a bow tie. "This is George Pollard, a colleague of mine who specialises in criminal law. You have my client here?"

Stafford knew Black and liked him. He recently informed Stafford that his parents had bestowed on him the middle name of Delius, after the German classical composer who once lived in the city. Black hated his middle name.

"You read about the death of Moira Nelson, Mr Black, the girl found dead on Ilkley Moor?"

"Yes, of course. Wait a minute. You're not saying…"

"No. But Tony Garland has admitted feeding her amphetamines on the evening she died. I suggest you go in and give him the benefit of your expertise."

"Are you thinking of charging him?" Pollard asked.

"I'm thinking of all kinds of things, Mr Pollard." Before the solicitors could shoot off more questions he left the room, determined to rid from his life the lump of meat slowly infecting his desk.

*****

By the time Jennifer Shaw escaped into the car park, she had absorbed a maw-full of Bradford's central police station. Her olfactory senses were better attuned to scent than sewage, but she knew a bad drain when she smelt one. The smell in the station was not a bad drain. Probably the mouldering carcass of a villain they'd forgotten about in some rancid cell. Sitting in her car, she lit up a Pall Mall and watched the downpour swallow up the rear lights of her brother's pigmy roadster as it disappeared into the city. Half-wit, she thought.

There was plenty of time to get to Leeds and she edged her car into the traffic. She and her husband were lunching at the Queens Hotel with the Mortimers. Frank Mortimer, a hosiery producer in Leicester, was an old pal of Stephen's and the couple were up in the West Riding for the day. The drizzle hampered visibility, and she fiddled with the controls to improve demisting of the Jaguar's windows. Some traffic lights had conked out under the earlier barrage of rain.

Half-way along the main road between the two cities, the stone of Bradford gave way to the dark red brick of its larger, neighbouring city. Her eyes were always drawn to Armley Gaol, a building whose outer appearance was so terrifying she wondered about the mental health of the prison service architects who had designed it. She wondered too if that was the place where they would hang Moira Nelson's murderer, if he was ever caught. By the time she was beyond the gruesome creation, the rain was bucketing down again, water puddling widely.

On the edge of the centre of Leeds, a diversion sign directed her away from the normal route. She could see, beyond the sign, that the tarmac was under some feet of flood water. In the rain, she missed the next diversion sign and found herself in a threatening maze of one up, one down back-to-backs. She didn't know where she was but took a stab at Holbeck or Hunslet. She'd never been here before. Why would she have been?

Eventually, she took one wrong turning too many, and the Jaguar's bonnet finished up facing a cul-de-sac, closed off by a high wall. A gasometer loomed above her like an evil vision from the imagination of H G Wells. How was this possible? While minding your own business, travelling from one big city to another less than ten miles away, you end up in a God-forsaken place that made a Belgian coal mining town look like Barbados. She liked that image. A good job the weather was grim. If it wasn't for the rain, she'd be manoeuvring the car in a tangle of clothes lines with street urchins kicking footballs at the windscreen.

As she was starting her three-point turn, an old lady walked in front of the car, and Jennifer Shaw halted the manoeuvre. The woman was bent into the wind, her head covered by the kind of shawl that had virtually disappeared in Ilkley. She was clutching a toilet roll.

She watched the woman hobble diagonally across the road towards the brick barrier at the end of the street. She noticed now, a row of wood and brick structures in the corner that were obviously privies. The old woman reached up to a handle at one of the doors and tugged feebly at it. It didn't budge. She then shuffled to the next one and managed to release the latch. The bottom of the door trailed off in a jagged, sloping edge, the wood broken away. Shaw could see, through the gap, the woman's feet and the lower part of her legs as she turned to sit on the toilet seat. Then she saw the woman's bloomers slip down to her ankles.

By the time Shaw found haven in a parking slot alongside the Queens, she was running late. She spotted the Mortimers' handsome Alvis saloon across the road. It was under a big wall advertisement for Reg Park, local boy and former Mister Universe, promoting Park's bodybuilding magazine. A handsome face, she considered, though not as nice as that of her husband.

Outside the white, slab-fronted hotel, built less than twenty years earlier, bell hops in their distinctive black, broad-brimmed hats busied themselves stacking luggage into the outside service lift. She marched through the jazzy art deco interior, painted as if the designer suffered from some wonky imagination. A couple of small posters, in neat frames, advertised Harry Corbett. Sooty, his glove puppet, nuzzled up to Corbett's neck.

In the luxurious Palm Court lounge, the three were sitting at a corner table. She greeted the Mortimers and offered a quick low-down on the police interview. She couldn't give a fig what her husband's friends thought of her brother. What mattered was what she thought of him. Not much right now, as it happened. They had bought drinks at the bar, the other side of reception, and had carried them across to the lounge, possibly to the disapproval of a clutch of matrons ingesting non-alcoholic beverages at the next low table.

"I've got you a gin and tonic." Stephen handed over a long glass. "I've booked the French restaurant rather than the Grill. Dover sole is off but everything else is on." He picked up the menu, all in French which he could understand but she could not. "I'll go through the list."

"Don't bother, Stephen. Order for me. Anything at all."

"That's a first. Your brother's antics must have got to you after all."

"Anthony? You must be joking. I've already forgotten he exists. Well, for the time being. I'm off to powder my nose. Won't be long."

In the magnificent black-and-white tiled powder room, Shaw washed her hands while staring at her face in the mirror. She couldn't get the old lady out of her mind. There was something so heart-sinking about the tiny figure, shambling across the cobbles to a bank of tumble-down privies exposed to the elements. A world of hovels built with no toilets inside or out. God, we still had an empire, she reasoned, and I've spent half an hour among slums that would shame Naples. Perhaps it was the weather getting her down.

Shaw decided to break out of her gloomy mood, or else she would end up killing the lunch. She dried her hands on the over-starched towel, dowsed her wrists in the hotel's cologne, and delivered an over-cheery hello to the woman entering the Ladies as she departed. At the table, the natural equilibrium in her outlook on life grafted back into place.

"Before we start, I must tell you about the policeman who interviewed Anthony," she said conspiratorially, leaning over the linen tablecloth. "A detective inspector. Extraordinary looking. He's the size of a door, with an almost square head. But that's not the most surprising thing. He has a scar, not a wide one, running down one side of his face. Whoever did it to him obviously just missed his eye."

"Sounds a brute," said Pamela Mortimer who was born in Leeds and had retained an astoundingly rough, local accent. Her shoulders were draped in a lilac bolero stole, fashioned in some shimmering material. Shaw liked her, but was not pally enough to say she dressed too much like an over the hill good-time girl from Wolverhampton, or some other equally dismal place.

"Could be. My brother referred to someone in the interview as looking like Boris Karloff. I thought he might be goading Stafford. That's the policeman. It's just the kind of thing Anthony does. But it didn't register with the policeman at all. In his late thirties, I would think. Very young for a detective inspector. Funnily enough, he is quite handsome somehow, though he has sad eyes. He's a bit like a misshapen Howard Keel. Difficult to tell whether he's a kind man or not."

"Do we want kind policemen?" Frank Mortimer said. "Some of those crooks could do with a good lathering."

"One thing I do know. Ray Stafford is an absolute liar. His office reeked. He said it was the drains. It wasn't. It smelled like rancid meat."

The waiter was ready with the starters. "Terrine de Joue Cochon," he said in a curious Yorkshire-Italian accent.

"That's me." Pamela Mortimer turned the plate in front of her. "Mmmm, pig's cheek paté. Looks really yummy."

CHAPTER 16

The following days were absorbing ones for Ray Stafford. The day after the Garland interview, he motored up to the Dales. He craved some robust fell-walking, but rain cascaded by the bladder-full all Sunday. He managed a mile or so on a track near the Ribblehead viaduct but then gave up.

He hot-footed it into the Station Inn at Ribblehead and took shelter in the main bar. It was packed to the ginnels.

At the far end of the bar, he found a slot near a window and wedged himself in below a "Wm. Younger's Edinburgh Ales" poster. The rain was absolutely stair-rodding. One or two battle-hardened walkers were still striking out, climbing over the stile at the back of the pub's car park and heading off into the gloomy wilderness. Across the car park, he could just make out children's faces in curtained windows punched out of the side of a van. A man sat at a small table in the middle of the Bedford while a woman heated a pan on a small stove.

A few hardy cyclists leant against the car park wall, munching sandwiches under their rain capes. A group of scouts had taken refuge in their stumpy coach, a Guy Arab with its Red Indian Chief mascot standing proudly on the radiator. The vehicle's roof included a large and curious dorsal fin with ventilation ducts. Two scoutmasters were battling through the rain, ferrying to the coach trays of lemonade bought at the bar.

Stafford peered at the viaduct's massive but now indistinct shape, and could just see the rear of a train slowly crawling across it like a black caterpillar. A fault in the window glass, coupled with the sheer volume of raindrops, gave the 'caterpillar' a distorted shimmer. Rain was crossing the fells at a slant, like dense fishing nets thrown across the terrain. The heaving bar smelled of dampness and heat.

"Big structure, isn't it?" The man standing next to him owned a jutting chin below a small mouth tightly gripping a pale brown pipe. He was small but muscular, obvious even under the covering of a drenched black cape. The man looked like a bat.

"Yes, it certainly is." Stafford took a sip of beer. He didn't want to converse, but after a minute or so felt it was too rude not too, so added, "You live close by or are you out for a fell walk?"

"Both. I live in Hawes though I am originally from Sheffield." The pipe smoke almost blanked out his face. "It's a marvellous piece of civil engineering but, you know, there's a parish church down the hill where over a hundred of the workers who built the viaduct and a nearby rail tunnel are buried."

"I didn't know that. Sounds to have been a very gruelling job." They had to readjust their positions as a group of women on some kind of club outing, now washed out, jostled into a space that didn't exist. The women's faces were ruddy and raw, but one of them had a kind of lean attractiveness and Stafford watched her until the man tapped his pipe on the window ledge.

"The Midland railway built wooden hut settlements all over Blea Moor while they were constructing the viaduct. There was a thousand men, women and children up here. No sanitation. Rats. About two hundred died. They even had a smallpox outbreak."

"I think the Midland railway built one of the hotels in the city where I live."

"There you go. Building those monuments to capitalism while they were killing the workers. It makes you wonder why we're not all committed socialists."

Stafford looked at the man. "I'm not sure about that."

"Bagster Waggett. Historian and fellow traveller." The man held his hand out and Stafford shook it and introduced himself.

"What did you do in Sheffield?"

"Local trade union official mostly, steel industry. The same in York but it was confectionery there."

He bought Waggett a pint and chatted a bit about the plight of the working man. Waggett possessed cunning, darting, little eyes, and expressed entrenched views on almost everything, which Stafford began to find irritating.

"We need a complete rebuilding of our housing stock, but we can't do that while we're spending a tenth of our economy every year on defence. For what purpose? This so-called communist threat is just a big load of nonsense."

At one point the rain and wind halted abruptly. It stayed like that for about half a minute, then they started up again, if anything even more ferociously. It was as if the wind had lost its way and travelled down the wrong valley before realising its mistake and returning. Waggett was like a cross between a teacher and a scrap dealer. The man didn't offer to reciprocate with a drink. Stafford soon left the Station Inn, noticing on the way out that the attractive woman had started up a conversation with a man who already had a hand on her shoulder.

He drove down the hill to Ingleton, the main local centre for potholers and walkers, and decided to enjoy an afternoon tea in one of the village's cafes. Once inside the Copper Kettle, he opted for a high tea and ordered a plate of ham and fried eggs. The tea room was jammed and its stone floor crazy-paved with water stains from macs and boots.

On the way home he wondered if Bagster Waggett was a member of the Communist Party. He also wondered whether a file was open on him at one of the security services. He wouldn't put it past them. He arrived in his driveway in the early evening, thinking he'd had a day without achieving much. Then he thought, There's nothing new in that.

At the start of the following week, more reports crept in about the evening Moira Nelson's lifeless body was dumped into the crack of an isolated rock on a stretch of secluded moorland. The notes said a girl fitting Moira's description, but probably with dark hair, was seen coming out of a late-opening coffee bar. A group of men were making a bit of a din further up the street. A motorbike, with a girl on the pillion, was noticed on a road nearby. More interviews with neighbours and friends threw up nothing. It was as if she had simply vanished. Repeated trawls of jewellers and pawnbrokers unearthed no sign of her missing belongings.

On the Tuesday, a coat, eventually identified as Moira's, turned up in a ditch near the main road between Bradford and Ilkley. The coat was spotted by dustbin men riding on the rear platform of a municipal dustcart. One of the men had stowed the coat in the lorry cab, he said to give to charity, before realising what it might be. That explanation provoked knowing smirks in the station. Stafford visited the site, the coat went off for examination, and local police stepped up investigations nearby.

Stafford received a hand-written note from Moira's grandfather, informing him of her wake on the Wednesday. He was surprised to discover that the wake always took place before the funeral. Another officer went instead. The following day, he joined mourners at Moira Nelson's burial. A few relatives arrived from Ireland, but not many. It was a long and arduous boat train trip, especially if they lived out in the bogs, Stafford surmised, and a flight from Dublin would have proved cripplingly expensive.

Moira's father stood, rather stooped, next to his wife. He seemed worn out and dishevelled. A piece of furniture in that state could be reasonably described as dilapidated. His eyes, and those of Emer Nelson, impassively traced the descent of the coffin into its resting place, paralysed countenances born out of broken spirits. Jennifer Shaw and a man he guessed was her husband stood a little to the side, their demeanour one of concerned outsiders. Dressed head to foot in black, with a face veil and a swooping hat like a flying saucer, Mrs Shaw projected an exotic presence disassociated from the humble and unkempt church grounds. She was like the wedding guest whose aura overshadows the dowdy bride. Jennifer Shaw's husband eventually strode over.

"Inspector Stafford?"

"That's right. Detective inspector. You are Mr Shaw?"

"Yes." The man glanced at the graveside gathering. "Tommy Nelson is one of our best managers. He looks crushed, the poor fellow. He had to fly back from Pakistan. He only got back yesterday."

"Yes, I know he was there. Selling or buying?" The textile baron swung his head back and cast his eyes down the length of the graveyard.

"We might be recruiting workers from there."

"Really? Why?"

"It's a long story, Detective Inspector." He looked a little wistful, and then he turned fully to face Stafford. "Probably not the right venue for such a topic."

"You're right."

Stephen Shaw exuded a natural mien of authority. He possessed the bearing of an admiral, Stafford thought. A Roman version of Anthony Eden, though without the Foreign Secretary's moustache. He caught him tracing the line of his scar as he looked up into the policeman's face. His wife would have mentioned the odd-looking copper who had grilled her brother.

"Do you have to attend funerals like this very often?" Stephen Shaw was turning back towards the grave.

"No, I don't. Murder is a very rare event, though we seem to be caught up in more than our fair share at the moment."

"Could I ask, Mr Stafford, how the enquiry is going?"

"We're giving it everything, Mr. Shaw. A lot of it is down to basic, time-consuming police work."

"I think I heard that television policeman say just the same thing the other night."

"Fabian? Everything Fabian knows, Mr Shaw, he learnt from me."

The man turned back to face Stafford and smiled, administering a friendly pat on his upper arm before heading back to his wife's side. She had gone over to speak to some of the relatives. They were flocking around her, like autograph hunters surrounding Greer Garson or Anna Neagle.

Other officers at the funeral chatted quietly with members of the family, checking if anyone had turned up there they didn't know. Stafford told his colleagues he would make his own way back to the office, and he left the grounds of the church and walked down the hill. Only a few vehicles were about, including an electric milk float crawling up the incline towards a dairy depot. After a few minutes, he reached the gates of Undercliffe Cemetery and stepped through them. This was a bizarre municipal burial ground, many of the interred there lying under outlandish headstones and fantastic mausoleums. Below extraordinary lumps of masonry, many mimicking Egyptian sarcophagi, would lie the remains of a local butcher or bakery owner. He had come here several times after his wife's death, the place curiously comforting and calming.

Stafford rested against one of the structures, a plain, pointed obelisk squatting on a robust platform. He stared out over the diorama of the city, losing himself in private thoughts. Soon his eyes saw nothing, his brain so absorbed in itself it had no capacity left as a visual receptor. Shaking himself free from this mental state, he glanced down to identify the person he had been standing on. "In Memory of John Wilman", it said. "Brush manufacturer of Bradford".

He picked his way down through the cemetery, occasionally absorbing some of the inscriptions he passed and which were becoming familiar to him. "John Richard Burrows, Rag Merchant", said one. There was the burial spot of William Mawson, 1889, "Architect of Bradford", whose partnership with Joseph Lockwood fashioned so much of the city's appearance. Others were just those of mildly amusing names, like Joseph Nutter or a certain Job Cheeseborough Pratt.

If Stafford had not strolled through this whimsical Victorian burial hill, he would not have found himself embroiled in a nasty, if, for him, rather pleasing incident. Exiting the cemetery by a lower gate, he could see the roof light flashing on a police box, calling the nearest policeman on the beat. Stafford walked over briskly, used his special key to open the door, and picked up the telephone before identifying himself.

"Suspected burglar in Appleton Road, sir. Would you please attend."

"Where is Appleton Road? How far is that? Are you sending a car?" He dropped the receiver into its cradle.

The road was only fifty yards further towards the city centre. He ran down the hill and then along the front of the small semi-detached houses in the mercifully short street. Making his way along a snicket to the back of the semis, he asked himself why they hadn't called one of the squad cars at the Nelson burial.

At first, Stafford could see nothing. Houses appeared lifeless. No lights were visible. Windows seemed tightly shut. All he could hear was a distant scraping sound. Probably someone dragging a dustbin. A gentle breeze disturbed the bushes, but silently as if reinforcing the stillness. If there had been a crime, the perpetrator had probably legged it.

Then he saw a man easing his way out of a bathroom window, where a drainpipe conveniently offered a short conduit to the roof of a tool shed. The man toted a large cloth bag. Hugging the garden walls, Stafford edged himself forward to a position next to the rear gate of the house the burglar was doing over. A high wall provided cover. He could see the burglar through the branches of a tall bush. A nasty-looking character with a muscular slab of a face featuring a broken nose and heavy brow. Another able-bodied criminal who chose crime rather than a job.

Stafford did not have his ebony truncheon. Plain-clothes officers were issued with these – about half the length of a standard issue truncheon for a beat officer – but usually only on special raids, not in normal duty. What Stafford always did carry was a short lead pipe, sheathed in a sock. He stored it in an inner raincoat pocket. It was a disciplinary offence to arm oneself with such a tool. Stafford sometimes wondered whether other officers at the station used a home-made cosh, and whether they guessed he did. He gave a quick scan of the houses and snicket. He couldn't see anyone else about.

The detective inspector hunched behind the wall, his hand gripping the metal instrument. At last the burglar appeared through the open gate, sticking his head carefully into the open. Stafford swung the pipe across the bridge of the burglar's nose. The man yelped and his swag bag fell. Stafford struck him a second blow in the kidneys which dropped him to his knees. He then kicked him hard in the thigh, disabling the leg. He considered kicking him again but resisted the temptation.

Using his knee in the crook of the man's back, Stafford wired the burglar's hands behind him, using rope he always carried, and secured the restraint with a naval bowline knot. Anyone looking down the snicket would have noticed him whispering in the man's ear, though wouldn't have known just how threatening that whisper was. Stafford then extracted his whistle, ready to blow it when he saw the police car he knew was on its way.

*****

On Friday morning, the day after the funeral, Stafford completed the simple paperwork on the burglar, wandered around the officers assigned to the Moira Nelson case, and quit the station. Back at home, he loaded the Vanguard's rear seat with a few of the larger pictures his wife had painted. Diana had been an amateur, self-taught water colourist, and his sister wanted a few paintings from the two dozen or so he had kept, to add to the cluttered walls of their small cottage.

He opened a Hormel tin of Spam to make sandwiches for the trip. "Cold or Hot, Spam Hits the Spot", the label said, and he filled the bread with thick slices of the almost pure one hundred percent pork. He'd already put his nephew Peter's presents in the boot and added a bag containing a metal sandwich box, flask of Typhoo and a couple of Aero bars. He reckoned it would take seven or eight hours to get to Somerset and was glad to be pressing the starter button on the car's dashboard before midday.

He passed the local cinema – one of forty picture houses in the city, this one showing *20,000 Leagues Under the Sea* with James Mason and Kirk Douglas – and was soon clear of the suburbs and heading towards Derbyshire. The drizzle was gentle, a big help because the Standard Vanguard's wipers were only one-speed. He'd chosen the car partly because the cabin space easily housed his frame. Designed as the vehicle of choice for the military, the car boasted massive headroom. Stafford knew that the boss of Standard, Sir John Black, had despatched designers to secretly camp outside the US Embassy in London during the forties, and sketch designs of all the American cars they saw coming and going. The Vanguard resembled a downsized version of a Plymouth yet, despite its size, the moveable bench front seat was as far back as it would go to fit his legs.

After a couple of hours, he parked in a lay-by and ate most of the sandwiches. South of Tewkesbury, he stopped at a transport cafe, slotting his car among the lorries in the huge cinder car park. He needed a break from the car and queued for a tea. It was brewed in a metal cylinder the size of a small ship's boiler. The table he sat at offered three bottles of the same brown sauce. The air was thick with cigarette smoke and the smell of fried fat. Windows dripped with condensation, water running down them in blackened rivulets. Serving staff wore aprons that must have once been white but were now an oily yellow.

He opened his paper and skimmed through it. The suspension of Comet flights filled a lot of column inches. Boeing announced it was getting ready to test fly its first passenger jet aircraft, the 367-80, to be known as the 707. A US biker film starring Marlon Brando and called *The Wild One* was heading for a ban by the British Film Board. More complaints were coming in about the love scene on the beach involving Burt Lancaster and Deborah Kerr in *From Here to Eternity*. He made a mental note to try and catch the film.

Stafford sensed some of the drivers looking at him. He knew what they were thinking. Thug or policeman? He finished his tea and stretched his legs around the perimeter of the A One Cafe's car park. Groups of navvies were climbing out of glass-panelled vans, joking and laughing in their strong Irish accents. Alongside, two low-loaders were parked up, both carrying several old-fashioned, drab-green caravans. The caravans, for the next few years, would be these men's homes, Stafford guessed, as they worked on some new civil engineering project. He climbed back into the car, shutting the door on the pungent stink of diesel fumes outside.

On infrequent long journeys like this, he wished he had put his hand in his wallet and bought a wireless for the four-year old Vanguard. One was not even offered on the options list. An Ekco could have been retro-fitted, but only at the exorbitant cost of over thirty pounds.

Resurfacing work was underway on a stretch of the A38 and the car pitched and lurched on the ribbing, a fault of its high but short body. Stafford was forced to make continuous small adjustments of the steering wheel on even the straightest of roads because of the car's narrow track and cross-ply tyres. An Automobile Association rider, patrolling in the opposite direction on his yellow and black motorbike and sidecar combination, spotted the AA badge on the Vanguard's radiator grill and gave Stafford a salute.

Once he was south of Bristol, the imaginary aroma of over-ripe apples and cow manure invaded his senses, just as real as if his nostrils were detecting actual odours. He began to feel his childhood. Off the main road, he crossed the moor towards the ridge on which North Curry stood. A patchwork of fields and of ditches known as rhynes, the moor was part of the Somerset Levels. The land was overflowing with water and the road partially flooded, but the Vanguard, with its high ground clearance, waded through comfortably.

Parking the car right outside the cottage, Stafford felt the weight of tiredness on his shoulders. He would have enjoyed an hour on his own in a hotel room. But he could see the front door opening, even in the fast fading light, and Peter flew out like a pinball.

The boy hugged him just above the knees, and Stafford felt guilty at how little he had seen of him. He pretended to heave the boy over the bonnet and Peter squealed. "Uncle Raymond. Stop. Stop. Stop."

His sister and her husband had followed Peter down the stone path.

"Hello, Ray. At last." May kissed him, and he shook Clifford's outstretched hand.

"How's the great detective?" his brother-in-law asked.

"Up to my neck in human manure, as usual. And you?"

"Up to my neck in cake mix and fondant. As usual."

May's husband was a supervisor at Stanton's, the large bakery in the village which used a fleet of vans to supply the surrounding area with breads and cakes. Stafford liked him, but a really close rapport between them was absent. Nevertheless, they chatted happily while May worked at the range. Just before their late tea, Stafford extracted his case from the car boot and noticed that one of the Vanguard's semaphore indicators was stuck in the 'out' position.

May had roasted a wood pigeon, delicious if slightly overdone. She had also conjured up a pie from the last of the previous season's apples she stored in trays in the shed at the back, each apple kept apart from its neighbour to delay fresh rot. The pie was tart, and he followed it up with a chuck of Cheddar cheese.

The big tin bath was still in the back room, the water, heated on the range in pots, now lukewarm. Stafford helped Clifford empty the bath and then stow it on the metal pegs poking from the outside back wall of the house, next to a wooden ledge supporting a stack of Lifebuoy soap bars. The family sat around the remnants of the coal fire and caught up

142

with their news. Peter sat on Stafford's lap, his arms wrapped round his uncle's neck.

Stafford was given Peter's room, which fortunately came with a full-length but single bed, while Peter slept with his parents. So small in relation to his size, the room felt as if built for another species. The wallpaper was made up of dense patterns of soldiers in red tunics and busbies holding rifles with bayonets. There were no pictures, save for a see-through diagram of a Lancaster bomber and one of a Mosquito. A dap bag holding Peter's plimsolls hung from the back of the door.

He slid open a wood pencil box containing Osmiroid school pens, and then closed it. He was tired but fidgety, and wanted to read something, though nothing serious. Delving into a tatty Brock's fireworks box stuffed with Peter's books, he picked up a *Dandy* annual featuring Korky the Cat on the front cover. He read a Desperate Dan, and Helpful Henry strip before tossing it back in the box. Underneath, he discovered a Dick Barton, Special Agent book, and he lay under the cover with the thick volume. Within a few minutes, he was fast asleep.

The following morning, he enjoyed a late breakfast of bacon and eggs while Clifford worked in the garden shed and May tapped out an article for the parish magazine on her portable typewriter. She had come to a stop, creatively defeated for a few minutes while she got her second wind.

"What's it about?" her brother asked.

"The thriving commercial life of North Curry. I am petrified I'll leave somebody out. They'll never talk to me again. It really is amazing that with a population of a thousand, including nearby hamlets, the village can support more than twenty businesses, and that is excluding the farms. You hardly need to go into Taunton. You know, you can still buy suits at Brownsey's."

"Are you including the churches as businesses?"

She turned around to look at him. "Of course not, you oaf. Honestly, you are such a sceptic."

Stafford cleared up his plates, washed them, then drove the Vanguard to Squires garage where a mechanic adjusted the indicator. He then parked the car outside the post office and general store and started a circuitous stroll of the village. Foster's garage, dispensing National Benzol in competition to

143

Squires' BP and Shell, seemed very busy, and Webb's nearby had laid out bicycles in racks for sale outside its front door.

Stafford went into Hutchings', a newsagent and haberdashery, passed the time of day, bought a paper, and then walked past three butchers and two shoemakers and repairers before entering the graveyard of St Peter and St Paul, a church complementing the village's two chapels. He sat down on a bench and opened the *Daily Telegraph*. Reams of words on the Comet filled the front page. A piece by an industrial writer reported that the planes were subject to explosive decompression, the fuselages literally blowing apart at the seams and shredding their aluminium skin. This was just half a millimetre thick. Speculation was rife about problems with rivets and the design of the aircraft's windows and communication hatch.

A photograph of Cadbury's Bournville factory stared out at him. The story said the chocolate maker was now using electronic calculators for invoicing, the first British company to do so on a large scale. A medical report about treatments for cancer caught his eye for a second, but he couldn't face reading it. The article made him close the paper.

He strolled through the graveyard and along a path towards the wetlands. Within a short distance he felt the earth giving way to mud and he retraced his steps. Back in the heart of the village, he had a look at the small billboard on the Bijou Cinema, where customers sat on converted bus seats and which the village believed was the tiniest picture house in England. The Bijou was showing an old film, *The Outcasts of Poker Flat* with Dale Robertson.

Walking past the auctioneers and land agents, Morris Sons and Peard, he turned into Knapp Lane, past the White Hart pub and along the road with its high-banked hedgerows. A tractor came along, a blue Fordson, and he stood to one side to let it pass. By the time he was back in the village, he had made way for three other pieces of farm machinery.

Everyone knew him, and he tried to keep chats to a minimum. "Hello, Morris. Just taking a constitutional. Talk to you later."

"Hello, Stanley. Might see you in the Bird in Hand."

He didn't want to slip into endless conversations on the same subjects of policing and 'up North' and myxomatosis.

Old Miss Chedzoy pulled up alongside him in her car and they had a chinwag about her terriers, Binky and Trip. Miss Chedzoy was one of those people lacing every sentence with phrases both ancient, and, in the case of the elderly former hospital matron, surprisingly modern. Everything was "handsome as handsome is does" and "the devil take the hindmost" and "catch as catch can".

She was vexed at something to do with the village's roads, though Stafford couldn't concentrate much on what she was saying. At the end he did get: "Anyway, I told the local MP to put it in his pipe and smoke it. I've got to go now, Raymond, as I'm seeing a big cheese in Taunton to try and get it sorted out. Might as well strike while the iron's hot. I'm telling you, Raymond, someone is going to take the rap for this." At last, she was on her way. Binky and Trip clung precariously to the top of the car's back seat as the Austin staggered away, the dogs bracing themselves as Miss Chedzoy crashed the gears.

He walked into the Radio House and inspected the electrical equipment on sale, deciding to buy a television with a bigger screen once he was at home. It was early, and the Bird in Hand was almost empty. He ordered a pint and took a corner seat. Along the wall was pinned the fixtures' list for the Taunton Brewers' skittle league. A building attached to the pub housed an eighty-foot pitch board, and there was a match that night with Isle Abbots.

Stafford continued along past the Angel, the village's third pub, and completed a circuit back to the tiny green. He inspected the war memorial which incorporated the names of six men from in and around North Curry who had died in the Second World War, and the twenty-five dead in the First, a number Stafford could still hardly believe. A Leyland Lion now filled the forecourt of Foster's garage. The passenger door of the coach was open, and someone was kneeling down, cleaning the burgundy-coloured moquette upholstery.

A chequerboard of mud, cowshit and grass caked the soles of his shoes. In Bradford, claggy industrial dust peppered the air but the pavements were spotless. Here, the air smelled of nature in its purest form, yet underfoot it was like a milking parlour after an outbreak of bovine diarrhoea.

He'd stayed away from the house while they were setting it all up for Peter's birthday. He thought his body would just get in the way. Now he extracted his nephew's wrapped presents from the boot of his car and slipped back into the cottage.

Within an hour, the back garden was alive with children, cramming sandwiches, cakes and Thayers ice cream into hungry mouths. It was all washed down by Corona pop in its distinctive bottle with white metal-clip top. The yelps, screams and tantrums mirrored those of any children's party.

"Harry is stealing all the orange."

"Where are the skipping ropes?"

"There's not enough room for a piggyback race."

"I like angel cakes and there aren't any!"

He caught May staring at him, worried about her brother no doubt, but she quickly smiled and waved the locket hanging around her neck in thanks for the gift.

Stafford took some cake and pop and talked to the parents who had arrived with their kids and never left. One or two of the children stared up at him. Occasionally, he said "boo", but gently. The air's early morning sweetness was giving way to a single smell of newly-mown grass from the garden next door. Mr Partridge was using his Ransomes Ajax to administer a short back and sides on his already prim lawn.

After the party, Stafford embarked on a circular drive along the narrow lanes with their high hedges. He ended up drinking down another pint at a pub near Stoke St Gregory. May cooked a chicken for dinner. The boiled potatoes, dug out of the ground that day, tasted of nutty earth. Several hours were spent playing whist and pontoon, and they listened to *Educating Archie* on the radio. Stafford always found the voice of the ventriloquist's dummy freakish and unsettling.

On the Sunday morning, they talked about seeing *Titanic* in the afternoon at the pictures in Taunton, but decided instead to go for a drive and a picnic.

"We'll be in trouble with the chapel again." May was loading Clifford's old Morris Ten with a wicker picnic basket bulging at the sides. "The minister pops round every so often to see how we all are, bless him, but what he's actually doing is poking about to see why we don't attend more often. Actually, the last time we were there everyone afterwards was talking about Billy Graham and that big Christian rally, or whatever it was he had in London. The minister can't make head nor tail of it."

They all clambered in and drove up through the Quantocks to the coast at Watchet. With four on board, the car struggled to make more than forty miles an hour when confronted with even a hint of a hill. A strong wind at Minehead rather scuppered the idea of a proper picnic, but they had one, nevertheless, sitting in the car. Lean beef sandwiches, except for Peter. He was the only boy Stafford knew who demonstrated a continuous craving for Shippam's fish paste. Dark clouds, occasionally separated by beams of sunshine, filled the sky, but they contained so little water the day remained entirely dry. By the time evening light started drawing in, Stafford was looking forward to leaving where he belonged and travelling back to a place that was both foreign and his home.

He steered into his driveway back in Yorkshire on the Monday while it was still light, in time to catch his neighbours airing the caravan for spring. A mug of cocoa in hand, he climbed the stairs to listen to the bedside radio. As he closed the curtains, he noticed that mattresses and removable cupboards from the caravan's kitchen now littered the neighbour's rear patio, along with saucepans, bunk bed sheets and travelling crockery. It looked like a flea market. He was asleep before finishing the drink.

*****

Across the city, a highly agitated man sat on the edge of his bed and looked out on to a ring of flickering lights. When he was young, his dad had hung him by his feet out of the very same window, after thrashing him with a belt until his skin split. He'd had his revenge on his father. The man twisted the purse bag in his hand, feeling the cheap jewellery inside. He eventually threw it back in the drawer, kicking it shut so violently the thin wood face splintered. He got up and went closer to the glass. He really wanted to hurt somebody. Anybody.

147

CHAPTER 17

The following day opened with the familiar rhythm of routine. Stafford picked up his paper as usual from Bairstow's. The owner was grappling again with an unwieldy cardboard promotion for a new comic. This time it was for the *Tiger* featuring Roy of the Rovers. "They're springing up like mushrooms," Alfie Bairstow remarked rather despondently.

At lunchtime, Stafford wandered off in search of a novel attracting approving reviews in the newspapers. He first slipped into the Prudential Assurance to check one of his insurance policies; the idiosyncratic pile, employing twirly terracotta brickwork that was a company hallmark, stuck out from Bradford's blackened sandstone like a dull pimple. Leaving the Pru, Stafford made his way to a nearby bookshop. Like many retailers, a wind-away awning sloped down above the window. Unusually, the shop's name was written across the canvas. The interior of bookshops always harboured one of two smells. Either a warm "sawdust" aroma of paper and cardboard and new publications, or one of dampness, mould and old tomes. Geldart's had the former.

The woman behind the counter, a brassy redhead in her forties, offered him a smile.

"Afternoon." She spoke with a pronounced East Riding accent, somewhere around Hull. He had noticed her before, out and about, and he could feel her eyes on him while he examined the fiction section. Finding what he was looking for, he moved to the counter. She smiled again and he gave her a couple of coins for the copy of *Lucky Jim*. He made a point of smiling broadly and she widened hers. The top three buttons of her blouse were undone, revealing a substantial cleavage. She handed over the book, wrapped loosely in brown paper. He used it to tap the back of her hand. "Thanks a lot," he said and left.

Part of the afternoon was absorbed with one of the regular station-wide reviews of the Nelson case. Stafford went straight home at the end of the day, giving himself time to make a dinner of pork chops and tinned peas. He was keen to watch the BBC's first live television news broadcast. A mug of Lyons coffee in hand, he switched on the box.

The first half of the broadcast was made up of static pictures, covering truce talks in the Indo-China war, a Russian espionage scandal in Australia, an item about the Swedish royal family and a coal miners' conference. Then came moving film. Stafford had to concentrate hard on poor quality images of raging floods in Texas to get any sense of what was happening. About two hundred people were dead. A slot about Britain's National Rifle Association followed. "Rifle shooting is becoming increasingly popular with women," the newscaster announced. "But they're not shooting rabbits," Stafford said out loud. A spot of trouble on the border dividing Israel and Jordan was the next item, and then a description of a production line in Northern Ireland. "Already, this factory employs nearly six hundred workers making radio sets for export. The sets are assembled at the rate of one radio set completed every seventy seconds, five hundred sets every day."

A map of Tunisia then swallowed up the tiny TV screen, the commentary explaining the arrival of three battalions of troops from France as another of its colonies went up in smoke. "Terrorist attacks have been increasing," the newscaster said. "Last week, fifteen people were killed or wounded, and last night a city councillor was shot dead in Tunis, the capital."

Stafford went into the kitchen and, on a slice of bread, layered Stork margarine and savoury duck, a local name for haslet. He switched off the box and lay on the settee, legs dangling over the end, opened the Kingsley Amis novel and continued reading until he started laughing. He stopped, wondering whether merriment was a bit sacrilegious given that his station was getting nowhere with two murders. Reading on, he gave up trying to muffle his glee.

The following morning, he sifted through more reports. Stacks of material were piling up and Stafford had the feeling his colleagues were all treading water. He felt the same. He scrutinised the latest droplets of information from the Ilkley sub-station. The analysis of the murdered girl's coat was on his desk, revealing nothing. Bored, the detective inspector went out for a walk, strolling along the town hall, entering a few shops, browsing but buying nothing. Then he stopped dead in his tracks. Turning about too quickly, he shouldered into an elderly nun as she walked past him, an empty flower vase in her hands. "Mother of God." He apologised and legged it back to the station.

In his office, Stafford pulled out one of the reports he had just read, and then walked into the incident room. He rooted through the growing number of paper stacks. Some piles were so hefty they risked teetering over. Sheets were sticking out haphazardly. He drafted in a constable to help. Eventually they found what he was searching for. In his office, he placed the two sheets side by side. He then telephoned the Ilkley station.

"Ilkley police, Sergeant Rishworth speaking." Rishworth sounded more like an army drill sergeant than a policeman, the sound a bark rather than a voice.

"It's Detective Inspector Stafford here at Bradford. I want to know about a report you've just sent us concerning a three-wheeler car seen close to the site where Moira Nelson died."

"Yes sir. I handled that myself."

Stafford flicked through the papers. "Did Mrs what's-her-name, Lumb, say what colour it was?"

"Let's have a look at my notes." Noise of shuffled papers came down the line, then the crash of something falling and "bugger" delivered in a shout. "Right. No. Here they are. Ahm. Yes, she said it looked like a dark colour, possibly red. Didn't know the make. It was nearly pitch black at the time, but as you probably know, Mr Stafford, there's a row of street lights just before you turn off as if you're going to Hebers Ghyll."

"Why did it take her so long to come forward?"

"You know how it is, guv. This kind of stuff comes in for weeks after. In this case, Mrs Lumb went to relations in Southport the day after the girl was found. She has only been back a few days and it has taken that long to get her bearings."

"A red three-wheeler was seen near where Nelson disappeared here in Bradford. Follow it up at your end. I'll try and get a list of owners in the area."

It was something, Stafford thought. Perhaps nothing. But perhaps something. He grabbed a phone book, scribbled an address, collared Norman Feather, and they left together in a squad car.

The Wolseley picked its way through the city centre. The Ritz was advertising *Hondo* with John Wayne. At one junction, lorries loaded with wool bales snaked down the road in static queues, exhaust clouds billowing from idling engines as the wagons waited their turn outside a yard entrance. Another strip of lorries was doing the same across the other side of the road. The police driver hit the switch for the car's gong, the sound of the clanging bell, feeble as it was, delivering a warning to everyone close by as the car crawled through the gap.

"What won the sweepstake?" Stafford asked Feather.

"Chimney Chump chokes in Catacomb Catastrophe. I thought mine was better."

The roads were now quiet, but people clustering in and out of small shops and countless public houses lent the pavements a lively air. Lights in pub windows were warm but devious invitations to interiors of manky carpets and stale beer smells. On a derelict piece of land where housing was being cleared, workmen tossed wood on to a large bonfire. The car then pulled off into a cobbled lane on the edge of the city, across from the big sheds of a busy trolley bus depot.

Sugdens' was a sprawling, unkempt site. A big sign, written in double-lined, black and yellow paint, read: "Berkeley Caravans, three-wheelers, motorbikes and Vespas. Save On Your Tax". Curiously, underneath the words was a stylised image of a palm tree on a kind of Caribbean island, painted in pink and blue. The two officers skimmed round the pools of standing water on the forecourt and entered a long thin showroom, seemingly fabricated out of plyboard. A short man with a tweed flat cap had been observing them from behind his desk. He stood up and held one arm out straight, the hand in the police 'stop' position, a fag between the yellowing index and middle fingers.

"No offence, officers, but I don't sell anything big enough to fit either of you. Unless it's a caravan you're after, but the size of the bunks might be a problem."

The man introduced himself as Victor Greasby. His hair was so black and slicked in cream it looked like treacle. A pronounced widow's peak bestowed a sinister aspect. His countenance though was entirely friendly and his face open and jolly. He was like a stumpy version of Tommy Trinder, with a Bela Lugosi wig.

Greasby explained that he ran the place, having married the daughter of the man who founded the business. Stafford told him they were making routine enquiries and needed a list of all three-wheelers he had sold, or serviced, or just knew about.

"Bond or Reliant?"

"Both."

Greasby sidled over to a grey filing cabinet, yanked open a drawer with some force and pulled out a book.

"It's all tabulated here since the time of the Flood. Well, six years. It's not a long list. I'll get Marjorie to type it out for you. What's happening?"

A woman of indeterminate age and shaped like a triangle resting on two pegs, emerged from another office and took the list. She banged into the door frame as she went back out.

"We're looking for a red one, or at least a dark colour," Feather said.

"I'll see what I can remember."

Greasby caught Feather glancing up at a picture of Geoff Duke. The owner shook his head in a dismissive manner. "The greatest motorbike racer Britain has ever produced. I almost tore the poster down last year when he signed for Gilera. Siding with the Ities. It's already hit my Norton sales."

A woman with high Slavic cheekbones and bottle-coloured hair so blonde it looked like custard, bent her head round the office door seeking assistance.

"I'll be out shortly, luv." Greasby took a stride towards her and placed a hand in the small of the woman's back. "To keep it simple, the Reliants have car engines, the Bonds use smaller ones from motorbikes. You can get a reverse gear on some of the Reliants but, generally speaking, the Bonds don't have reverse."

"No gear reverse?"

"No. You want them to go backwards you just push them. They can turn, though, on a sixpence. I'll be out with you in a minute."

The woman stared at Stafford, smiled, then frowned and disappeared back into the showroom.

"At these prices she's lucky the car comes with a bloody floor." Greasby leaned back in his chair.

"We'd like some photographs if you have them," Stafford said.

"I've got a couple of promotional brochures. I wouldn't mind them back."

"Very large site you've got for selling all this stuff," Feather pointed out.

"You're right, but we're expanding all the time. Look, there are forty makes of motorbike produced in Britain, and I can supply just about every one. And have a gander at this. We'll be getting them next year, I hope. We'll sell loads of these."

He chucked some sheets of paper over the desk. The photographs were of micro cars. Drivers and passengers climbed in by tipping a glass roof or by pulling open the whole front.

Feather pulled a face. "They look like tin bubbles."

"Well let's hope that name doesn't catch on." Greasby reached over to retrieve the literature.

Back in the office, the two policemen decided the first thing to do was show witnesses photos of the peculiar bug-like cars to see if the model, if it was just one, could be identified. Then vehicle owners would need interviewing.

As he was leaving, Feather unwrapped a Cadbury's Wholenut bar and headed for the door. He rested his hand on the doorknob, then turned and remarked: "That burglar you nabbed, sir. Amazing what damage you can suffer just getting arrested." A knowing smirk was already travelling across his face as he stepped into the corridor.

*****

A small vessel on the far horizon was the sole blemish on a seascape so mesmerisingly natural and intoxicating it could have been lifted from a travel brochure of the Adriatic.

A cornflower blue and cloudless sky met in a perfect line a sea that bestowed on the word 'azure' the rights to its own brand name. The sun's rays beat down at an angle that did not yet confer on the small ripple of waves even a hint of a steely twinkle. That granted the view a more vivid composition, creating out of two tones of one colour an illuminated splendour of such intensity you couldn't understand why water was ever the colour of mud.

Or at least that's what Jennifer Shaw thought, sitting on a public bench on Scarborough's South Cliff, the North Sea becalmed in front of her. With the Italian Gardens stretching out below, the radiant grandeur of the vista reminded her of Capri. Yet it could not raise her spirits. For someone whose genial disposition was usually bazooka-proof, this was unsettling.

It wasn't as if they were not having a belting time of it. She and her husband had come up the day before for the Friday night ball, held every year by the worsted trade. They'd been lucky enough in the association's room-draw to nab a seaview apartment at the Crown Hotel, the white stucco confection in a Regency terrace on the Esplanade. The room had been recently done out in cream, with cornices and window surrounds picked out in pale green. The management incorporated in the decor a handful of framed prints of adverts from the past. One was for Spa water in soluble form known as Scarborough Salts. Another was for "Dr Rooke's famous oriental Pills and Solar Elixir".

In the triple-size doctor's bag she had bought from a tannery in the northern Italian town of Arzignano, the initials JS stamped on it personally by the tannery owner, she had toted up two of her new purchases. She eventually opted for the Balenciaga in China silk rather than the Christian Dior sheath. The Crown was the venue for the ball so it was just a simple stride down the stairs. The orchestra was top notch, the food passable, and she'd managed a long chat with Nellie and Georgina Dixon. Known collectively as the Misses Dixon, they ran the Crown on behalf of the Hudsons, its owners. She'd known the two for years.

The Shaws had even enjoyed one of those priceless moments that, as a tool for etching memories, was light years ahead of a classic restaurant steak or a breathtaking hotel bathroom. Stephen had placed his brogues outside the suite's door in the early evening for a clean and polish. He'd first checked the service was operating, given the way the ball was stretching the Crown's resources. Half of the other guests on the corridor had the same idea. In the morning, he opened the room door to collect his wife's *Daily Telegraph*, his *Times* and the shoes, only to discover he'd been left a pair of black brogues instead of his pair of browns.

A quick call from the bedroom on the newly-installed electric bell system produced a maid who ran off for the boot man. On arrival, the boot man – unbelievably, it said Hector Heck on his name badge – identified his mistake and knocked on the door opposite. A pugnacious male answered, a specialist small-scale wool dyer whom Stephen vaguely knew. He was wearing Stephen's brogues.

"I'm sorry, sir. I left the wrong shoes outside your door this morning," Hector Heck informed the resident of room six.

"I know, I'm wearing them".

"Er, these are your shoes here, sir."

"Yes, they do look like mine."

"I think the gentleman across the way would like his own shoes back."

"Do you want me to change them?"

"I think, sir, that would be a good idea."

"Well, if I must."

It was incomprehensible. She wondered what would have happened if she'd left out a pair of her fanciest footwear. Would the man have strolled into breakfast dressed in a double-breasted suit, tie inscribed "Bradford Dyers' Association", and three-inch heel boots with tiger skin piping?

Shaw pulled her still sleepy mind back to the present, left her seat and walked back along the Esplanade towards the Crown. Scarborough Castle was startlingly clear on the hillside above the small harbour. She could see in front of her the massive bulk of the Grand below, the biggest hotel in Europe when it was built. Its bizarre design, she knew, aped the calendar – four turrets, twelve floors, fifty-two chimneys and three hundred and sixty-five bedrooms.

Stephen was already sitting in the Bentley. She climbed in and they set off. The bright weather was bringing out the day-trippers. A few charabancs had already arrived from industrial towns up the coast. Small shops were selling beach balls and buckets and spades from brightly-coloured outside displays. A few people were in shorts and regulation brown socks and sandals. They passed the local picture house, *Roman Holiday* with Gregory Peck and Audrey Hepburn on the billboard.

"I've had an extraordinary conversation with a building contractor in the hotel lounge," her husband was saying. "They've just opened a bunker somewhere close by as an RAF radar station. Keeping tabs on the Ruskies, I suppose. Not much security if you get told all this over a cup of coffee."

The road heading west was almost devoid of traffic, but vehicles came thick and fast in the opposite direction towards the coast. Full loads of adults and children were crammed into some of the vehicles, their little engines working overtime. She rested her head on her husband's shoulder and started to nod off. She was in that almost asleep condition that never entirely felt right when it wasn't even midday.

The other side of Malton, her husband was forced to step on the anchors at a roundabout. His wife slid off the shiny leather seat, only just saving herself from being dumped in the footwell. She straightened up, ran her hand through her long hair, and let her head roll on to the door window. "I must look like the wreck of the Hesperus."

"You're always gorgeous, darling."

"This morning, I don't think so."

"You just look like someone who's knocked back half a dozen pink gins and a bottle of Chablis, with a full cooked breakfast as a chaser. Come to think of it…"

"Don't remind me. Actually, it was a very good do. I just feel a bit distracted."

"Oh? With what?"

It was amazing what clarity thirty minutes of even broken sleep bestowed on a flagging brain. Jennifer Shaw knew what was bothering her. What was bothering her was that she didn't know what was bothering her. And that bothered her. She wasn't intuitive. She didn't believe in a sixth sense. That's why the feeling of apprehension was so foreign.

She should have been full of the joys. They had decided to go away for a full week, leaving Yorkshire on the coming Monday for a couple of nights in the south before flying to France and meeting the Tomlinsons at the Westminster, the hotel they always stayed at in Le Touquet. But she definitely didn't feel carefree. More apprehensive. She extracted a Pall Mall.

By the time they arrived home, Pennymore was locked up. Mrs Williams and her husband had been given the weekend off and were in Derbyshire visiting relatives. The building crew worked only in the morning that day, but Archie Tyzack had persuaded them to return for the whole of Sunday. Jennifer Shaw had vaguely wondered whether working on Sunday broke some by-law.

She let herself in, checked the post and put her head round the door of her new kitchen. One unit, sliced in half to accommodate the new Prestcold refrigerator, now blended in perfectly. Only a few days of work remained. In the kitchenette, she put a full kettle on the two-ring camping stove and ascended the stairs to run a bath.

As soon as she entered the bedroom, she could smell it. A hardly perceptible but nevertheless unpleasant aroma. She lifted both toilet lids, but she knew the source did not lie there.

"Can you smell it?" she said, as her husband entered the room. "A faint trace of a pungent odour."

He flared his nostrils. "Can't detect a thing." He kissed the back of her neck and disappeared into his bathroom.

Standing in the middle of the bedroom, she realised what it was. The room had been infiltrated by someone with no business there. Her senses were detecting the remnants of body stench.

Quickly scanning the room, her eyes lit on an empty space next to the bed where her silver box should have been. She went over and placed her hand on the surface where the antique container always sat, as if checking that it might still be there but had somehow turned invisible. She then flung open all the cupboard doors, tearing through her clothes, opening jewellery and watch boxes, even though they were always kept locked. Nothing else was missing. Stephen exited the bathroom, a towel over his shoulder.

"We've been robbed, Stephen. The Victorian box next to the bed. It has taken a walk."

He put his hands in his pockets and stared at the empty expanse on the bedside table, sharing with his wife the first experience ever of being the subject of a theft. Then she went downstairs to call the police.

CHAPTER 18

Wilfrid Oldfield pedalled his Humber 'police special' slowly up the hill. The bicycle was built like a tank and weighed as much. His knees creaked, his neck ached. The weather had turned cold and damp again. Thank goodness for the chill, Oldfield thought, but he knew his face would now be the shade of beetroot. At one point, the incline became noticeably steeper and he conceded defeat, dismounted and started pushing.

He'd never been to Pennymore, and when he plodded through its imposing gates that Sunday morning, Constable Oldfield was dismayed at the length of the driveway. It twisted between the garden's humbling foliage for another ankle-aching sweep. He trudged up, his hands sweating on the rubber-covered handlebars. Two builders' vans were in the drive with a large motorbike nearby. He wasn't sure where the house entrance was and took the wrong route. A motorcycle enthusiast, Oldfield made time to admire the large Norton Dominator, panniers either side of the rear wheel, that was parked on a stretch of garden paving, before he ended up down a side path. A tall woman was standing behind a long, thin glass door as he rested his bicycle against the wall. He obviously startled her. Then she smiled and swung the door open.

"Good morning, officer. Jennifer Shaw."

"Morning. I couldn't find the front door. Long drive you've got there."

"Yes, sorry about that. Come in please."

The constable wiped his face and stepped into a long hall. Mrs Shaw switched on some more lights and steered him into a living room as big as a lounge in a middle-sized hotel. She beckoned him over to a mammoth armchair, and he slumped into it.

"Would you like some tea and biscuits?"

"No thanks, Mrs Shaw. Constable Oldfield, that's my name. On second thought, could I have some water?"

"Of course you can. What about some orange?"

"Champion." The constable stretched out his legs and got his breath back. Retirement was a month away and he was counting the minutes. The chair was so comfortable he could easily have dozed off, but the woman returned with a long glass. He drank it in one go. It tasted of pop but smelled of perfume.

"Sorry we couldn't come yesterday, Mrs Shaw. I think the station told you but we've been really snowed under with this poor girl's murder up on the moor."

"I quite understand."

"Now, let me get my notebook and pencil. Lovely room Mrs Shaw. Smashing view. Here we are. Now. You reported a silver box missing from your bedroom."

"That's right. It's very important to me. Can't believe its gone. It's hallmarked Birmingham, eighteen ninety-four, Thomas Hayes."

"Hold on a minute. Let me get this down." Oldfield, who was an elderly sixty-year-old, had left school when he was eleven. He could write adequately, but slowly and in capitals, which meant he often pressed too hard. The pencil point broke. "Oh, sorry. Let me get another pencil." He kept about ten in his uniform pocket, all over-sharpened.

"Could someone have just moved the box somewhere else in the house, Mrs Shaw?" The constable licked the point and eased up on the pressure his hand applied to the pencil.

"Definitely not. I have a housekeeper, Mrs Williams. She is away at the moment, but I rang her at her relatives last night just to check. Anyway, she would never do anything like that. She would never move it. Nobody in the house would. We have a building firm on site. We've known Mr Tyzack for years. He even has a set of keys. They've been here for weeks."

Oldfield knew Archie Tyzack. He virtually knew everyone in the area, outside the nobs.

"Any sign of a break-in?"

"None that we can see. I suppose the house doors are unlocked when the builders are here."

"Could I see the bedroom?"

"You want to see the bedroom?"

"Always good to see the scene of the crime, as it were, Mrs Shaw."

By the time he'd got back into the corridor and noticed the sweeping staircase dog-legging into the sky, he wondered whether he should have bothered. He followed her up, his head in a stream of scented vapour. He gripped the banister and willed his joints to work. She waited for him on the landing. She could have been Lauren Bacall's elder sister. He wondered how much older he was than this lovely woman. Not all that much probably. He wished she wasn't looking at him. By the time he joined her, he would have sacrificed half his wage packet for an oxygen cylinder.

Constable Oldfield did his best to regain his breath as they walked along the landing. It was amazingly wide, and the scattering of chairs and sofas made it seem like another living room, half suspended in mid-air. In the bedroom, he noticed too late that his size-tens with heavy ribbed soles were making faint, dirty patterns on the white carpet. He hoped Mrs Shaw hadn't spotted that.

"It was taken from there." She pointed to the bedside, her arm aiming one way but her head the exact opposite, obviously tracing the track he'd just laid across her bedroom. He winced and, more out of embarrassment than anything else, peered out through the bedroom window. A birdwatcher, Oldfield settled his eyes on various corvine birds searching for food in the Pennymore grounds. The crows and rooks were padding about like old men. But it was not these little black beasts that really caught his eye. On a dark-stone patio, the builders were sitting around, mugs of tea in hand. Sixty years of hardly ever reading a book had left him with perfect sight. He watched the group for a moment. One of the men was of particular interest to Wilfrid Oldfield. The constable frowned and moved closer to the window. Then he brought his pencil up to his face and repeatedly tapped it against his lower lip.

"Very good view from up here, Mrs Shaw. I think I have seen all I need to see." He deposited more size-ten treads as they left the bedroom.

*****

On the Saturday of that weekend, Stafford rolled out the Webb Whippet from the shed and mowed the long lawn, even though the grass was still damp. The sun shone and the temperature was warm. He weeded the beds, a job he despised. In the evening, he took himself off to the pictures to see *The Big Heat*. A morose feeling swept over him for several minutes as he watched Glenn Ford enjoying some very cosy domestic scenes with his wife in their big through-kitchen. It was painful watching, and he felt the loss of Diana again so acutely his concentration slipped.

Then people started getting tortured and murdered. Boiling coffee thrown in the face seemed to be a favourite of the director. Brutal but enjoyable, Stafford thought, as he got deeper into the film. It was especially satisfying seeing one nasty heavy getting his just rewards when his kisser ended up burned and scarred. The police surgeon on the screen droned on about the mentality of psychopaths. Stafford wondered whether that was what he and his colleagues were up against. He checked the credits for the name of the vicious sidekick. He'd keep his eyes open from now on for anything featuring Lee Marvin.

He ventured out on a trip to Swaledale on the Sunday but the weather was buckling, snatching away the first taste of spring. He stopped in Skipton, at a hotel with a Morning Coffee sign outside, and enjoyed a pot of the beverage with hot milk and some tea biscuits before deciding to turn back. He couldn't face another day of driving Dales rain.

Back at home and feeling that aggravating condition of listlessness mixed in with overwhelming restlessness, he decided to fill what was left of the day by conducting the last of the interviews he had assigned himself.

He grabbed his raincoat and left the house. Across the road, two men were pasting up a new Brylcreem poster, dominated by the head and dinner-jacketed torso of Denis Compton. As he reversed his car out of the drive, Stafford caught sight of the long-handled brush pushing into place the last piece of the paper jigsaw, revealing the hair of the legendary cricketer and Arsenal footballer. The hair was immaculately plastered and slicked-back by the emulsion of mineral oil and beeswax. Down the hill, the lights in a municipal hall blazed a cheery welcome for the kids heading to Sunday school.

At the bottom of the main road to Manchester, hundreds of children milled about on the wide pavement outside the Odeon picture house. A 'meet the stars' event for the Belles of St Trinian's. Stafford wondered how they got a Sunday licence for that, the kind of thing usually held at children's Saturday morning cinema shows.

Half a mile further up, the road started jamming with cars. Pavements were crammed all of a sudden with pedestrians. As it was an early evening kick-off, Stafford expected to avoid the crowds now pouring up towards the Rugby League Cup Final replay at Odsal Stadium. He'd obviously mistimed it. Supporters huddled against the drizzle as they gang-walked up the hill. They all looked the same. All men. All about the same height. All wearing dull-coloured macs. An image of a herd of gnus he'd seen on television's *Zoo Quest* sprang to mind. Police had arrived in numbers, in the force's own paddy wagons, to deal with crowd control. Stafford turned off near a cluster of these Black Marias and weaved his way through the back streets up to the city's Wibsey district.

He found the house without too much trouble and parked a few doors away. As he climbed out of the car, the smell of roast pork wafted out of an open window somewhere. Three young boys were hanging around the corner of a wide snicket beyond which Stafford had left the Vanguard. One was sitting on a wall, his nose in an *I-Spy* book. The other two were playing Cowboys and Indians, one with a headdress, the other kitted out with a kid's version of a ten-gallon hat and a gun holster. The detective inspector approached the boys.

"Hello there. Are you having a good game?" Under the cowboy hat, a look of pure malevolence confronted Stafford.

"It's alright," said the Indian, but his chum offered no response, blank eyes staring from a flat and freckled face. Then the Cisco Kid drew one of his six-shooters and plugged Stafford repeatedly in the chest. The cap pistol issued loud cracks as the roll of explosive material wound its way inside the plastic barrel. The kid was jabbing the gun forward as he shot, as if he really meant it. "You're dead," he screamed. "I've killed you." Stafford wondered how many years it would be before he'd see Hopalong Cassidy down in the station, manacled in real handcuffs rather than the fakes hanging from his belt.

"Play quietly now," Stafford said rather uselessly. As he turned, freckle-face shot him twice more in the side.

The three-wheeler was standing on a patch of grass in the garden. It was red and feeble-looking and had just one door, for the driver. It looked like an ugly ladybird. A man was kneeling down scrubbing the Bond's floor, a bucket of sudsy water next to him.

"Good afternoon, sir. Are you Henry Crabtree?" The man got up, a cloth in his hand. "I'm Detective Inspector Stafford." After Stafford showed him his police card, Crabtree actually took the wallet out of his hand and stared at it for several seconds. He had a totally vacant demeanour, and Stafford was eventually forced to retrieve his identification from the man's sweaty paw.

Crabtree was probably in his early thirties but looked older. His left shoulder was noticeably wider than his right. A long body sat atop short legs. The head was large and sweating profusely, perspiration trickling in several streams. A comb-over flapped in the breeze.

"Could we go inside, sir? Just some routine questions." The man looked so bemused at the appearance of this stranger in his small garden Stafford felt almost apologetic for disturbing him.

Stafford followed him into a small kitchen. Crabtree went to the sink. He washed his hands and lower arms in a thorough, obsessive repetition that went on for about half a minute. He had a snub nose with nostrils facing directly in front, and blue, piercing eyes. His skin was the colour of suet. He looked like a piglet.

"Henry, is there someone in there with you?" A female's sharp voice came from the next room.

"Just a minute, Mum."

Stafford trailed him into the back where a woman, probably in her late sixties, sat in a rocking chair, knitting something in pale brown.

"Oh, who's this?"

"Detective Inspector Ray Stafford of Bradford police. Mrs Crabtree is it?"

"Yes. I'm Henry's mother." The woman lodged the knitting in her lap. She had neat, well-cut, pale grey hair and a face powdered to alabaster white. Her red dress was finished in white frills and her black shoes were decorated with tiny bows. She looked as if she was ready for a pensioners' tap dancing class.

"I've just got a few questions for your son, Mrs Crabtree. It's just routine. Nothing to worry about." He turned to Henry Crabtree.

"We're interviewing people who drive three-wheelers. One was seen close to where a young woman disappeared a few weeks ago. You might have seen newspaper reports. Moira Nelson."

"No, I haven't." The man's face was as blank as a peeled spud.

"You don't read the *T&A*?"

"No, I don't."

"Nobody mentioned the case to you? At work perhaps?"

"No, they didn't."

Boredom was descending again on Stafford's brain. He should have stayed at home. He extracted a picture of Moira Nelson and handed it to the man. "This is the girl."

Crabtree held the photograph, bent his neck forward, then raised his eyebrows, bestowing on his face the first signs of emotional definition. Stafford stared intently at the man. Then Crabtree said, "I didn't do anything to her. She wasn't nice to me, but I didn't do anything. She got on the back of a motorbike. I think she was drunk."

This was followed by a few seconds of silence while Crabtree looked at his mother, then turned towards Stafford. Mrs Crabtree sat frozen, before springing from her chair in a movement belying her age. The knitting landed on the carpet. A dog barked somewhere. Crabtree still held the photograph. They were all standing in the middle of the room. Stafford heard a clock ticking. An indistinct thud came through the hall shared with the next door house. The living room windows rattled.

"You did what, Henry?" The mother glanced at the photograph. "You talked to this girl, Henry? Why were you talking to this girl?" She discharged the questions with such venom it was as if Henry had broken a taboo, crossing a line into behaviour she found unacceptable, even despicable.

"Wait a minute. Let's be calm. When was this, Mr Crabtree?" Stafford retrieved the photograph.

"A few Mondays ago. I always go to the radio club on Mondays."

"When did you come out of the club?"

"It usually finishes about eight-thirty. She was resting against a lamppost, swinging her handbag and smiling."

"Smiling? You talked to her?"

"Not then. I went and got my car. When I drove back she was still by the lamppost."

They were all standing in the centre of the carpet, as if it was a sherry party. Without the sherry. Or the party. Stafford noticed for the first time a shelf, above the fireplace, supporting scores of tiny glass animals. Crabtree's mother sat down without averting her piercing stare, now boring into the side of her son's head.

"Are you sure it was this girl?" Stafford offered him the photograph again but Crabtree didn't take it.

"Yes, I'm sure."

"So then what happened?"

"I stopped and asked her if she needed a lift somewhere."

"A lift? And what did she say?" His mother fidgeted in her chair.

"She came over and put her head through the side flap. She didn't like my car. I don't suppose you can blame her. She said it was about as much use as a lifeboat with a hole in it. I remember her saying just that. She slapped the roof. I'm not sure she really meant to."

"Did the motorbike arrive straight away?"

"No, about ten minutes."

"You sat in your car and watched the girl for about ten minutes?"

The clock seemed to be ticking louder. The mother was staring at her son, her face a crosshatch of animosity and bafflement.

"I must have done."

"Who was on the motorbike?"

"I don't know. How could I know? It was a bloke in leathers. I couldn't see his face."

"What kind of bike was it?"

"I don't know. A big one."

"Did she look as if she knew the rider?"

"I don't know. I don't think so. They talked for a few minutes. Then she got on the back and they went off."

"Did you go to Ilkley that night?"

"Ilkley? Why would I want to go to Ilkley? I came straight home, as I always do."

A sense of resentment was wrapped up in that last sentence, Stafford felt. Crabtree looked rather guileless, completely uncomprehending about Ilkley, responding to the questions directly, total unconcern written in his piggy eyes. Stafford didn't know what was going on between these two. Having thought for a second that he was cottoning on to something, he felt the trail now turning cold.

The mother stood up again and Stafford turned to her. "Can you remember, Mrs Crabtree, when your son came home that night?" He rested his hand on her shoulder to get attention. Her mind was obviously running off somewhere else.

"Which night? Anyway, he always comes home about nine or nine-fifteen when he's been to the radio club."

Stafford realised that in his enthusiasm he hadn't tied the date down, but before he could say anything, Crabtree said, "Mum always writes it down, don't you, Mum? In her diaries. I know you do, Mum." Another squirt of resentment there.

"You keep a diary, Mrs Crabtree? Would you go and get it, please?" Stafford smiled at the mother. She remained rooted for a few seconds before hurrying off upstairs. Stafford could hear at the front of the house the shout of a rag-and-bone man, a convoluted noise best described as a deep-throated shriek. A tabby cat walked along the back wall of the garden, body in stalking configuration. Henry Crabtree sat down on the settee, leaving Stafford standing on his own. The detective inspector could see, the glass animals on the shelf were all horses, lined up in one direction like a miniature army.

Mrs Crabtree returned, her hand clutching a book the size of a paperback and in a green material. Stafford gave her the relevant date, and she read the diary entry. "Nine-thirty. That's when he got back home."

"Could I have a look at that Mrs Crabtree?"

Her son stood up. She held the book to her chest before reluctantly handing it over. Stafford flipped through it. It was a standard diary. He turned back to the page Mrs Crabtree had been reading from. It was the correct date. It read: "Henry left for work at half-past seven, as usual. Made him ham sandwiches for lunch with mustard. He only wanted one – not enough. Gave him two. Mrs Spink says Norma Bulshaw is in the family way. What can you expect from that crowd? Told Broadfoot his stand pies were filled with too much jelly and not enough meat. Next door's whites don't look clean. Skimping on the soap flakes I'll bet. Miserable cow! Told Mrs Howroyd for the third time to get her husband to fix the shed door. Useless clod. Still banging in the wind. Got Henry a lovely malt loaf from the bakery. He'll love it. Saw Mrs Boocock in there. She looks ropey. Like a used Woodbine. Henry back from work at ten-to-six. Nice piece of halibut in egg and bread crumbs for tea. Left at half-past six for radio club. Back at half-past nine." Then there were some names, including English Electric, and initials and numbers.

"What are those at the bottom?" Stafford asked, although it hardly seemed relevant to anything. Mrs Crabtree looked at the page.

"Companies Henry is thinking of buying and their prices. You know, the shares in those companies."

"Your son buys stocks and shares?" Stafford, aware of what he had done, turned to Henry and asked him the same question.

"Well I don't," Henry Crabtree said. "The stockbroker does it for me. He's in Leeds."

"You have a stockbroker?" Stafford thought about the feeble contraption laid up on the grass outside. It was proving a laborious job getting a handle on this duo. One thing was certain. To get up to Ilkley, murder someone and dump the body on the moor, and then get back to Bradford in the time available, would have required rocket propulsion. And Crabtree drove a car with the horsepower of a broken washing machine.

The unsolved murder of Katy Follows the previous year lay in the back of Stafford's mind. The anonymous telephone call in that case originated from close to this part of Bradford. He asked Mrs Crabtree if she had kept a diary for the previous year.

"What for?"

"I just need to check something."

She came down with another diary, and he gave her the date Katy Follows died. Not a glimmer of recognition in either pair of eyes. She found the page. He avoided the personal nastiness, though he did catch one sentence: "Burt Humpage had egg stains on the front of his trousers which makes it look like he had an accident." The entry for Henry showed he was visiting a Mr Raistrick in Leeds, for a 2pm appointment, and got back at home at 4pm.

"Who's Mr Raistrick?"

"The stockbroker," Henry Crabtree said. The entry removed any suspicion that might have hung over him about the Follows murder, providing the entry was true.

"Where do you work, Mr Crabtree?" The man did not answer. He turned round slowly and walked to the window. He rested a hand on the curtain and stretched his neck by repeatedly lifting, then lowering his chin.

"At Jowett's," he eventually said. "I've just lost my job with the takeover and all that. After all those years with them."

"Sorry to hear that." Stafford felt uncomfortable and wondered how much money this 'couple' had stashed away for a rainy day. He was already concentrating though on the motorbike. This was probably the lead they were looking for. Nevertheless, everything here needed tying up.

"Look, I am sorry to bother you with all of this, Mr Crabtree, but could I see your room before I go?"

It was startling how people hardly ever challenged the word of a policeman. Stafford couldn't remember the last time a law-abiding member of society had seriously questioned a request he'd made. He followed Crabtree out of the living room and had to duck under the frame of the stairs, before heading up them into a large bedroom.

The room was shipshape, bordering on compulsively neat. A large poster of a Flash Gordon-style spaceship, surrounded by multi-coloured planets, adorned one wall. The other walls were bare. No sign of a book or a magazine anywhere, though a stand-alone bookcase rested to one side of the fireplace. Its shelves were packed with boxes, all in neat rows, with exactly the same gap between each box. Coloured paper was attached to the end of each container. The boxes ran three orange, three blue, three yellow, three green. Then they repeated the colour sequence down the rows. "What's in the boxes, Mr Crabtree?"

"All electrical things. Radios are my hobby."

Through the window, Stafford could see the tabby now clinging, spread-eagled, thirty feet up a tree, trying to get its claws into squirrels taunting it from above. The cat was stuck, no way to go except down. In a heap.

Several models of wireless, in various states of disrepair, filled a work desk. A clutch of screwdrivers as well as other tools were laid out in parallel ranks on a blue cloth. Then Stafford caught sight of the rolls of electrical cable. Just what you'd expect with this hobby. But still. He took a decision he should already have made. The house, the garden shed, the apology for a motor car outside would have to go under the microscope. His instinct told him there was nothing to be found here. But relying only on instinct was plain stupid. Boy, was he going to be popular, asking for manpower now on one of the police's busiest days.

"I need to go down and use your phone."

"It's in the kitchen."

A screech Stafford could just hear told him the cat had parted company with the tree and was heading nose first for a heavy landing on the grass.

Back in the station, a note from Ilkley was waiting for the detective inspector. They had eventually traced the three-wheeler seen near the moor. It was owned by a plumber, over with his wife from Skipton to visit relatives. It wasn't even red. It wasn't even a Bond. So that seemed to be that. Stafford was clutching a statement made freely by a man who had simply talked to a murder victim on the night she died. And an entry in his mother's diary provided a perfect alibi. And that was all. Stafford was right. He wasn't the toast of the station.

He was hungry but couldn't think of anywhere on a late Sunday afternoon serving food in the city centre. Come to think of it, he couldn't think of anyone serving anything anywhere. He went through the motions of typing out the two Crabtree interviews. It was only when he was in the interview room, going through the statement with Henry Crabtree, that he understood the man could barely read, if at all. Crabtree was beginning to look resentful, but did everything he was told.

The mother remained agitated, especially about the neighbours. "What are they going to think with you people ransacking our house when we've done nothing wrong?" Exasperation and anxiety were written all over her face.

Stafford knew. Mr Humpage with the egg stains and Mr Broadfoot with the meat-free pies and the Bulshaws and the Boococks would be spouting back the same bile in the same fish and chip queue. "I don't think they'll be thinking anything," Stafford reassured her.

The one conclusion out of all this was that they had to trace the motorbike, and its rider, that Crabtree said he had seen taking Moira Nelson away. That would be the main priority for tomorrow other than what he had to do in Bradford's sister city.

Stafford didn't fancy going home. Taking his car north, he eventually found himself on the Chevin, the wooded hillside area about a dozen miles from the centre of the city. Lights in a stone-built pub in the semi-rural landscape caught his eye, and he parked the Vanguard and went inside. For a few seconds he wished he hadn't. Both bars were heaving, the snug with a mixture of the elderly and, unusually, a noisy element playing 'devil among the tailors'. He had thought table skittles was dying out.

Stafford walked round to the other bar and stood behind a two-person deep block of drinkers trying to get served. Waiting patiently, he made no attempt to get attention. He then moved into a slot at the end of the bar and waited again for some minutes before ordering a pint of Tetley's. He negotiated a route across the room and leant against the frame of a door that led into the pub's backyard. He took a large mouthful and surveyed the scene. A jumble of groups clustered around small tables, the space between the tables saturated with vertical bodies constantly manoeuvring in order to let people past. Stafford drank too quickly, the pint gone within five minutes. He needed to relax a bit and try and enjoy himself, but he wasn't really in the mood so had to force himself back to the bar.

Conscious, all of a sudden, of a woman standing next to him, he deliberately turned to look at her. She smiled. About thirty, quite tall with a soft, attractive face and a rather pointed nose, she was using no make-up, save for lipstick. Blue rings under her eyes suggested she was not getting enough shuteye.

"You wonder whether it's worth it sometimes," she said to him eventually, as they waited their turn. "Having to elbow your way to the bar when you could be at home relaxing and drinking pretty much the same stuff." She owned an educated voice with a soft northern accent. He just stopped himself from saying that she looked as if she needed sleep.

"I guess people come here because they enjoy the company," was his lame reply.

Neither of them made any attempt to shuffle closer to the staff working flat-out behind the pumps.

"I noticed you when you came in," she said. She glanced at him and then looked back. He felt blood shoot to his face, and something surge through his body as if he'd been injected.

"Oh? It must be my distinctive raincoat."

"Are you visiting the area?"

"No. I live not too far away. As you probably can tell, I'm from the West Country."

They were still making no attempt to get served, and a couple of people pushed in front of them. He noticed her hands were devoid of rings.

"We used to have a few holidays in Sidmouth. I have an aunt there. Are you a policeman?"

"That's perceptive. Maybe it's that raincoat again."

"You're just up here for a drink on your own?"

"That's right. Drink on my own. Live on my own." He immediately regretted saying it like that.

She smelled of soap, and he wanted to lean across and kiss her neck and kiss under her chin and put his arm around her. He thought of telling her that but didn't. Instead, he said, "What do you do?"

"I'm a teacher. English and PE. All-girls school."

They were still showing no interest in waylaying the bar, and had slightly angled themselves so they partly faced each other. He was glad his scarred side was furthest away. Their bodies were just touching.

"I better get these drinks in for my friends. They'll be champing at the bit. One minute."

She took out a pen and paper from her handbag. "Here. This is my telephone number. Call me if you can."

The note said Margaret Kendall. She'd also written out her address. The writing was large with bold, simple strokes.

"I will. My name is Ray Stafford."

"Please to meet you, Raymond Stafford."

He put his arm round her shoulder, took one pace forward into a gap a bit too small for his body, and said to one of the barmen, "This woman has been waiting quite a long time." She got served straight away, and as she left with her drinks on a small tray, he rested a hand on her shoulder. She slightly leant into him. "Bye for now," she said.

He bought a half pint and headed for the snug. Before leaving the room, he turned round. She was looking at him and they smiled at each other. He drank the half rapidly and left.

At home he made something to eat, picked up a framed photograph of Diana and stared at it for a few moments before sitting in front of the television. David Attenborough and another installment of *Zoo Quest*. This time it was bats and how they generated ultrasounds which bounced off objects so they could pick up echo locations, like radar. This gave them absolute knowledge about where they were and where they were going. Lucky bats, Stafford thought.

CHAPTER 19

Park Square in Leeds, a little green haven in the heart of the city, was created in the eighteenth century as a residential estate for merchants and lawyers. In a place bred to make money, commerce quickly got its sticky claws into it. At one end of the square, an ornamented warehouse and cloth-cutting works built by the founder of the city's mass produced, ready-to-wear clothing industry. Its outer walls were topped by an extraordinary façade, the design of its elaborate corner features lifted, by its local architect, straight from the Orient. Across from John Barran's grand edifice stood Wakefield Chambers, fronted in terracotta brick and tiling with rose motif. Anyone approaching the chambers, as Detective Inspector Ray Stafford was doing that Monday morning, could see from there the top of Leeds Town Hall, a gigantic slab of stonework designed by the same architect responsible for the Grand Hotel in Scarborough.

Stafford entered the revolving front door and worked his way down the nameplates on the hall board until he came to "L. Raistrick & Assoc. Stockbrokers." He climbed to the second floor and walked through a set of double swing doors into a small reception area. A woman in her late thirties was sitting behind a semi-circular desk. A curiously unformed, rather featureless face was topped by hair of a washed-out nothing colour, tied in a severe bun.

"Good morning. Raymond Stafford. I have an appointment with Mr Raistrick." The area was over lit with harsh neon strips. The walls were blank save for a clock with Rhodes and Son, Bradford, inscribed on its face.

"Oh, yes. Mr Stafford. Mr. Raistrick is expecting you. I'll just see if he's free." Her voice was baby-like and she talked in a semi-whisper, not conspiratorially but more as if she just didn't want anyone else to hear. She took half a dozen steps and poked her head round the nearest open door. A man in overalls, perched on a stepladder, worked an industrial-sized screwdriver on one of the door's hinges. The offices were over-heated as well as over-lit. Stafford took off his mac and attached it to a peg on an ornate coat stand, the stand canting over from the weight of the lead cosh in one of the pockets.

The receptionist returned and half-whispered that he could go right in. He thanked her and walked across the wooden floor which gave way to a thick, spongy carpet.

"Detective Inspector Stafford. Good morning to you. Goodness me, you're a big fellow." Lionel Raistrick held out his hand. He was neat and unremarkable looking and well into his sixties. He was wearing one of the new-style, narrower-cut drape suits, no doubt made locally, but with an old-fashioned waistcoat and watch chain. An elaborate gold tiepin adorned a sober dark blue tie.

"Take a seat. You better leave that for a few minutes, Mr Knaggs. Go and get a cup of tea." The handyman grunted and stepped off the ladder.

Raistrick turned back to Stafford. "Got to find out what's mithering that door. It's not hanging right. Would you like some tea, Mr Stafford?"

"No thanks. But thank you for seeing me at such short notice."

"Not at all." Raistrick sat down and was swallowed up by a huge burgundy-coloured swivel chair.

"Well now, I've dug out the diary for last year as you requested on the phone." It was a fat and handsome leather-covered book, gold lettering on the front and spine.

"Here it is. You'll see Henry Crabtree was here on the day you are interested in, from two to three in the afternoon. He definitely came because, as you can see here, in the margins, these notes I took at the time, telling me of the client's requests, together with my scribbled thoughts. He always takes up the full allotted time with me. I think he likes being here. As you can see I had another appointment right after."

A gold ring, faced with a crest of some kind, adorned the index finger Raistrick was using to point all this out. He turned the diary round and slid it over. There was the entry, followed by marks and squiggles and notations.

The phone rang and Raistrick answered. "Oh thanks, Vivien, put him through. Won't be a moment, Mr Stafford, but I have to take this call." A photograph was propped up on a window ledge, the stockbroker smiling with a woman about his own age, standing on the deck of a small cruiser. It must have been shot quite a few years earlier. Windermere or the Norfolk Broads, Stafford guessed.

"Morning, Mr Shovel." Raistrick winked at Stafford. "You'd like to what? Japanese companies? Mr Shovel, I'm afraid I don't know a thing about Japanese businesses. If I were you, I'd stay well clear. Well, alright. I'll see what I can do, but I don't even know whether you can buy their shares. Will do. Bye bye, Mr Shovel."

"Wonderful name that," Raistrick said as he put the phone down. "Shovel. He actually owns a company making those giant scoops for draglines. Often wondered whether he changed his name by deed poll to help the business."

"The Chief Inspector at my first posting was called Stuart Steeler but with a double 'e'. We called him 'Gestapo' because of his initials. And because of other things."

"Names can be so important in so many ways."

"Anyway, back to Mr Crabtree. I can assure you it is just routine. He is not involved in anything. We're just tying up loose ends."

"Well, I'm glad to hear it. He is a remarkable man. You know he can't read. Sorry, I shouldn't have revealed that nugget."

"I know about that."

"Well, Henry Crabtree has a spectacular record at picking shares. Truly remarkable. Hardly ever gets it wrong and never ever comes a cropper. I think it's a sixth sense, I really do. Anyway, I'm talking too much again about a client."

"So he was here for a whole hour, and can you remember whether he came under his own steam?"

"Steam is about it. Have you seen that food mixer he drives? I can't understand why he doesn't buy a decent car. It looks as if it wouldn't power a torch. He always comes in it. I always, I mean always, make a point of looking down to see whether he's forked out on a nice new motor. Needless to say he never has."

"Your car the Lanchester outside?"

"It is. I've just bought it. Rather old school but that's me as well."

Stafford shook hands. Henry Crabtree could not possibly be involved in last year's unsolved murder, and had an alibi for Moira Nelson's. The search of his house yesterday evening had turned up nothing. The cabling did not, in the end, match that found round her neck, neither by colour nor size. The chairman of the radio club had confirmed Crabtree's presence for the whole of the meeting on the evening they were interested in. The police force had been bowled another googly.

"He's such a strange man, that Mr Crabtree," the receptionist volunteered as Stafford put on his coat. She had her volume turned low and made jabbing motions with her index finger towards her boss's door. "I think Mr Raistrick gets all his tips from Mr Crabtree and then passes them on to other clients."

"Vivien, I can hear you." Raistrick's voice boomed through the open door. The stockbroker might be getting on a bit, Stafford thought, but his bat-like sonar was obviously in tip-top shape.

Outside, Stafford walked through the square to a general food emporium. He didn't catch the name of it as he went in, and was surprised to discover rows of tightly-packed items he had never heard of in a bewildering array of colours. Since his wife's death he had little interest in shopping for anything other than basic provisions. Looking along the rows, it dawned how little he knew of the way things were changing, even amongst the most basic items. Daz and Surf washing powder were new to him, as were Sugar Puffs and Kellogg's Frosted Flakes. Maxwell House 'instant' coffee he had never seen before. A small demonstration was under way for Brooke Bond tea, served through paper bags full of holes. He watched, rather surprised, as the demonstrator poured hot water on the midget bags. She was a middle-aged woman plastered in make-up but wearing a long white coat, as if she was a technician in a laboratory.

Today, he liked the idea of being in the shop and of shopping. He knew that was because of Margaret Kendall. The case might be getting him down but he felt, in other ways, elated.

He bought his groceries and entered a newspaper and sweet shop next door. Even more cardboard poster-promotions for new products were on display than in Bairstow's. One was for a new *Jack and Jill* girls' magazine. A young woman was returning glass pop bottles and the shop assistant handed over three pennies for them. Stafford bought two chocolate Wagon Wheels and walked back, eating one of the sweet biscuits on the way. He noticed for the first time the name above the office outside of which he had parked his car. "Quickmire Gravel Extraction", it said.

At the police station in Bradford, Stafford went into the incident room to see how far they were getting re-checking interviews connected to the sighting of motorbikes. A note on his desk only reinforced the detective inspector's perception of Henry Crabtree as an entirely innocent man. A visit by officers to Jowett's, shut down as a car maker but whose factory was still open, revealed that the company had never used the wiring with the peculiarly-coloured outer casing found wrapped around Moira Nelson's neck.

He opened the local paper and read on the front page that one hundred and two thousand people had passed through the turnstiles at the previous day's rugby match, coughing up the colossal sum of close to nineteen thousand pounds. Another story that caught his eye was about the new craze for smokeless zones. It said the average factory chimney in the city produced over four hundred times more filth than a domestic chimney, and in a typical twelve month period, each domestic chimney generated seventy-eight pounds of pollution. A quarter of a million gallons of sulphuric acid fell on Bradford yearly.

Sunlight streamed into his office in defiance of this murky blanket. Through the side window, he could see two of the new German-made Rolodex card files sitting unloved

177

on a desk top. Just delivered in the hope of better sorting material held for on-going cases, it seemed as if no one was venturing near them. The mini mountains of material for the Nelson investigation were now encased in old Fyffes banana boxes.

Stafford stretched and yawned and felt in his jacket pockets for the note Margaret Kendall had given him. It wasn't there so he tried pockets in his coat. Not there either. He could feel his heart racing as he went back to the jacket. After finding the note in a pocket he'd already just tried, he transferred the telephone number to his desk diary. He then picked up the phone to call the Ilkley office. Sergeant Rishworth's bark greeted him.

"Stafford here. Just to thank you for digging up the info on the three-wheeler, sergeant. It's all turned out to be a wild goose chase. What I..."

Rishworth stopped him mid-sentence. "Mr Stafford, hang on a minute. We were just going to call Bradford. Something has come up. As you are on the phone, just hold on, please."

Stafford waited, watching the sun's rays casting temporary patterns on the metal partition walls. A fly buzzed somewhere. He screwed up a piece of paper, then aimed at but missed a bin. An officer walked over to inspect one of the Rolodex files and then wandered off. It was warm and Stafford loosened his tie. He fancied another Wagon Wheel and started reaching over to his coat for the remaining biscuit just as Rishworth's bark came back on. Stafford listened.

Before the call was over he was standing up. Lucky for him he'd rung Ilkley at that very moment. He called the Chief Superintendent's office. Then he left, seeking out Norman Feather and another officer before commandeering a marked car. It was the Riley and the driver with the oversized gloves.

As the car began its journey, Stafford explained the call. The atmosphere in the saloon shifted immediately. Everyone went quiet. It was the quietness of anticipation mixed with a dollop of nerves. Sometimes tension helped focus the mind. Sometimes it did just the opposite, dispersing concentration into fragments, brain cells latching on to small, irrelevant subjects. Stafford tried, but failed to stop his mind wandering off in that direction. Passing the Essoldo, he saw the *Creature from the Black Lagoon* had been superseded by the *Beast from 20,000 Fathoms*. He'd seen that number before and his mind hunted the thought down, increasingly exasperated that it couldn't recall where.

They passed a recently closed ironworks and then motored alongside short streets of three-storey eighteenth century houses with rows of almost slit-like windows. The car turned into a green, a lonesome church, with a boarded window, standing like a moody sentinel at one end of the muddy grass. They then exited into a narrower road. This was densely packed with so-called 'tunnel-back' houses, a single storey-high aperture every second house leading to communal yards each with four privies, two for every pair of houses.

The Riley made its way into a more leafy neighbourhood with larger homes and a mixture of commercial buildings and grim, blackened chapels. It then turned down a cobbled street and came to a stop at the front of a two-storey stone house somewhat wider than most. A local squad car was idling outside, white smoke issuing from its exhaust in jerky spurts.

The house came with a half-raised basement and six steps to the front door. They were met there by a constable. Down the ground-floor corridor, Stafford could see a basic kitchen with a scullery running off. A faint if rather repugnant smell of sour, cooked food pervaded the air.

At the top of the steep, narrow staircase, Stafford and Feather were met by Sergeant Twelves and an elderly constable who moved around with a slight limp. They were taken into a large bedroom and shown the items, carefully wrapped in a scarf. The clover leaf pendant with M.N. etched on the back. The butterfly brooch with the inscription on the inside. The scarf was dark green with a blue stripe at both ends. They had all been found in a purse bag stuffed into the bottom of a cheap chest of drawers. One of the drawer fronts was broken. Small bundles of used clothes nested in the unkempt room's nooks and crannies. A fetid stench of old sweat lay everywhere.

Stafford looked out from the bedroom window on to a quarry about twenty yards from the edge of the garden. Great chunks of sandstone, of the type used to construct the imposing buildings of the city centre, were being loaded on to a large, bright-yellow dumper. The driver seemed to have some kind of white cloth wrapped round his head and knotted under his chin. A ring of coal-fired braziers emitted dots of incandescent red, even in the daylight.

The haul of Moira Nelson's things, on its own, simply proved this man had the dead girl's possessions. But Stafford and the other officers knew it felt much more than that. One of the police drivers sprinted up on to the landing to inform them that the Bradford station had now confirmed the location of the man they were seeking. The officers returned to their vehicles. The local car pulled out from the cobbled side street first, and led the way as those officers knew where they were headed. Roads were quiet, and both cars refrained from using their gongs.

It was a beautiful mid-afternoon, the wrong weather for this, Stafford thought. He tried to relax. People were going about their normal business. He could see women queuing in a butcher's, peering down at the displays of meat behind glass counters. Children in shorts clustered in small groups, hurrying to their schools' sports fields. A tanker carrying sulphuric acid crossed their path at a main traffic light junction.

Feather took out a Terry's chocolate apple and held it up. "They've just stopped making these for good." No one responded and after taking one bite, Feather thought better of it and put the rest of the chocolate back in his pocket. At the other side of the town centre, a coal lorry loaded with sacks delayed them as it reversed into an alleyway, the driver's eyes startlingly white in a pitch-black face.

The two cars drove through featureless housing and then rose up between ever more grandiose homes until they turned in between mammoth stone pillars, Pennymore written in black and gold on both. The drive wound up through near-parkland, bushes and trees densely packed and giving only brief glimpses of a manicured lawn big enough for a football match. Birds in large numbers swooped between treetops.

They came to a stop outside a big garage, its doors in white-painted wood with black metal studs. As Stafford climbed out, he could see Tony Garland standing at the side of the drive, one foot on the low wall of a raised flower bed. He led the small phalanx of officers as they walked towards him. Garland was dressed like an ageing model on a cigarette advert. A supercilious expression stretched across his face, feeding off the majestic surroundings of his sister's home, Stafford imagined, but that expression was beginning to fade into one of puzzlement. The detective inspector reached him, offered him a slight nod, and proceeded up to where the builders appeared to be working on new outside piping.

A stone arch partly obscured the building team. Supporting neat stacks of flowerpots, a small table rested against the stonework. Over to the right, the colossal lawn in Cumberland turf was clearly visible now, stretching down between the trees. It had been cut in wide, angled stripes like a cricket field. A large Atco mower with articulated roller and seat was parked up at the side. A pungent smell of grass and wet vegetation filled the air with a slightly sickly tang.

As he got past the arch Stafford stopped, pointing to the left at a powerful-looking motorbike, with side panniers, resting against a tree. He just caught a flickering sense of movement out of the corner of his eye. Then something heavy smacked him in the side of the face, the percussion generating a dull vibration, coursing down his spine and into his legs. Almost in slow motion he watched his own body arcing over an object, hard and awkward, then saw the wheelbarrow coming up at him as he fell. His mouth caught on a sharp ridge and he felt it rip open. A rapid injection of acidic bile filled his mouth just before vomit shot up his gullet. His skull slid rather heavily on to a stony surface. Before he disappeared into blackness, his last memory was of scuffling noises and the taste of blood and puke.

CHAPTER 20

The bath was never the most comfortable resting place for Ray Stafford, his body too long for the enamel cocoon. Now it was even more awkward. The force of the blow to his face had hurt his spine, and he couldn't find a restful position for his neck as he lay in the water. Torsional stresses on ligaments, tendons and other internal cabling jarred his nerve ends.

He decided to extricate himself and stood up gingerly, then tugged a towel off the rail. He dried himself slowly. Dressing posed surprisingly few difficulties, but he was careful buttoning his shirt. The injuries were a good excuse to go into work without a tie. He then removed the towel draped over his head. The pain in his face meant he couldn't rub his hair so he just combed it wet. He walked down the stairs slowly, holding on to the banister and keeping his head level. Light seeping through the coloured glass in the front door was a little painful for his eyes.

Stafford had spent the previous night in hospital after regaining consciousness in the ambulance on the way there. Drifting in and out of sleep in the bare hospital ward, his mind kept focusing on his wife. He'd discharged himself that morning and then slept for several hours in his own bed. Now he was determined to go into the station, even at this late stage of the day.

In the living room, he switched on a radio but music only offered a grating din. The last straw was Rosemary Clooney's *Mambo Italiano*. He switched off the wireless and put on the television. In his mood, total silence felt funereal. *Watch with Mother* was broadcasting *Rag, Tag and Bobtail* rather than *Andy Pandy*, the curious cloth child who lived in a wicker basket with Looby Loo. He watched a little story about Rag and his two chums, the puppet animals squabbling over a bed made of leaves. Realising his brain was heading over the edge, he turned the 'off' knob and saw the picture collapse into a white dot and finally disappear. It was time to get out of the house.

He examined himself in the oval mirror above the sideboard in the living room. The side of his face where the heavy-duty spade had crashed into his skull was not just swollen but wholly misshapen. Facial distortions made it look as if he was chewing a plum. Swellings stretched the skin around one eye, giving the skin a thin, almost transparent sheen. Once arrow-straight, the long scar now careered off at right angles. Tearing the corner of his mouth on the edge of the wheelbarrow had required eleven stitches to repair. The slit tugged one end of his mouth down into a grimace. Another swelling hid the bridge of his nose and, for some reason, a long cut had opened the skin between nose and mouth. Gravel indents on his forehead had faded, not that that made much contribution to a more congenial kisser. Tony Garland's Boris Karloff. All he needed was a bolt through the neck. Actually, the bolt was superfluous. He thought about Margaret Kendall, at the same time happy but cursing his luck.

Stafford stretched his back circumspectly, but that hurt. Twisting his pelvis from side to side and turning his head was no easier. He didn't really know what exercises he should indulge in, so he stopped. Out of the front window he could see the woman next door returning home after a shopping trip. She was leaning over slightly, pulled by the weight of the bulging rush-bag with which she had trudged up the hill.

He walked into the hall, eased on his shoes, then rested one foot on the fourth step of the stairs and carefully tied the laces before doing the same with the other shoe. He took his jacket from the back of the chair in the rear ground floor room, still set up as a dining area but which had remained unused since his wife's death, and slipped it on.

At least the man who had redesigned his face had taken a whack himself, leaving him with a shattered eye socket. Yesterday, Stafford wanted Terry Packard dead. Today, he wanted to carry out the killing himself. He opened the door to the cupboard under the stairs and selected the lighter of his two cricket bats resting against the wall. His kitbag lay on a shelf, and he pulled it off and lodged the Gray-Nicolls in the bag. The bat smelled strongly of linseed oil. It was a little uncomfortable carrying the holdall and he unloaded it very slowly on to his car's back seat.

The police thought they had got their hands on Moira Nelson's killer when they visited Jennifer Shaw's magnificent home. Now they knew they had. Feather had paid Stafford a visit in hospital and had also telephoned him at home to give him the latest dollops of information. A watertight case was under construction. All that work the police had embarked on, yet the hero of the day was a constable with arthritic knees and on the brink of retirement. Old Willie Oldfield thought he was on the trail of a thief who'd half-inched an antique box. He was, but he had also identified the man who had strangled the life out of Moira Nelson. The Bradford police force would be wallowing in a bout of self-satisfaction, which Stafford could share. On the other hand, his mug looked like that of a leper suffering multiple abscesses of the teeth.

Driving the Vanguard should not have proved a problem, yet somehow small stretches, pulls and twists of the arms and wrists pressured his body, pumping up the pain in his spine and limbs. In the police car park, he carefully placed a scarf around the lower part of his face. He hoped he could steer a course to his office without requiring any communication with anyone. The three teeth smashed, then removed in the hospital, made his voice whistle. Fortunately, the lost teeth were at the back of his mouth.

Stafford arrived behind his desk without making conversation and removed the scarf. He put the holdall with the cricket bat under a spare chair. The groceries purchased in Leeds were still there. He rummaged around in the bag in search of anything soft. He hadn't eaten all day. The only suitable comestible was a chunk of crumbly, white Lancashire. After breaking off a piece and dropping it into his mouth, he slowly masticated the cheese. It was just bearable. Feather came in.

"Jesus Christ, sir, you'll frighten the kids. It has really ballooned up."

"Thank you, sergeant. That really makes me feel ready to face the public."

"Still talking as if you've got a harmonica in your mouth. Should Larry Adler be worried we ask?"

"Just fill me in on where we are. Is he talking yet?"

"Not a peep out of the cretin. He's absolutely certifiable, sir. He was so aggressive when we brought him in some of the lads wanted to manacle him to the radiator. Four of us were having to restrain him."

"That's when his eye socket got done?"

"No. During the arrest that. Twelves from the Ilkley station. I don't know what he used. You owe him a pint."

"So where are we with it?"

"We've got the maniac bang to rights. I told you last night there was no sign of that type of cabling in Packard's work bag. You know, the type found round Moira Nelson's neck. But we found some in the shed at Packard's home this afternoon. That's a critical piece of evidence, though we still don't really know why he used the cables.

"He carries all his equipment in his motorbike's panniers and he doesn't remove the panniers during the week, according to his mother. The cable has the same green and orange striping. Packard's mother says he recently finished a stint as a temporary electrician at an industrial boilermakers. Whitehead's in Stanningley. We are checking up there now to see what cabling they use. Even better, we've shown his photograph to cafes around the area where Moira disappeared, and we've got two cast-iron identifications that he was around that night. One is from the owner of the Sorrento. That's put him right at the spot. Funnily enough, he looks a bit like a Teddy Boy, but he isn't one. Doesn't belong to any group. The bastard doesn't seem to have an allegiance to anything."

The dull pain at the top of Stafford's cheekbone now transferred to the back of his jaw. He stopped chewing, carefully trying to mine with his tongue a piece of cheese embedded in a gap vacated by a tooth.

"And then look at this." Feather handed over a couple of sheaths of paper. "You can see from his charge sheet why Willie Oldfield taped him when Mrs Shaw reported that antique missing. Oldfield knew all about Packard. Still don't know yet why Tyzack's, that's the building company, employed him as an electrician. Packard didn't complete his electrician's apprenticeship, but the company did have another qualified electrician on the site. Maybe they didn't know about his background, and it's as simple as that."

Stafford examined the paperwork. A first formal warning from the police for bullying, at the age of fourteen. He'd rabbit punched someone in the playground, the other kid needing medical treatment. Broke someone's jaw in a pub fight. Two other charges of assault, one an unprovoked attack at a bus stop. All interspersed with minor thefts. He'd served eighteen months in total. Bending his neck to read the papers hurt so he raised them to eye level. That only pulled on a nerve cluster in his shoulder, if anything making it worse.

"The house he lives in is his mother's. She moved out about six months ago to live with a sister. We traced her quite easily yesterday afternoon. She said his temper was frightening her. Packard's father is dead, but his mother said he once broke his dad's shoulder with a hammer. That was never reported to the local police."

The tear down the side of Stafford's mouth was now stinging. He wondered whether he'd dislodged a stitch. He also thought he could taste blood and wondered whether eating the Lancashire had been altogether wise. "No sign he knew Moira Nelson?"

"That's a funny thing. We've talked to Tony Garland. He told us he's staying at his sister's house because she asked him to keep an eye on the builders while they are away for the week, you know, since the Shaws suffered the theft. Anyway, Garland said he once brought the girl into the house when his family wasn't there. But it was only for five minutes while he collected something, or so he says. They were off for a drink or such like. Unhealthy relationship that is, or was, if you ask me. He's more than twice her age. To get back to the point, he thinks the builders were there. It was only a couple of weeks ago. There's nothing to suggest though that Packard talked to her or even saw her. Packard only occasionally went to those Bradford cafes. I think it was probably a random pick-up."

Stafford caught his image in the side of the metal ashtray on his desk. He could also see his face if he moved his torso slightly to the left. It appeared as a reflection in the shiny office partition wall as the sun swept across the front window.

"Packard is not talking, other than the effing and blinding you'd expect from a maniac like that, so we don't have a clear motive. She probably just refused to give him what he wanted." Feather threw a sweet wrapping into a waste bin.

"And he kept some of Moira's things?"

"That's right. How often do we see that? Plenty. Homicidal nutter but also a greedy bugger. We recovered Shaw's box, as you know. Taking all that stuff and just squirrelling it away. He could have tried arguing that he'd stolen it from someone else. He didn't even try that. He is one of the nastiest pieces of work I've ever seen."

Feather took out a canister of Nuttall's Mintoes and offered Stafford one. His colleague frowned and pointed to his chipmunk face. "Oh, sorry guv." Stafford was surprised Feather's uniform came with a pocket big enough to secrete a Nutall's can.

"Another thing. Remember what McCrone reported about the wounds on her neck, that the perpetrator might have small hands? Packard has small hands. Really small. The lads say all we've got to do is make sure Packard doesn't get sent to Broadmoor or some other cushy number, but gets the big drop instead."

Feather eased his bulk from the chair he was sitting on and plonked himself on the corner of Stafford's table. "One thing you should know, sir. When we were looking through all the interviews yesterday morning related to motorbikes, we came across a note where a witness had mentioned seeing a rider who he thought was called Packard."

"Bloody Hell."

"It doesn't get any better. He also said he thought he rode a Norton. It just got lost in the paperwork."

"Do you know who was responsible for not following that up?"

In his exasperation, Stafford was opening his mouth too far, intensifying the pain and sending his voice whistle up an octave.

"We don't know. It's not clear from the duty sheets. No one's owned up. We were all sifting through the information so perhaps it's collective responsibility. Maybe the sheet of info just stuck to another sheet, so we kept missing it. At worst it possibly delayed the outcome, that's all."

The room was flooded with sunlight now. It seemed to make the various aches in Stafford's face much worse. Maybe it was because he was screwing up his eyes. It didn't help that he was largely in charge of the investigation so missed opportunities, like the one he'd just heard, were more his responsibility than anyone's. That made everything painful.

"We've kept it from the press today but we'll tell Moira's parents this evening?"

"That's about it in a nutshell. It was assumed you wouldn't want to do that yourself."

When he was on his own, Stafford got up and stretched and, using his fingertips, gently prodded around the globe of distended flesh now forming half his face. He gazed out of the exterior window and pictured swinging the Gray-Nicolls and depressing the top of Terry Packard's skull. The handle of the bat was now poking out of the kitbag and he pushed it back in with a foot. Stafford draped the scarf around part of his face and checked down the corridor, but a lot of officers were still about. The duty man controlling the outer cell doors was still at his post.

He did the same thing twenty minutes later, but the station was still busy. When he eventually tried it a third time, it was much quieter. The duty officer near the cell doors had vacated his seat. Probably in the canteen as usual at this time, getting his tea, Stafford thought.

Stafford strode along the corridor again. He then went down two steps to where the keys for the outer cell door were kept in a drawer, unlocked the door, a barred gate in a barred wall, and walked past the cells to the bottom. He checked there were no officers malingering down there. Then he retraced his steps to cell nine and took a look along the corridor again. It was deserted. The man who had crashed a spade against his head was at the other side of the door. Stafford didn't even know what he looked like.

He released the metal viewing flap. Packard was sitting on the edge of the bed, a truculent, malevolent face staring at a blank wall. The face was quite still, as if in a trance. His untreated eye socket was now swollen to the size of a tennis ball, giving one side of the head a gruesome, coloured

188

scarring. It was like a dose of atomic radiation you saw in a horror film. Moira Nelson's killer had not heard the opening of the viewing flap, and Stafford looked at him for a long time.

Then he angled his mouth, his own disfigurements largely hidden, and whispered, "Packard. Listen to me. You are a fucking animal, and you're going to swing for this until you're dead."

Totally unprofessional, but pleasurable, Stafford considered as he walked away. He'd only gone a few steps from the door when he heard a foot crash against it, the creature in the lock-up expressing his deranged personality in one of the frenzied ways he knew. Stafford locked the outer cell gate and deposited the keys back in the drawer.

In his office, and against his better judgement, Stafford popped another piece of cheese into his mouth. Feather came back in, carrying his own kitbag which he propped on the edge of the chair.

"Look, sir. I'm not sure you should be playing cricket in your state. It's only a bit of pre-season net practice after all." Feather wrinkled his forehead and gently shook his head.

"You might be right, sergeant. I'll see how I feel. It's a pity they don't make some kind of protective headgear for batsmen."

"A helmet? Playing cricket with a helmet? I think that blow affected you more than you think, sir, if you don't mind me saying."

Stafford had no intention now of joining in with cricket practice for the police team. He selected the exact change for a *Daily Telegraph* and let the coins fall into his coat pocket. He then picked up the two bags and left the office. After depositing the bags in his car, and with the scarf round his face, he walked into town. There was just time to buy a newspaper before all the newsagents shut.

Council workmen were stringing bunting between lampposts ready for tomorrow's visit by the Queen. He entered the paper shop and handed over the exact change. In asking for the paper, he discovered that his voice hardly whistled at all if he kept his lips close together. The man behind the counter offered him a quizzical look, something he would have to put up with for the next month or two. In truth, that had been a feature of most of his adult life. He wondered again how tolerant Miss Kendall would be of these new, albeit temporary disfigurements. Perhaps he should wait a few weeks before contacting her.

As he left the shop, Stafford could see the Limbless Ex-Servicemen's Club across the road. A special meeting of some kind must have been scheduled, probably in preparation for the Royal visit. A group of old men, some with leg stumps and crutches, others with arms missing, were gathering outside the entrance. He could hear the chatter even from a distance. A few of them were patting their old comrades on the back. Slightly ashamed of the concerns he harboured for his own injuries, he removed his scarf, walked across and gave them a cheerful greeting.

As he strolled back to the station car park, his thoughts returned to the murder of Katy Follows. That had all the characteristics of remaining an unsolved crime. The investigation was petering out, and they had got nowhere. But at least they had cleared up another murder. His mind concentrated on Moira Nelson. The Nelson case was his as much as anyone's. It was he who had interviewed her mother. It was only right he broke the news to the family that they had taken Moira's killer. It wasn't the job of other officers. Back at his desk, he made a few internal calls to ensure he would be carrying out that task himself. Before he left to do it, he opened his desk diary, read off a telephone number, and made the call. On the fifth ring, Margaret Kendall's voice came on the line.

CHAPTER 21

"Anything in the paper?" Jennifer Shaw asked her husband as she stood in front of the mirror and adjusted her clothing. She had decided, after all, to buy a Chanel cardigan suit. She'd gone the whole hog and purchased one in bright lilac with a black collar and belt.

"It says here that the preferred colour of Parisian street walkers this year is lilac with black collar and black belt."

"What?" She lobbed an empty packet of cigarettes in his direction, missing him by several feet. She retrieved the packet and took it over to the kitchen bin. "What time must we leave to catch the flight?"

"About two. It'll take less than an hour to get to the airport. Are we all packed?"

"I think so. Apart from your shaving gear. Curious looking thing, your new electric razor. How long do you think you're going to be?"

"A couple of hours at most. It'll take that time to sort it out. Still can't believe we've had a boiler explosion. Lucky no one was hurt."

"Does it affect production?"

"Not much. Just the mill's heating and the lifting equipment. Here, take the paper. I'll get another one."

Jennifer Shaw let herself out of room 302 at the Grand apartment hotel in Folkestone. The room was really a capacious suite with living room and big kitchen, and came with a seaview above the Leas, Folkestone's graceful cliff-top walkway. When the town was a watering hole for the rich, that particular suite and nearby rooms had sometimes housed Edward the Seventh and Eighth, their queens and members of the Royal entourage.

She was going to walk down the stairs but the lift door was open when she arrived at the end of the corridor, so she stepped right in. Her companions in the lift, two men with thin moustaches and Midlands accents, were engaged in a business conversation, though they were obviously on some kind of holiday break. Both wore slacks and heavily-patterned pullovers.

"It's a sound deal, Eric, I'm telling you," one was saying. "We can shift more scrap metal, and at twice the speed, doing it this way. It's money for old rope. Charlie is on tenterhooks waiting for the details."

One of them leered at her and winked. She managed a slight twitch of the mouth in acknowledgement and then escaped into the foyer when the lift hit the ground floor. The great Edwardian days are definitely long gone, she mused.

The Grand was nearly full and the foyer really bustled. She walked through the Palm Court, the name used by scores of prestigious hotels in a collective failure of imagination. This Palm Court retained a folk history more interesting than most, as she had learnt for the first time the day before even though she had often stayed at the Grand.

"It's where the term 'monkey business' comes from," the receptionist had informed her. "A lot of the men in the Royal parties wore beards and when ordinary people walked past and looked into the Palm Court, they could see all these people. The locals referred to it as the monkey house. Then, because of all the shenanigans with the Royal family, you know, the mistresses and all that, this term 'monkey business' was dreamt up. Personally, madam, I don't believe all those stories about the Royal family." Personally, I'm not sure I believe your story, Shaw thought.

Out on the Leas, she sought out a bench and sat down. This was the second time within a week she found herself in an idyllic spot gazing out on the briny. A peacock-blue sky with wispy clouds rested, this time, on top of a muddy sea with a surprisingly spumy surface driven by a weak breeze. A few large ships were ploughing across the watery expanse.

The atmosphere was so clear Shaw could trace the French coastline from Cap Blanc Nez to Cap Gris Nez.

The cliff top pathway was surprisingly busy with strollers enjoying the late morning sunshine. She shared the bench with a woman in her twenties who was dressed head to toe in black. The young woman held the handle of a giant Royale Newport and rocked the pram gently forward and back. She was like a character in a Dickens novel.

Shaw lit up a cigarette and opened the paper. The first item on the front page that caught her eye was the report of a press conference given by the health minister, Iain Macleod, accepting the work of a scientist, Richard Doll, four years earlier that proved a link between lung cancer and smoking. "Mr Macleod chain-smoked throughout the event," the paper said. Shaw blew a cumulus of cigarette smoke into the air and laughed.

"Something funny in the paper?" the woman next door asked.

"No. Not funny at all really. Just me being silly. Nice-looking baby. What's its name?"

"Sidney."

"Oh." The girl was very pretty and innocent looking. Rebecca of Sunnybrook Farm, dressed for a funeral.

"Beautiful view, isn't it?" Shaw said. "Amazing how clear the French coast looks."

She turned back to the paper and her favourite column on new words. "An occasion at which, typically, young people dance to amplified pop records, usually compered by one person playing the records, and featuring special lighting effects. Discotheque." What an eccentric word, Shaw thought. "Discotheque," she said softly.

Saying "cheerio" to the young Mary Poppins, she walked along the pathway towards the centre of Folkestone and climbed into the tiny red and white car on the funicular that ran down the side of the cliff. The water made a swooshing noise as it was released into the car's five hundred gallon tank which gravity-powered the contraption along the track. The block was eased off the huge brake-wheel in the building at the top of the cliff, and the car descended to the seafront, passing its sister car rising smoothly in the opposite direction.

Once out of the vehicle, Shaw leant on a railing and smelt the salty air. The immediate surroundings were not too salubrious, but the seaside put her in a holiday frame of mind. She could feel her composure returning after the horrible events of the past few weeks. She had always eased through life so confidently, protected by some miracle shield from the hazards that afflicted others. Then to discover that the daughter of someone who worked for her husband and who knew her brother had been done in by a criminal thug working at her house. It was if it had all been stored up by the Gods as a kind of retribution for the effortless life they had bestowed on her.

She and her husband had heard the news of Terry Packard's arrest two days earlier, while they were holed up at London's Park Lane Hotel. Owned by the Bracewell-Smiths, part of the Yorkshire business tribe that Stephen was part of, the Shaws were small investors in the hotel, received advantageous room rates and put up their senior managers there. Sitting in the hotel's smoke room, its ceiling a copy of the Reindeer Inn in Banbury, Shaw had been thinking about poor Tommy Nelson. Then the message came through that someone was being charged with his daughter's murder.

When she found out who, she was flabbergasted, though she did remember his mean face. At the time, she was decked out in a Norman Hartnell evening gown and Roger Vivier shoes, set off by clutch bag and jewellery put together for her at Cartier's main Paris shop in the Rue de la Paix. She was so distressed she wouldn't have minded descending into the hotel's magnificent art deco basement ballroom togged in Mrs Williams' gardening clothes. Well, she thought as she looked out across the English Channel, I hope the Gods are satisfied with their revenge and don't come back for another bite.

She wondered for the first time whether the large policeman with the scar down his face had been involved in the swine's capture. Perhaps her brother knew, but she couldn't bear speaking to him just now. Her mind slipped to the peculiar smell in Ray Stafford's office, her olfactory senses and memory generating, on the spot, a replica odour almost as pungent as the real thing. Shaw left her vantage point at the railing and began a congenial stroll along the front. She then chose a cliff path, stopping every so often to sit and admire the view. The walk made her hot, and she undid her coat with its shawl collar and deep sleeves.

By the time she arrived back at the Grand, the Midlands businessmen were outside with their wives. One was a buxom, platinum blonde who Shaw would have sworn was Diana Dors. It was only when she got closer that she could see the woman was twice the age of the young actress and poster girl. The group was loading a picnic basket and fold-up chairs into the boot of one of those new cars with garish two-tone paintwork and acres of cheap chrome.

Shaw's husband, brow creased in a frown, was in the 'monkey house' reading a newspaper, a pot of tea and a vanilla slice in front of him. She put her hand on his cheek and sat down opposite. "What's up?"

"Nothing, really." He took a drink from the china cup. "It's just seeing other industries having troubles. It's not just our game under pressure. This story is a round-up of all the problems this year in the car industry. I know you are not really interested but look at this." He tapped the article he was reading. "Lea-Francis, the company that makes the shooting brake used by our Bentley dealer, you know you saw it on the drive, has gone under. Venerable old firm. What a shame. Joining poor old Jowett. Kaiser-Frazer is on the point of calling it a day in the US. Ford is giving up in France and selling its factory to Simca. Bugatti is chucking in the towel. Nash and Hudson are having to merge, and Packard is throwing in its lot with Studebaker. That's Packard the car, not Packard the man."

"Oh my goodness, let's not try and think about him. Didn't we have a Packard hire car in New England?"

"Yes, we did. Well remembered. What a holiday that was. Wolfeboro and the lake and the inn. And you thinking that man at the bar was Gary Cooper when it turned out to be the local bakery owner."

"I do occasionally come unstuck on identification, I concede that." She ordered a pot of tea and immersed herself in the *Telegraph's* fashion pages.

The car was parked in the road between the Grand and the Metropole Hotel, the other gigantic red brick block that dominated the top of the Leas. The bill paid and the luggage safely stored in the boot, the Shaws shut the doors, exchanging the sea air for the heavy smell of polished cowhide in the Bentley's dark cabin. The nearest lamppost boasted a sticker advert for *The Barefoot Contessa* with Ava Gardner and Rossano Brazzi. They had gone to see it at a local cinema the previous evening and had both nodded off before the end.

The coast road, winding its way west to Lydd Airport on the Kent marshes, was largely free of traffic and the car was soon out into the countryside. "Such a strange landscape," she said. "Like I imagine the moon, except with grass."

"Yes, It is a bit eerie. We've got plenty of time. Let's pull into one of these lay-bys and I'll take a photograph."

He drove the car into a parking area on Romney marsh, and they walked down a sandy path to a wood platform set up for bird watchers. It was a creepy vista, enveloped in an unearthly silence, punctured every so often by the sound of wildlife. A plain wooden information sign with hand-chiselled writing was staked into the earth. The odd laughing sounds they identified from the board as marsh frogs in their breeding season. Neither of them knew much about birds, but they recognised the grey herons and the noise of the peewits. They expected to see more gulls but the calm weather was probably encouraging them to stay over water.

"Everything sorted back at base?" she asked.

"I think so. A new boiler is coming up from Birmingham tomorrow. Tommy Nelson is settling back at work now. Oh, I didn't tell you. He's persuaded me not to set up a system for recruiting workers from Pakistan. Instead, I'm going to spend a pile of the company's reserves on updating our machinery. I get the feeling that's not what the rest of the textile brethren are doing. The decision has given me a cold sweat. Let's hope it's right."

She rested her head on his shoulder. "You always make the right decision, Stephen. How did he take the news that they've got someone for the murder?"

"I thought that was all off limits while we are away?"

"Well, that is what I said."

"Look, I think it has eased his mind. He's a very level-headed kind of fellow but there's definitely a slice of venom there. He said the family will feel much better if he hangs."

"It makes my flesh creep," she said. "Perhaps we should have the Nelsons over for dinner one evening. If they can stand each other's company. And being in the house where that villain worked. On second thoughts, we'll take them out to a restaurant. I'll be thinking about that man, Packard, every time I go into our new kitchen."

"Don't think like that, Jennifer, for Christ's sake. Let's do what you suggested and put it out of our minds for the time being. This little jaunt has come at a perfect time to get your mind off things." He opened the Braun Paxette and took a photo of his wife, dressed as usual like a mannequin but with a landscape backdrop more suited to boots and a hacking jacket.

They continued the rest of the short journey, turning on to the narrow airport road and across the Denge marsh. He parked the car close to Lydd's white, two-storey control tower.

Inside the airport, built in six months and brand new, they showed their air ferry tickets and were directed through to the passenger hall, with its drinks bar and outside seating close to the runway. He found a table in the open air while she went off to buy him a beer and a brandy for herself. At the table, they sat quietly, enjoying the sunshine and watching the activity. A few planes of Silver City Airways were loading up or under preparation, before starting the twenty minute door-to-door hop to Le Touquet. Cars waited in a short line, ready to be driven into the gaping mouths of chubby, converted Bristol Freighters in their metallic-effect livery. Across the other side of the marsh, she could see the tops of seafront houses behind the huge shingle spit that ran round to Dungeness.

Eventually, someone in uniform came over to the cluster of tables, busy with people enjoying their drinks, and informed everyone of the next flights. The Shaws walked out to their car and drove it on to the edge of the runway tarmac, a traffic officer guiding them through customs and immigration. The car's documents were inspected at the booth run by the Automobile Association. Jennifer Shaw watched the Bentley as it was driven up the ramps into the belly of the plane, the second of the two cars to be chained down in the hold. Then she and her husband walked across the runway to board the aircraft.

It was a cosy, not to say tight fit, the cabin housing fifteen passenger seats. She thought about opening the paper but it would have required too much of a performance, so she just gazed out of the porthole. Feeling life was falling back into its natural rhythm, she nevertheless let her mind wander, but only for a moment, to the Comet and those horrible accidents.

A uniformed official appeared from the terminal and strode briskly towards the plane. He ascended the few steps to the low-rise door at the rear and walked down the aisle to talk to the crew on the flightdeck. The pilot emerged and stared down the aisle. Shaw could see that he seemed to be eyeing her and her husband. Goodness me, now what, she thought. He walked towards them, gave the Shaws a smile, then slipped down on his haunches close to her husband. He then rotated towards the little boy sitting next to his mother on the seats in front of them.

"I'm sorry, madam," the pilot said. "We are overbooked by one person. Would you mind if we sit your boy in the cockpit? I'm sure he will enjoy it." The boy, who was about ten and dressed in a blue V-neck sweater, white shirt with tie and black short trousers, looked expectantly at his mum. "Of course he can. Off you go, Simon." The boy unclipped his belt and followed the pilot, clearly delighted at this turn of events.

There was a delay of a few minutes. Then she could hear someone approaching down the aisle from the back of the plane. She could tell immediately who he was as he got to the vacated seat. One or two of the other passengers craned their necks. He was holding his hat across his chest and smiled at the mother.

"I think this is me." His drawl was as deep in real life as on the screen. "I hope I haven't been too much of an inconvenience to everyone." He then eased his long body into the seat in front of Stephen, who grinned at his wife, nodded and winked. Gregory Peck sitting in front of you was a fabulous story to have up your sleeve when dining with Janet and Herbert Tomlinson. She couldn't believe their luck. Well, they deserved a change on that front. Jennifer Shaw snuggled deeper into her seat.

The aircraft began taxiing and then its twin, two thousand horsepower, Hercules engines lifted it off the ground and over the coast. Within minutes it was cruising, briefly, at one hundred and sixty-five miles per hour, twelve hundred feet above the sea, before starting its descent towards the French resort. With a Hollywood film star seated inches away and the prospect of an evening at the casino, Jennifer Shaw's breezy confidence returned as bright as the sunshine. She thought of one of the new expressions for 1954 in the *Telegraph's* column on new words that morning. "Far out," the Sphinx thought. "Far out."

*****

1954

BIBLIOGRAPHY

1950's Scrapbook (The) – Robert Opie

A Pedlar's Legacy – Patrick Beaver

Allen's English Phrases

Architecture in Bradford – John Ayers

Autocar motor magazine

Boeing 377 Stratocruiser – Nicholas Veronico

Bradford Corporation Motorbuses – J.S. King

Bradford Region (Studies in its Human Geography) (The) – C. Richardson

Buildings of Bradford (The) – George Sheeran

Comet (The) – Arnold Kellett

David Hockney – David Hockney

Fifty Years of Pakistan, Volume 1, Fed. Bureau of Statistics, Islamabad

Foul Deeds and suspicious Deaths in and Around Bradford – Stephen Wade

History of Aviation – Kenneth Munson. And John Taylor

Jowett – Noel Stokoe

Kitchen (History, Culture, Design) (The) – Feierabend

Little Germany – Rosemary Ashton

Look of the Century (The) – Michael Tambini

Memories of Bradford

Odsal Odysses – Phil Hodgson

On Ilkla Mooar Baht' AT – Arnold Kellett

Railway Years in Chapel Le Dale (The) – Gerald Tyler

Sovereign Statues of Bradford City Hall (The) – John Stolarczyk

Twentieth Century Fashions – Valerie Mendes and Amy de la Haye.

Unsolved Yorkshire Murders – Stephen Wade

Yorkshire, The West Riding – David Pill